COLLEGE JOCKS
AND FRAT HOUSE BROS

Gay, Erotic Stories from University Life

MATTHEW COOPER

For more information contact:
Riverdale Avenue Books
5676 Riverdale Avenue
Riverdale, NY 10471.

www.riverdaleavebooks.com
Design by www.formatting4U.com
Cover by Scott Carpenter

Digital ISBN: 9781626016835
Trade Paperback ISBN: 9781626016842
Hardcover ISBN: 9781626016859

TABLE OF CONTENTS

Introduction

You've heard the comment that college is the 'best four years of your life.' That's what they say to every high school graduate heading off to continue their education. With a pat on the back, millions of young men are sent off to live in dormitories or frat houses. Most are out there on their own for the first time in their lives.

College is a time to learn who you are, try new things, sow your wild oats. You're young, horny, ready to discover what your body can do, and then they throw you onto a campus filled with thousands of other hot, young dudes, all eager to experiment and find out what their bodies can do, too.

Maybe you milked every drop out of your college experience and never stop reminiscing over all the crazy memories of those passion-filled years; or maybe you look back and wonder why you didn't push the boundaries of your dreams and fantasies while you had the chance. For me it was the latter, and I still look back and wonder why I didn't burst out of my shell early enough to make the most of all four years of campus life. I've since made up for it, which explains the stories that come out of me.

When I signed on to edit an anthology of erotic stories set during the college years for Wilton Springs

Press, it sparked my own creative juices, and I ended up writing a bunch of stories about jocks, nerds, theater queens, and frat boys. When I finished work on FRAT BOYS AND DORM ROOMS, that anthology of erotic short stories, my juices were still flowing. I realized there was more inside me that had to come out.

And so here we are now. I took that idea and kept writing, and story after story poured out of me. Before I knew it, I had a book full of my own stories collected and ready to be shared with all of you.

If you read FRAT BOYS AND DORM ROOMS, you'll recognize a few friends you may remember from those stories. Jeremy the R.A. from *The Jock in My Dorm Room* is back to have his own fun, and this time he gets his own dorm room action.

My good friend Brady Books introduced us to a hot, little blond frat boy named Tyler in his story, *Tag, I'm It!* I was so aroused by the fraternity antics in Brady's story, I asked him if it would be all right if I borrowed Tyler for a story that was brewing in my mind. Brady and I are a bit obsessed with our randy creation, so you might hear about Tyler again someday. Trust me, he's up for anything.

I hope you enjoy all the stories collected here. It's been a lot of fun writing them. Whether young, college-aged characters are your thing or not, I hope you can find the hot, erotically charged energy of their antics inspiring.

Some of the stories you'll find here are just great, hot hook ups. Others have the added element of new love and budding romance. But whether it's a one-night stand or a deeper connection, my goal is to celebrate gay sexuality and gay sex.

What you won't find is stories of hazing, excessive alcohol consumption, or post-coitus regret. My hot young characters don't do anything they don't want to do. They celebrate their sexuality and squeeze every ounce of joy and eroticism out of their college years.

So turn the pages and come back with me to cruisy libraries, frat parties, dorm rooms, community showers, and Hot Gay Sex. If you enjoy these stories, find me on Facebook at AuthorMatthewCooper to keep in touch and hear about my future writing projects.

Enjoy,
Matthew

You Owe Me

Josh was behind the wheel of his shitty car driving in circles. He was so frustrated, he was fuming. He cursed the college, the administration, his decision to go to a school so close to home, and most of all the jam-packed parking lots of his suburban university.

His parents were more than happy when they found out he would have no option but to live at home once he had signed his letter of intent and decided to attend this particular school. He thought it was the prefect distance from home, just under 20 miles, so that he would be able to have his freedom, live on campus, but get home often on weekends and holidays.

But what he didn't anticipate was the campus was too small to accommodate all the students that wanted to live in the dorms. Even now in his sophomore year, he was not even allowed to live in the dorms. Anyone who lived within 25 miles was not allowed to live on campus. And it was not a nationally well-known school, so most students came from this half of the state, and over 70% of students commuted to school every day.

Which is why yet again, Josh found himself driving around in circles... looking for a free parking space in one of the lots on the over-crowded campus. Fortunately, he was used to the hassle, so he'd arrived over an hour before his Tuesday night class. It met once a week, so it was a long one. Three hours, from 6 to 9. But he liked that. Most of his other classes were typical two- or three- times a week with shorter periods, but this one he liked. Once a week, then plenty of time to study before the next lecture.

Fall was sliding by, so sunset was earlier and earlier. So, while it was only five, the sun was already low on the horizon, and the shadows were getting longer and longer as he drove up one row of parked cars and round again to the next. Not a single parking space to be had.

Just as he got back to the closer spots and started over in the second row, he saw something that made him almost slam on the breaks. His head swiveled right around to keep his eyes locked on the vision ahead of him. There just a few feet ahead lit up by the headlights of his car was a beautiful, round ass and the V of a muscular back. He could not take his eyes off the stud walking down the row of parked cars. All he had was a view from behind, but it was more than enough to cause a stir in Josh's stomach. And best of all, that round bubble butt was stuffed in a pair of tight, grey sweatpants.

As his car crept even with the stud, his eyes would not stop staring at the body which walked with purpose passed one car then the next. As he came up even, he was still staring, and the guy turned to look over. Josh stared face to face at a complete stud. This guy had a military haircut, high and tight, Josh quietly named it in his head. A square jaw was this guy's most obvious feature with a strong jawline that could probably slice through glass.

Josh and the guy locked eyes. Josh crept forward, but his eyes were lost in the big puppy dog eyes of the muscular stud in sweatpants along the side of his car. Just then he noticed a female student step out from between two cars a little ahead, and he had to hit his breaks. Nowhere near hitting her, Josh was still a bit freaked out, and the girl glared at him like she was about to scream.

Brought back to reality, Josh put his foot back on the gas pedal lightly and crept a little further. In his rearview mirror he could see the stud. His eyes were locked on the rearview mirror looking right back at him. He was shaking his head, and Josh could tell he was snickering about the close call. He felt like an idiot. He could have hit that girl because he was ogling a hot, muscular, straight dude in the parking lot.

Chastising himself, Josh turned the corner and came around to the next row. Still not a space to be found, Josh grunted loudly. Until he noticed the stud come out from between the cars ahead of him. Now in the next row over, he approached from the front, and Josh's headlights flooded his entire body in light. If the butt was hot in the sweatpants from behind, Josh near about fainted as he saw what was swinging back and forth in the front between the guy's legs. Fuck he loved gray sweatpants and how freely college dudes flaunted their goods. And what goods that must be.

Again, Josh made eye contact, and the guy, Mister Sweatpants, was staring right at him with a huge grin on his face. But they ended up side by side again, and Josh kept crawling forward. Again, he looked in his mirror and got the vision of the guy's curving back muscles again. Just then Sweatpants turned his head and again looked back at Josh. The guy had a huge grin on his face. He knew what Josh was going through unable to find a parking space, and he was obviously enjoying seeing someone else go through the struggle of campus parking wars.

At the end of the next row, Josh again turned around

3

to head to the next row in his futile attempt to find somewhere to park. For a third, very lucky time, he again was going to get to pass by the muscle god in sweatpants.

Whether by coincidence or other miracle, the stud was again walking along in the next row of cars. But this time he was walking down the middle of the lane, blocking the way as he strolled slowly. Josh was directly behind him and had to slow down to the hot dude's walking pace. He could not stop staring at the beautiful round ass in front of him, so he was not even pissed off at the guy blocking his way.

Then the guy stopped. Josh had to hit the break. He slowly turned and acted like he hadn't realized he'd been blocking the car trying to go down the aisle. He stared Josh right in the eyes. *Fuck*, thought Josh, those eyes are so fucking dreamy. *I've never seen this guy on campus before*. The two guys stared each other down, but it wasn't challenging. Sweatpants had half a smile on his face, a smile that had a bit of playfulness twinkling just at the corner of the guys' eyes. Josh took in the vision in front of him and let his eyes unlock from the guy's gaze so he could wander his eyes down the man's entire body. Tight T-shirt. Backpack straps framing a wide rounded chest. Tight stomach. And that bulge hanging there.

The guy nodded, and Josh brought his eyes back up to the guy's face. He came around to the driver side door and pointed at the window. Josh hit the button, and his window dropped. Turning his head, Sweatpants was still standing straight up, so Josh got a face full of that hot significant bulge. Was the guy playing with him now? Because there it was right in the open window in front of Josh's face. Finally, Sweatpants leaned down and put a hand on the door.

4

"Looking for a space?" he asked through a toothy grin. His face was now inches from Josh's, and he could sense a warm, friendly tone of concern.

"Yeah, this is impossible. Any chance you're pulling out?"

The guy stared right into Josh's eyes. It was a long stare that made Josh wonder. Guys don't typically look at another guy as long as this guy just did. Josh noted. After an awkward silence, the muscular stud finally offered, "Yeah. So how about you drive me to my spot, and then you can have it?"

Oh man, Josh was so relieved. "Fuck, yes. Thank you. Why don't you get in?" As the unbelievably hot guy walked around in front of the car, Josh realized what was about to happen. Fuck, this gorgeous muscle stud was getting in his car with him.

As the guy crossed in front, Josh's mind started going to all the porn he'd watched online in the last few years. He pictured how this could play out in amazing, sexual fantasy. *Well*, his mind invented, *how can I repay you*. The guy's cock would get hard in his pants, twitch and tent straight through that seemingly thin piece of cloth separating Josh's face and the man's bulging cock. He would reach down and grab it. *Well, you could always suck my cock.*

He heard the metallic clank of the handle of his passenger door, but it didn't open. The guy was leaning in and looking through the window. He called out, "You want to unlock the door?"

Josh, flustered, reached for the button and clicked it open. The lock opened with a quick pop. The guy pulled the door wide and flopped down in the passenger seat. "Ah, this is great, dude. A free ride for me, and a space for you. Promise you won't hit anybody?"

Josh looked over. He stared into the big wide, almost innocent, eyes and took in the big smile the stud offered. "I know we just met," Josh said. "But fuck you."

Sweatpants kept smiling over at him. "I'm just joshing you."

Josh put his foot down on the gas pedal, "Hey, how did you know my name?"

"No, shit. Well then, Josh. I'm in your hands.," the guy joked.

"So where are you parked," Josh asked.

"Auxiliary 1," he said.

Josh almost hit the brake and had half a mind to kick this guy out. "Are you fucking with me? That's why I'm looking for a space here. That's not even on campus. You're on the other side of the park?"

The guy now looked a little sheepish. "Well, don't knock it, dude. A space is a space. You know you're never gonna find one this close."

Josh sighed, "So I have to leave campus, drive down the avenue, and pull around to the other side of the athletic fields, and walk all the way back? I never park all the way out there."

The guy shrugged, "You want the space or not? Way I see it, you owe me big time for this. Even if it's a trek."

Josh's pervy mind went to all the porn set-ups he watched. *You owe me.* Fuck, fuck, fuck, he could not risk getting beaten up by a big muscle straight dude at this point. But this felt like one of those videos. *You owe me…* what could he do with that?

Josh made light of it as he drove off to the back gate of the campus. "I'm not paying you for your parking space," he objected.

The guy laughed and slouched a little in the seat,

making himself comfortable. "Nah, nah, dude, I wouldn't make you pay me. But I think you could admit you really appreciate this. And we get all this quality time together."

Josh said, "Yeah, of course, I appreciate it. I was just avoiding having to go all the way out there, you know."

"This fucking campus is the worst. I can't stand the fight, so I always just go out there and walk back. It's far and all, through the fields and the park, but at least I'm not driving around and around and around. Like you were."

"Yeah, yeah," Josh smirked. "I get it. But you never know when someone might be leaving."

The guy leaned his head to the side and looked over at Josh who had to keep his head forward to watch the road as he steered out of the parking lot onto the access road to the back gate of campus.

"Well, it can get dangerous all that driving around. You almost hit that girl."

"Fuck I know. I didn't see her. She came out of nowhere." Josh looked over quickly to see the guy still staring right at him.

"Cuz you were staring at my ass," he said.

Josh froze. He had nothing to say. He kept his eyes on the road and didn't respond. Fuck, he was caught. What should he say? Should he admit that he was? Was the guy flattered? Was he offended? He was basically saying, *I know you're gay.*

Josh pulled out of the back gate onto the side street behind campus, all while unable to say a single word. *You were staring at my ass.*

The auxiliary parking lots were overflow space for just this reason, but he hated going all the way out to them. He had to turn down the main avenue through town and come around behind the baseball and soccer fields, and on the other side of a town park, the college had additional parking, but when you parked there, you had to walk back through the park and fields. That was going to get even worse once winter started.

"Well," the guy in his passenger seat finally said. "I do appreciate the ride, and now you'll get to park this clunker."

Josh turned to look at him. He was smiling. Those lips, those teeth, this guy must know how hot he is. "Are you making fun of my car?" Josh asked.

"Well, it is pretty beat-up. And old," he said.

"You can always walk."

The guy laughed. It was adorable, and Josh's stomach leapt. "I'm just kidding you. But hey, you do kinda owe me, don't you think?"

This again, Josh thought. Did this guy watch as much porn as he did? Was he putting that out there for Josh to take the bait? Josh realized his cock was getting warmer and lengthening in his pants. Josh was already taking the bait whether he knew it or not.

He went for it. "Well, I do really appreciate this. Bros gotta look out for each other, right?"

The guy didn't respond right away, but Josh could feel him sitting there, head tilted looking right at him. Josh was getting flush. Was the heat in the car rising, or was it just him?

"Yeah," the guy said. "Exactly. I'm taking care of you. So, then you can take care of me. Right?" Josh could not believe he said that. He had to know what he was implying. This guy, this hot incredible muscle stud, must be thinking what Josh was saying. Nobody said shit like that without knowing…

And just then Josh turned his head to look over at the guy. He was grinning right at Josh. Looking down, Josh saw one hand snake into the elastic band of those gray sweatpants. The guy pushed his hand down into his own pants and gripped the big piece of bulging meat between his legs. "So, you want to take care of me? Buddy?"

Josh did not hesitate. "Sure."

Sweatpants reached a hand up and slid it behind Josh's neck. Caressing it with his fingers, he said, "See, I knew you were staring at my ass."

He had made it down the avenue to the chain-link gates of the auxiliary parking lot. Pulling in, he had to laugh. "Fuck it all, would you look at this?" In the parking lot which could probably hold over 100 cars, there were only a handful of cars here and there. There were dozens and dozens of free spaces.

The guy was pointing to a car at the far back of the lot closest to the park path that led back to campus. "That's me over there." Josh pulled into a free parking space one down from the nice sporty car the guy was pointing at.

He put the car into park and cut the engine off. He turned to look over at the hot guy in his passenger seat. He was still staring right into Josh's eyes and smiling. And now the hand inside his pants was stroking up and down on what he could tell was a huge, fat cock.

Josh could not pull his eyes away. He took in the whole vision. This guy was slouched down in his passenger seat, staring right at him with big, puppy-dog eyes. He spread his legs slightly, and his hand kept sliding up and down inside those gray sweatpants.

Josh sat upright in his seat and felt slightly taller than his guest. And he had an idea. "You know what? Seems

I don't even need your parking space. So, I don't really owe you, do I?"

The guy continued to look at Josh. With his other hand, he pulled his shirt up from the bottom, uncovering his hard, muscular torso. He showed off his abs, then pulled it even higher to uncover his rounded, muscular pecs. Josh couldn't believe how smooth and muscular the guy was. He looked like such a straight muscle dude. But now, Josh realized he was the one in his own car, and this guy was now stroking himself in a stranger's car.

"You know what I think," Josh asked. "Seems I did you a favor driving you to your car. So maybe you're the one who owes me." It was Josh's turn. He leaned his hand down and pulled a lever releasing his seat. It reclined, and Josh slid backwards and down with it. He looked down at himself, reached his hands down to his own crotch and put his thumbs into the top of his jeans.

He turned his head back to his passenger who was basically half naked in his car. He wondered if the guy was gonna take the bait of his turning the tables on him. Josh unbuttoned his jeans, then pulled the zipper down. He mimicked the guy's action and reached into his own jeans and pulled on his cock. It was fully hard in his hand.

He looked right at the muscular guy next to him. Fuck he could not believe how hot he was. The guy looked down at Josh's crotch, at the hand pressed into the jean material, stroking. "Oh," he finally said. "So, you want me to…" he trailed off.

An awkward silence lengthened between them. Josh knew he had taken the lead, so he went with it. He reached his right hand up and put it behind the guy's head. He placed his hand on the back of his neck and left it there, giving a gentle, encouraging stroke of his thumb across the guy's neck. "Seems only fair, don't you think?"

Success. Josh had played it out just right. With a huge grin on his face, this hot, muscular, stud of a jock with the military haircut and the square jaw, bent down right away. As the guy's head descended, Josh pulled his jeans down toward his knees. His cock popped out into view just as the guy's head reached his lap.

"Oh fuck, yeah buddy," he said before opening his mouth and sliding down on Josh's hard cock. He didn't waste any time and slid all the way down on it, right to the hilt and back up again. Once, twice, a third time, he bobbed up and down on Josh's cock.

Finally, he let it slide out of his mouth. "Fuck, yeah, buddy," he repeated. "I knew you were looking at me."

Josh moaned. He could not believe this was happening. He had this stud bent down swallowing his cock in his car in a parking lot. This was as hot as any porn scene he could remember. "That's right, suck it, bro," he whispered. "Ah, yeah."

The guy went to work. Up and down on his shaft, sucking and slurping. With one hand he cupped Josh's balls. With the other he had pulled his own massive cock free, and he was stroking himself as he took Josh's cock deep down his throat.

He pulled up for a moment and looked around. "Sure, we're alone?" He asked.

"Yeah, no one around," Josh said.

"You've got a really nice cock."

"Thanks. But dude, look at yours. It's a fucking monster."

The guy smiled, all while practically drooling. "Yeah, it gets me in trouble. But dude, I can't believe you switched this on me. Everybody always wants to suck me off."

"Well, why don't you get back to it then," Josh smirked at him before he put his hand on the back of the guy's head and pushed him back down on his cock. He took a little more control this time. He pushed down on the back of the head between his legs. The guy let out moan after moan as Josh bucked his hips into the guy's mouth. With one push, Josh pressed him down on his cock and kept his hand firmly on the dude's head and held him down with his meat lodged all the way down his throat. Second after second after second, Josh wouldn't let him back up. The guy moaned in ecstasy. Josh kept full control on him. The guy moaned again and again until finally Josh could hear the change in the moan, a quiet gag. Josh let him up for air.

Coming back up for air, the guy gasped loudly, "Fu-u-ck, dude, that was so fucking hot."

"Glad you liked it," Josh said.

"I can't believe this is happening. Dude, this is so fucking hot."

Josh offered, "Never mind that big stick of yours. I think you're a natural cocksucker."

The huge grin that erupted across the stud's face showed without a doubt he agreed completely with Josh's comment. "Dude, please tell me we can do this again."

Josh immediately fantasized about making this big muscle stud into his personal cocksucker, Josh's very own, obedient boy toy. But he knew he also wanted other things, too. Like to suck him back, or maybe even to have this big bruiser fuck his brains out until Josh's eyes were rolling to the back of his head and they were both slick with sweat, panting. *But*, he thought, *another day*.

12

He leaned into the scene of what was happening now. "Tell you what," he said. "You bring this home, and you can suck me whenever your pretty mouth would like. Now make me cum. And take every drop, baby boy."

Suddenly the stud looked so eager at the dirty talk, Josh could tell he was in charge. In a split second, his head disappeared back into Josh's lap. He swallowed his cock and bounced up and down on it. Sucking and licking, the guy was a cock hungry horn dog.

Josh could not take it very long. He kept looking down at the hot muscular body wedged down in his front seat. He looked at the back of the head with the tight military haircut bobbing up and down on his cock. The reality of their situation was enough to make Josh erupt. Josh threw his head back and blasted down the dude's throat.

Moaning and enjoying every drop, the guy did not let up on Josh's cock. He kept it buried in his throat and took in every drop of Josh's eruption. His hand pumped furiously on his own cock. Finally, he bolted up and leaned back in the passenger seat.

Josh watched him lean back, furiously jerking his huge cock with two hands. The hot stud turned his head and looked Josh right in the eyes. He was panting heavier and heavier with every thrust of his hands.

"You're so hot, dude. I'll suck your cock whenever you want, OK?"

Josh nodded, "Yeah."

"I'll give you my number," the guy was losing his breath. His eyes looked filled with a desperate lust. "I'll be your boy, yeah? I'll be your good cocksucker. I promise I'll be good again. Can I be? Can I be your good cocksucker?"

"You already are," Josh said, smiling at him. "This is just the start."

"Oh fuck, yeah. Will you suck mine, too?"

"Yeah, baby. We're gonna have some fun from now on."

He smiled again. He was gasping for breath over and over and over again as he stroked his huge cock. "I'm Brandon," he said breathlessly.

"Josh."

He was loving the show and was amazed just how big Brandon's cock was in his hands. He reached over and caressed Josh's chest while the big hunk jerked himself off. As he leaned over to enjoy the feeling of the smooth, rounded muscles, Brandon also leaned toward him. Their faces came close, and Josh pushed closer.

He pressed his lips to Brandon's, not sure if he was going to be OK with kissing, but he didn't care. He wanted to feel those lips on his. Brandon opened his mouth wider, accepting Josh's mouth on his.

Josh pushed his tongue into his mouth and immediately could feel the saltiness of his own cum. Brandon moaned a final loud guttural sound and let out a huge wind of air from his lungs. Josh turned his head to look down and watched as the huge cock exploded all over the stud's muscular abs and chest. Blast after blast coated the stud.

Moan after moan, gasp after gasp, Brandon finally started to calm down. Josh looked over at him. He was completely covered in his own cum. "Fuck," he said. "You don't have a towel or anything, do you?"

Josh just smiled at him and shook his head. "No, guess you're just gonna have to wear that home like a good boy."

Brandon smiled and looked over at Josh. As he pulled his shirt back down over his soaked torso, he said, "I love the way you think." He leaned his head back on the headrest and looked over at Josh. "That was so fucking hot. So, we can really do that again, yeah?"

Josh pulled out his cellphone, tapped it on, and handed it to Brandon. "Here dial your number." Brandon tapped it in and handed it back to Josh who then hit a button to dial, and Brandon's phone rang in his pocket. "That's me," he said.

Brandon pulled his phone out and clicked on the call to end it. "Awesome," he said. "So. thanks for the ride. You have class?"

Josh came back to reality. "Night class. I should go. But yeah, let's do this again real soon, yeah?"

"I'd like that," Brandon said as he opened the passenger door and rose out of the car. As he walked over to his car, Josh just sat and watched him. He drove a new looking red Ford Mustang. *What a straight dude kinda car*, Josh thought. *And yet this muscle stud who drives a Stang was just gagging on his cock. Appearances can be deceiving.* Brandon revved the engine loudly, pulled out of the spot, and offered a smile and wave to Josh as he drove away.

Walking back to campus along the park path, Josh was in a euphoric haze of amazement at what had just happened. He heard a ding and looked at his phone.

Hey Josh, that was so fucking hot. Can't wait until round 2.

Me too!

What time is your night class over?

Nine.

Want to come over to my place after?

15

Text me your address.

He couldn't believe his luck. He read their texts over again. This guy Brandon was so hot, he could not believe it all really happened. With another ding, he looked at his phone and saw an address come through on the text thread, and a smile spread across his face as he walked back to campus.

Enjoy the Show

After two years of sharing a cramped, little, cinder block room with another student and dealing with shared, communal showers and bathrooms for the entire floor, I was finally a junior and able to get into the new apartment tower on campus. Well, it wasn't really an apartment, but that's what they called them. 'Apartment living' was the tagline, but that was such bullshit. There was no kitchen, and your room was still a single room. But at least we didn't have to deal with communal bathrooms. Don't get too excited though. The new dorm tower featured what they called 'semi-private suites.' All that meant was that between each two adjoining rooms was a shared bathroom. So while I didn't have to deal with a bathroom shared by 20 guys, I did still have to share with the guy in the adjoining room.

The annoying part was having to make sure you locked two doors when you left your room—the door to your room and also the door to your bathroom. I mean, I wanted to trust the guy in the other room, but you just didn't really want to take chances. You never knew who they might have over, and it's just a good idea to keep your room secure.

I shared my bathroom with a guy named Isaac. Our first day moving in, I bumped into him where you'd expect—in our shared bathroom. I was unpacking one of my giant cardboard moving boxes and pulled out my bag of toiletries. Stepping into the bathroom, there he was, my neighbor, standing in front of the mirror in just his bright white underwear, shaving his head.

He turned to me and smiled. His incredibly white teeth shone at me. I froze in place. "Hey, man. How you doing? I'm Isaac," he greeted me.

"Rog. Um, Roger, but everyone calls me Rog."

"Well then, hey Rog." He just stood there facing me. Isaac was, I don't know the word to use. Stunning? Gorgeous, maybe? The deep, dark, smooth skin of his torso was all I could look at. My mind went back to anatomy class, and my mind started naming muscles and body parts. Pectoralis major. Rectus abdominus. Tendonous inscriptions. Inguinal ligaments. Deltoids.

I might have spent too much time on that chapter, because Isaac just stood there. "Um, just shaving the hard candy shell." He pointed at his head, which was half shaven and half covered in shaving cream.

"Yeah, yeah. Sorry. I was just unpacking my toiletries. Um, guess we don't have too much storage room in here."

"Ah, it's cool, man, check it out. Here under the sink. I put two crates down here. You can use one." He pointed under the sink where I saw two plastic milk carton crates. One was half full of assorted bathroom items, and the other was empty. "Have at it," Isaac offered, pointing at the empty crate.

"Thanks, man." Without thinking I bent down on one knee to reach the crate, but it was a little close to my new bunkmate, and I found myself kneeling in front of him. I looked up from a very awkward and personal

18

position. Isaac was grinning wide at me. His deep, dark eyes were almost smiling. His big round lips parted, revealing those gleaming teeth.

There is no way Isaac didn't notice as my gaze trailed down from his smiling face down his rounded chest, pausing for every bump of his six-pack, and landed at the loose-fitting boxers that were inches in front of my face. There my eyes widened and nearly popped out of my head. There was a huge bulge right there. It hung to one side like a sausage in a bag, hanging down along one leg. I lurched back embarrassed.

"Oh, sorry. Sorry," I stammered. I tossed my bathroom belongings into the crate and leapt back to my feet. I had to make a joke of it, "That might have been a little close. I didn't mean to invade your space."

Isaac shrugged and turned back to the mirror to resume shaving his head. "Well, this is our space now. We're gonna have to get used to the closeness I think."

I stepped back toward my door. "Yeah, sure. Well, I guess we'll be smelling each other's farts for the semester."

Isaac laughed and pointed at a canister on the back of the toilet. It was air freshener. "Already thought of that, roomie." We shared a laugh, and I went back to my room but left the door open so we could continue the conversation, and well, not to be rude.

* * *

One night a few weeks into the semester, I had forgotten to brush my teeth. I'd spent a very long night studying in my quiet room and fell asleep with my face against my textbook. This class was killing me. I looked over at the clock, and it was 2 A.M. I tossed the textbook onto my desk and figured I better brush before getting back into bed.

I shuffled through the door into the little shared bathroom. I was already half-asleep and didn't want to jar my senses in the middle of the night, so I didn't turn on the bright, overhead light. As I got in front of the sink, I noticed Isaac's door was not closed. It hung open at about a three or four inch gap. I reached for the knob to pull it closed so I didn't disturb him, and that is when I looked through the gap and saw him lying on his bed. All the lights in his room were out, but his dark, smooth skin was bathed in a soft light.

My hand was about to pull the doorknob, but my brain said, hold up a second. It had noticed something and wanted to see more. That soft, dull light was coming from Isaac's iPad, which he held in his hand. And the skin it glistened off was… all his skin. He was lying on top of his sheets completely naked. I leaned a little closer to the door, so the gap revealed a wider view. In one hand Isaac held his iPad. The other hand, though, was wrapped around his huge cock. He was jerking off.

My brain was in charge. It told my hand to stop what it was doing, not to pull that door closed. It told my entire body to remain as still as possible. And it told my ears to listen a little more closely. They made out the sounds from the iPad even though Isaac clearly had it turned down to a barely audible level. I heard the moans. It was porn. Of course it was porn.

So yeah, I'm straight. But I'm also not above being a bit of a peeping Tom. No matter what, there was a massive, erotic thrill pulsing through my body of sharing Isaac's private, naked moment without him knowing. And if I'm being honest, I could not take my eyes off that freaking, massive schlong. I'd never seen one so big. Well, I'd never really seen any erect ones in person except my own. Sure, I'd seen them in porn, and even though those are usually pretty big, there was something very different about seeing one live in the flesh just a few steps away.

I made up my mind in an instant—this straight boy was gonna watch. The light bathed Isaac in a glow. It was almost magical, like he floated there in the dark room, suspended in a circle of light that only illuminated him. I watched his hand moving up and down along his thick shaft. I was so jealous of the bulges of his body, not just the cock. His chest moved up and down. His abs were held tight as he stroked.

My ears kept listening to see what they could make out of the video Isaac was watching. It was mostly just moans. I could hear a dude's sounds, moaning and grunting. Every now and then I'd hear the voice say stuff like, 'Oh yeah,' or "Oh yeah,' or 'Yeah, take it.' Very heady stuff.

I realized I was bulging hard and erect in my shorts. I felt a tiny bit of moisture at the tip of my cock as I pre-cummed a little. I reached down and freed my own cock from my clothes, pulling the band down and pushing it under my balls. I gripped my own cock and continued to watch. I'm such a perv.

That's when my ears really attuned to the sounds, or maybe, just maybe Isaac actually turned the volume up. I watched that huge cock in his hands, and then I saw him bite his own big lower lip, and that's when I distinctly heard the voice from the porn moan louder, "Yeah, take it, boy."

Boy. Boy? Wait. What? I heard it again. "Take it, boy." Holy shit. "Fuck me, sir. Fuck me." Was Isaac…

"You like that cock, don't you?" He was. Isaac was. "Fuck my ass, sir. Fuck me."

Isaac was watching gay porn.

My mind raced in the moment. I pictured the day we met. Me kneeling in front of him, that cock, that huge cock inches from my face in his tighty whities. I looked back over at him and started jerking off at a good rhythm. I stood there in the darkness spying on my hot, muscular roommate while he pulled on his huge cock and watched gay porn. I didn't make a sound. I could not let him catch me, but I couldn't peel myself away either.

Isaac jerked off. I jerked off. We were sharing that, but he didn't know it. That made it even hotter for me. Until after a while, I saw his eyes close and his head tilt back, and from between the grip of his hand, a blast of cum shot through the circle of light and landed all over his bulging abs. I watched one more shot before my own cock erupted in my hand.

Fuck, I thought. The ecstatic pulses coursing through my body were interrupted by thoughts of, *you have to clean this up, don't make a sound, he's going to hear you, don't moan out loud.*

As I took a step back, Isaac must have clicked off his iPad, because suddenly the light was snuffed out, and my vision of him disappeared into the full darkness that took over his room. I reached over and grabbed some toilet paper, bent down, and as quietly as I could, I wiped away the evidence of my giant load from the bathroom floor.

I thought there was no doubt I was successful in hiding my presence. I didn't make a sound, not a whisper, not a peep. I snuck back into my room, still half hard from the excitement of what I'd watched, and put myself to bed.

* * *

When I woke in the morning, I heard the shower running. So I stayed in bed, waiting my turn for the bathroom. I had over an hour before my first class, so I was in no rush. I could hear the water rushing and pictured Isaac showering. After a time, the water went off, and I could hear the sounds of his morning routine. Those were followed by the sound of Isaac's door opening and closing again. I still waited a while, because I did not want to come face to face with him.

I got up, arranged my books and assorted study materials, and put them in my backpack. I stretched and scratched myself and finally turned toward the bathroom. I opened the door to find the room warm and moist from Isaac's hot shower. Reaching the sink, I looked in the mirror and froze. There in front of my face stuck to the middle of the glass was a bright yellow sticky note paper. I read the words that were clearly meant for me, written by my suitemate. *Hope you enjoyed the show.*

Holy fuck. Yeah. Yeah, I had been caught. There was no getting around this now. But I looked back at the note and realized—there was a smiley face along with the words.

OK, so if he were really, truly offended, like if he were going to beat the shit out of me with all those muscles of his, he wouldn't have added a smiley face. Right? I mean, well, he's gay, so it's not like he would be freaking out by having another dude watch him.

That's when it dawned on me. Sure I made every effort to remain as quiet as possible while I ogled him and watched his private jack-off session. But that never mattered. Isaac was in a darkened room, and I had left the lights off in the bathroom. But the lamp in my room had still been on. I thought I was so slick staying so quiet and so calm, and the whole time I was backlit for him to see. He probably saw me even more than I saw him.

I decided right then and there that I was not going to bring it up. This would just be something we don't talk about. Unless he decided to. Besides, it was really his fault for leaving the damn door open anyway. He should have assumed that I might use the bathroom. He should have been more careful. Come to think of it—he was probably more embarrassed than I was. He's the one that got caught, not me.

* * *

Isaac never did bring it up. And I wasn't going to. He didn't seem to treat me any differently after that. Actually if I have to think about it, he was maybe more friendly. Well, yeah, of course he was. He was gay, and he was probably assuming I was, too. I started casually mentioning my dates to him, naming the girl I was going to hang out with. I introduced him to one or two, so he got the message.

I know. It was stupid. And if I'm being honest with myself, I think I was just overcompensating. We never talked about that night. It was water under the bridge. At that point, I thought he was probably more flattered than offended. And there was one detail that remained very obvious to me every single night after that. Isaac never fully closed his bathroom door. If he'd been pissed off at me for watching, wouldn't he have made sure it was fully closed and probably also locked? Yeah. I bet he liked being watched.

A few weeks went by. I was acing my classes and looking forward to the next year when I would finally be a senior. I'd hooked up with a few girls here and there that I went all the way with, so I was pretty sexually satisfied, too. One Friday night I was lying in my bed in my room. The dorms were super quiet, because about half of the place went home on weekends. I heard laughing in our bathroom and realized Isaac was not only still here for the weekend, but he must have company, because there was more than one voice.

I could hear a second voice. It was deep enough that I could tell it was a dude. They were definitely in a good mood. I heard the other guy say, "Are you sure?"

Isaac replied to him, "Don't worry. He's not here." Was he talking about me? Were they going to open my bathroom door to see if I was there? Cuz I was. They would find me frozen on my bed listening to them. The banter and laughter subsided as they went back into Isaac's room. I could only hear very low muffled voices and couldn't make out anything they were saying.

I was reading, and since the semester was winding down, I'd decided on a novel for pleasure. I needed a break from textbooks. And it being a Friday night, and the last girl I'd hung out with had gone off to her parent's beach house for the weekend, I decided on this quiet night at home with no studying allowed. I lay in my bed with a tiny reading lamp casting light onto the pages of my book.

It was probably about a half-hour after the voices in the bathroom when I heard a more distinct sound. It was a subtle little click. I turned my head to see the door of my bathroom slowly open. All I saw was a hand on the inside doorknob and an expanse of arm that grew larger as it silently and slowly pushed my door more and more open. Then it disappeared, leaving my bathroom door open wide enough to walk through. Light from the bathroom washed into my darkened space. I was definitely confused. Isaac had not appeared or looked at me or even said anything. He just opened the door to my room and left it there.

I turned off my reading light and stood. I leaned and looked toward the bathroom door without moving closer to it. The light in the bathroom clicked off, and it was pitch black. I stepped closer and saw all the lights in Isaac's room were on. It was lit up like a fucking Christmas tree. His bathroom door was also open. I reached the door and looked through the bathroom. His door was indeed open. I stood there in the pitch dark. His room was awash in bright light. I heard voices.

Well, I heard Isaac's voice. He was using a commanding tone as I heard him say, "Take your clothes off." That was all I needed. I slinked into the dark bathroom, kept close to one wall, and crept over to the other side. I lodged myself beside the sink outside of the beam of light coming through his open door.

I looked through and saw Isaac facing sideways. In front of him stood a really cute guy. He was so pale compared to Isaac's dark skin. His cheeks were rosy, washed in a pinkish hue. Isaac stood shirtless in front of his guest. The guest stared into Isaac's eyes. Isaac had clearly ordered him to take his clothes off, but this guy was just standing there not doing anything.

"Did you hear me, freshman?" Isaac said to him.

"Yes," the guy responded. "I…"

Isaac interrupted him. "I what!? Did you hear what I said?"

"Yes."

"YES WHAT," Isaac barked at him.

"Yes… sir…" The kid sounded meek and powerless, but I could tell from the way he looked at Isaac that he was right where he wanted to be.

"When I tell you to do something, you do it. Understood?"

"Yes, sir," the guy answered more quickly.

"If you hesitate, you will make it harder on yourself." Do you understand?"

"Yes, sir."

"Take. Your. Clothes. Off." Isaac spoke with such authority, I reached down and dropped my own shorts to the floor, like he'd been talking to me. As the freshman in his room bent down to pull off his shoes, I took the chance to peel off my shirt and reach down and pick up my shorts. I threw them through the door back into my room and stood there completely naked.

I watched this little guy pull his shoes off and his socks. He put them off to the side and stood back up straight. He reached to his waist and pulled his t-shirt up, revealing his slim waist then his smooth, flat chest. Isaac took the shirt from his hands and tossed it across the room toward his desk.

I took in a closer look at the guy. He had chestnut brown hair to go with his pale skin. He had big, round eyes, and an upturned pug nose. If Isaac were right around six feet tall, which is what I estimated, this guy was about five if not six inches shorter. He was so slim, must have been barely a 30-inch waist, if that. But his ass rounded out behind him. I mean, like I said, I'm not gay, but that was a juicy butt on such a skinny guy.

Isaac frowned a little. "What did I tell you to do?"

The guy's voice quivered. "Take my clothes off."

Isaac got right in his face, and lips to lips, he slowly stated, "You're still wearing pants."

This guy knew what he was doing. "I… er… what are you going to do to me?"

"I told you if you came back to my room, you *will* do what I say. You are going to service me, and I'm going to use you for my pleasure. Is that what you want? You can leave if you want to leave. But if you stay, you're going to do what I say."

Isaac just stood there. The freshman just stood there. I just stood there. At this point, I was the only one who was completely naked. I was also sporting a raging hard-on. Isaac was in complete control of this guy.

"You're still standing there."

"Yes, sir."

"You're still here."

"Yes, sir."

Isaac smiled. "Now do what I say, or I'm going to be upset with you. Take off your pants."

He still didn't obey. Isaac reached one hand up and rested it on the pale kid's chest. He took his nipple between his thumb and finger and squeezed. The kid's eyes closed, and he let out a whimper. Isaac squeezed harder. The boy moaned loudly. Isaac moved to the other nipple and squeezed again. The kid's face squinched up in a silent grimace until he couldn't take it anymore and let out another whimpering moan.

Isaac took his hands away and repeated himself, "Take off your pants." Finally the guy undid the button and zipper of his jeans, bent over, and peeled them off. I saw he wore a jockstrap. His cock was straining hard in the pouch, and his round ass stuck out between the two elastic bands. It was so smooth and so round pushed together by the fabric.

Isaac smiled, "Oh leave that on. That's nice." He reached around and wrapped each hand around an orb of that sweet ass. That brought his body closer to the guy's and their chests came together. This young freshman kid was so incredibly pale white against the dark black of Isaac's torso. They came together like Yin and Yang. Chest to chest, hands to ass. The boy leaned his head down to rest on Isaac's shoulder.

Releasing him and stepping back, Isaac said very simply and very directly, "Get on your knees." He responded immediately, sinking to the floor. Isaac added, "Take out my cock."

The guy reached up with both hands and opened Isaac's jeans. Folding the fabric open on each side of the zipper, I could already see the huge bulge of Isaac's massive cock, and the guy wasted no time pulling Isaac's underwear down, and the cock flopped out and hit him right across the face.

"Oh fuck," the guy gasped. He looked up at Isaac. The spell of their verbal play stopped for a moment as the guy laughed a little, "What the fuck did I get myself into?"

Isaac laughed, too, and for a moment, they both just smiled at each other until the guy shrugged, opened his mouth, and slid down on the huge member in front of his face.

"That's it, boy, suck that cock." Isaac went right back into his dominating tone. "Yeah, that's why you're here."

My hand was glued to my own cock, and I very slowly stroked myself. Pre-cum started dribbling into my hand, and I enjoyed the slickness it added to my jerking.

But Isaac didn't keep it going for long. Over and

over, the freshman tried to get more of Isaac's cock down his throat, but he couldn't. He kept pulling off with a loud gagging sound. Spit soaked his face and dripped down his chin. So Isaac stopped him with an order. "Turn around." The younger student listened. "Put your hands on the floor." He listened, and his round jockstrapped ass rose up as he went down on all fours.

Isaac turned to his desk and pulled out a tube. He squeezed a huge gob of lube onto his cock and stroked it in.

"If your throat can't take it, your ass will, boy."

The guy turned his head over his shoulder to let up at Isaac, "Yes, sir."

Kneeling down between his guest's legs, Isaac put two hands on the big round asscheeks pointing up at him. He positioned the head of his cock in between them and pushed forward. The pale guy screeched loudly, "Oh fuck!"

"Relax," Isaac urged but pushed forward. nonetheless.

The freshman panted loudly, expelling air from his lungs and breathing in and out heavily. With a long, "Ahhhhhh…" he dropped his head to the floor, and I could see a few inches of Isaac's cock disappear inside his beautiful round ass.

"Please. Please," the guy whimpered. "Please. Slower." But I could tell he was loving every inch after every inch that was disappearing inside of him.

"Oh yeah, baby, take it," Isaac ordered. "Take that cock." And after what seemed like an eternity, Isaac's hips pushed right against those soft, round mounds. His cock was buried deep inside the skinny, little freshman on his hands and knees on his dorm room floor.

"Oh fuck, you're so huge. It's so big. It's so big," whimpered the guy.

"You can take it." Isaac slapped his ass loudly with an open hand. The slapping sound filled the room. The guy let out a shriek. "That's for not listening right away."

"Yes, sir." And Isaac slapped him again before pulling his cock nearly all the way out of his ass.

"Tell me what you want," Isaac said.

The kid kept his head down toward the floor. He was breathing heavy. Half of Isaac's cock was still out of his ass. Neither of them moved for a moment until he said with a begging tone, "Fuck me, please." And Isaac pushed the entire length of his cock back into that ass.

Isaac started pumping hard in and out of the freshman. The guy whimpered loudly. Isaac's hips started hitting into his ass harder and faster. It started making a loud slapping sound. He was railing this kid good. And that's when he turned his head and looked right through the bathroom door. I'd moved a little too close, and my head was bathed in the light coming through. Isaac looked right into my eyes and smiled wide.

He kept piston-fucking the guy and looking into my eyes. I kept jerking off. He reached down and squeezed hard on the guy's nipple to elicit a wild moan. The guy arched his back up, and Isaac got an even better grip on the little round nib.

Isaac kept at it. In and out of that beautiful round butt. I kept watching. The freshman kept moaning. My roommate was a fucking stallion. He was going and going and going. I imagined what it must be like to have that huge, massive cock slamming in and out of your ass. I mean, for this freshman, what it must be like for him. Not that I was wondering what it would be like for me to be the guy on the floor getting pounded by this beautiful man. No, I mean, I'm straight. I just, you know, I liked

31

the show. I guess, if anything, I'm a voyeur. I'm sure you can understand that.

Isaac ended up putting his arms around this guy and grabbing him, and he spun him around onto his back. Still impaled on his cock. The guy was a fucking champ the way he took that cock. And with him now on his back, Isaac lifted his legs up and pushed them clear over his head, so the guy's ass was pointing straight up in the air. And standing over him, he shoved his cock straight down into the guys' ass pushing him hard against the floor. The kid was basically bent in half, legs fully over his head, ass up in the air. Isaac fucking plowed him like crazy until he started grunting like an animal. Finally he pulled out, and standing over the freshly fucked freshman, he exploded all over him. He aimed right at his face and shot a huge stream of jizz. He shot again and again, and I looked down to see the guy completely smeared in cum. It glistened all over his face, his neck, his chest. It was all in his hair.

That's when I couldn't hold off anymore and let loose with my own blast. I moaned way too loudly, and both of them looked over to see the end of my eruption. Four eyes were on me, and I freaked out and turned tail back toward my room.

"I thought you said we were alone," the kid screamed out.

Isaac called out loud enough so he knew I could hear, "Don't worry, he loves a free show."

My Room, My Rules

My gaydar is shit. I've had guys flirting with me like mad and had to have a friend nudge me and pull me aside and say, 'Dude, I think that guy likes you.' Fortunately I do have a few friends who have had my back in situations like that. My friend Jill, for one. She may be straight, but she loves gay men. She always says she'd rather hang out with 'her boys' than have to deal with some drunk, frat boy trying to get in her pants on a Friday night. I'm the exact opposite.

I remember this one frat house party. She and I had been very unimpressed with all the drunk, stupid frat boys and sorority girls packed into this off-campus house last spring. We were eager to finish out freshman year. We'd studied way too much, got good grades, but we hadn't partied enough. Neither of us had gotten laid. She kept telling me how many gay guys she ran into on campus. I told her she was confused—that there were basically none to be found. She would laugh at me and say things like, "You wouldn't know a gay guy if he were sucking your dick."

But she was no better. At least I had an excuse. We were basically surrounded by horny, straight college dudes 24/7, and her pussy was basically crusted over from lack of use. Her joke, not mine. But there we were, two

19 year olds ready to enter our sophomore year in college, and neither of us had gotten laid since high school.

I was nursing my third beer because I didn't want to get completely wasted, but Jill was on her fourth, maybe fifth, glass of a very questionable punch when the cutest guy in the room sat down on the coffee table in front of us.

"Hey," he said and looked at both of us. Surprisingly he was not that drunk, unlike most of the other people at the party.

Jill beamed at him, "Hey." I just nodded and took a sip from my beer bottle.

I'd never seen the guy before, which was not surprising since I spent most of my freshman year studying in my room or in the library. One look at him, and I regretted my life choices. Damn, fuck, hell, if there were guys that looked like this all around me for an entire year, and I wasted the whole time studying, I was mad as hell at myself. He was beautiful. And I don't mean that word lightly. He was so beautiful, he was angelic. His shiny, bright blond hair fell down over his face. I could tell it was natural, too, not some shitty dye-job. His big round eyes were full of life and shone in the dim light. His loose, button-down shirt hung around his torso barely touching him with just two of its buttons secured. From between the open folds of it, I could see the golden, completely smooth flesh of his slim body. He was looking back and forth between Jill and me, his full lower lip begging to be bitten.

"I've never seen you guys at any of our parties before," he said through a big smile.

"We don't get out much," I said with my beer bottle still in front of my face.

"That's too bad," the angel responded, tilting his head slightly. "We'll have to change that."

Jill nudged me. I figured she meant she wanted this guy who was obviously admitting to us that he belonged to this particular frat who was throwing this party. My gaydar powered down immediately. Guys in this frat were never gay, not even questioning. This frat was known for banging every girl on campus. It didn't hurt that it was full of unbelievably hot guys. It was almost like a requirement to join. Like they knew if the hottest guys on campus were in their frat, they would get all the attention. I swear, they recruited like it was like Abercrombie HR.

Jill nudged me again as the three of us fell into awkward silence, like none of us knew what to say. Blondie kept looking back and forth between the two of us. I guessed he was trying to figure out if we were together. Finally, he offered, "I'm Tyler."

"I'm Jill," my friend replied. "And this is my friend Seb." Ah, she got it. She had to establish right away that we weren't together. I wondered if this was the night she'd finally get lucky.

But Tyler didn't look at her. He looked right into my eyes and looked confused, "Seb?"

I got that sometimes. "Short for Sebastian."

"Oh, oh," he said awkwardly. "Sorry, yeah, of course. Well it's nice to meet you… Both" He added the 'both' as an after-thought. I think that was my cue to make an excuse and leave them alone. Jill's knee pushed into the side of my thigh as she downed the rest of her cup of punch. That was definitely her sign to me to fuck off. I swigged the rest of my beer, too.

"Hey, so I should go find another beer. Jill?" I

reached an empty hand out to her, and she handed over her empty cup. "Tyler, do you need a freshie?"

He looked back and forth from Jill to me, "Uh, yeah, yeah, definitely," he paused. He looked over at Jill for a minute then back to me. "But you can't carry all three. Why don't I come with you?"

Oh fuck. Poor Jill. This was not the plan. This kid had no game. Didn't he see how we were setting it up for him to have some time alone with her? I looked over at Jill. She was beaming at me, and I didn't know why. "I'll keep our seats warm. You two go."

"Yeah, sure. Makes sense," I said. Tyler was now smiling really wide at me. I edged forward off the couch cushion and felt like I was ruining her chances. "Uh, you sure you'll be OK here alone? I can manage."

Jill rolled her eyes and looked back and forth between me and Tyler. "Would you fuck off and get me a refill? I'm thirsty. Tyler, take care of this one, will you? Make sure he doesn't get lost."

Tyler stood, and as the coffee table and couch were pretty close to each other, he pressed forward right up against me as we didn't both fit well in the tiny space. I had the cup and the bottle in my hands, and the sudden pressure of his body in front of me pressured me backwards, and I was about to fall back down onto the couch, when his hand reached around my waist and braced me upright. "Careful there, stud," he said, our faces inches apart.

"Thanks," I said. I turned out from between the furniture and stepped away. I looked over at Jill, and as Tyler turned out away from her to join me, she was behind his back looking straight at me with wide eyes, and I could tell exactly what her lips were mouthing, *Oh. My. Gahhhhhhhhd.*

* * *

Tyler and I made our way through the packed house. It was nothing but bodies all pressed together. Leaning close to hear each other as they talked, dancing in packs and in pairs, grinding against each other, merging in circles to do shots. As we maneuvered through, sometimes getting stuck between the clusters, Tyler would grab my shirt or arm or put his hand on my back to keep us together.

When we finally made it to the kitchen, it was also completely packed with bodies, but they came and went. People would come in, grab a drink, and head back out again. We made our way around a handful of partygoers, and we found ourselves left alone as they all made their way out of the small kitchen, various beverages in hand. I found the punchbowl while Tyler went over to a cooler in the corner that was full of beer bottles. He turned away from me, and I snuck a peek over when he bent down to open it. Holy fuck, his beautiful round ass popped up. It looked like two perfectly round orbs stuffed in his jeans. I'm pretty sure if anyone looked at me at that moment, they would have seen clear through my wide-open mouth down to my tonsils.

I grabbed the ladle of the punchbowl and refilled Jill's cup as two guys came bursting into the room. They launched at Tyler and pulled him up and started groping him. "Tyler, Tyler, Ticklish Tyler," they sang out as their hands pressed all over his body.

"Stop it! Stop," Tyler cried out, but it was through an uncontrollable fit of giggling. The sound of it was pulsing right to my dick. The two dudes were crazy handsome and much bigger than either Tyler or me. "I've got beers in my hand! Stop," he begged, and they finally released him.

One looked over at me. "Hey man, who is this?"

Tyler pulled out from between them to step closer to me. "This is Seb."

"Hi," I said as I finished filling Jill's cup and putting the ladle back down.

"Hey, man. I'm Jack. This is Pete," said the one to me.

The other, Pete so it seemed, nudged Tyler one last time. "Tyler, I think you better watch out. I think this one was eye-fucking your ass when you bent over."

"What? No, what, no," I stammered. "We were… I'm getting a refill for my friend Jill. He was getting us beers."

"That hot piece on the couch," Jack asked.

"Would you not," Tyler reprimanded him.

"Sorry. She your girlfriend, Sebby?"

"What? No. She's just my friend," I offered. "She's… uh… she's single. If that's what you were asking." I'm nothing if not a very good wingman. Maybe she needed a little attention from a big, stupid frat dude.

"Then maybe we should go say hi," Pete suggested. "Come on, we'll go back with you."

I was just glad to be past getting caught ogling Tyler's ass. I hoped he didn't believe any of that. We made our way back through the crowd, now four instead of two. This time Tyler walked in front of me, and since he carried two beer bottles and I had the full cup of punch, he kept pressing arms and bodies away to make room for me to follow him, and he kept looking back at me to make sure I was able to follow.

Pete and Jack got there first, and they immediately

bookended Jill and sat down on each side of her and nestled in. They were already through introductions by the time Tyler pulled through the last bodies, and I followed. Not seeing any room on the couch, Tyler nodded to the coffee table, and we sat on it side by side facing the trio on the couch.

Jill pointed at Jack, "Pete?" Then she pointed at Pete, "Jack?" I think she knew exactly what she was doing.

Pete leaned into her. "No, I'm Pete. He's Jack. But you can call us Pierre and Jacques."

"Oh you're French," she asked.

Jack answered, "No, just nicknames."

Tyler leaned really close to me and whispered into my ear. "Uh oh."

"What?"

He leaned in even closer to me—so close his lip actually caressed against my ear. My stomach lurched, and I'm pretty sure he probably heard the exhale that came out of me at that intimate touch. "I think we need to save your friend," he whispered in my ear.

"Why?"

"Because. When they use those nicknames, they only have one plan in mind."

"What's that," I asked.

Tyler kept his lips so close to my ear, I could feel his breath on my neck. "They have French nicknames, because their favorite thing is… the Eiffel Tower."

I was at first confused, not understanding, "In Paris?"

"No dummy. The sexual position?" He paused. It was beginning to click in my head at that moment, and I really didn't need more of an explanation, but Tyler kept going in my ear. "They like to fuck a girl together. Both of them. At the same time. You know, both ends at once."

I was unable to respond. Part of my mind was laughing so hard inside thinking that Jill did not know what she was in the middle of right now. Part of my mind was, I don't know, maybe jealous of her? Tyler took my silence to mean I wasn't getting it. "You know, tag team, spit roast. Then they hold hands over her, you know, like making it look like the Eiffel Tower."

"Yeah, yeah, I get it. Stop, I'm gonna hurl," I laughed. "Oh my god."

Tyler leaned back away from me, he said, "OK, I was wondering if you were totally oblivious or just a prude."

I didn't like either of those monikers. "I got it. I got it. Jill's gonna get it."

Tyler added, "From both ends if she wants it."

"Who wouldn't?" I couldn't believe I'd said that out loud. I immediately flushed with heat. Oh fuck, what did I just say? I looked over at Tyler. He was grinning at me so widely; I didn't know what to say. I had to make it into a joke. "I mean, Jill. Or, like any girl. Right? I mean, um…"

Tyler just smiled at me, letting me awkwardly flounder with my words. "Maybe we should save your friend."

"You know what," I suggested. "I don't think so. She's a big girl. She can make her own decisions." This was something my friends did to each other often. When one of us was in an awkward situation, instead of helping, we'd leave them there and joke about it later.

"Oh, so you are bad after all," Tyler said. "Come on," he added and stood up. He nodded away from the three on the couch who were now so close to each other, I knew Jill was about to have to make that decision. On her own.

I stood up and followed Tyler out of the crowded living room. He made his way over to the far wall of the room where I saw a doorway. He opened it, looked back over his shoulder at me and nodded, stepping through the door. I followed him. It was a stairway down to a basement. When we got to the bottom, I realized it was a fully furnished basement, not a dank space at all. There were hallways leading around a bunch of rooms. There was a room with a pool table, another with a bar and a foosball table. There was a room with a huge television bigger than I'd ever seen with a couch and several recliners. This was such a frat house. But there was no one down here at all.

"We don't let parties come down here anymore. We learned our lesson with how much damage can be done. This is just for the brothers."

But Tyler passed all these options. He walked past the television room to a small area in the back where there were three or four closed doors. Opening one he walked through. I followed him into a very small bedroom.

He looked at me. "This is my room. It's not much. It's in the basement. But at least it's private. I'm just a freshman, so I'm stuck down here, but when I'm a senior, I'm gonna run this place." He smiled and tossed himself backward to sit on his bed. His shirt which had already barely clung to his body, held in place by just those two buttons fell down off one shoulder and opened wide in the front, revealing more of his golden torso.

I stood in the middle of his room, not sure where to sit. I looked over at his tiny desk and took one step toward his one chair. "No," he blurted out and patted the bed next to himself. "Here. That chair's not. uh… comfortable."

I turned back to him. He was so hot, so beautiful, so… half shirtless, I could not think. I just responded to his cue and sat down next to him.

I didn't know what to say, "Um, I'm sorry if you were trying to get with Jill, and those guys beat you to it." He just stared at me and after an awkward moment let out a gasping little laugh.

"You are fucking daft, aren't you," he asked.

"No," I snapped back.

He reached over and took the beer bottle out of my hand, and along with his, he put them down on his nightstand. Turning back to me, he said very bluntly, "Pete was right, wasn't he?"

"About what," I asked.

"You were eye-fucking my ass."

I stopped breathing. He stared at me. I stared at him. He would not let me off the hook. The silence lingered between us. I sat there. He sat there. We were frozen in time. I had no idea what to say. I'm such an awkward fuck. "It's a really hot ass," I finally said. I'm such an idiot.

He stood up from the mattress, pivoted his body until he was standing right in front of me. He tilted his head and looked at me with a devilish grin on his angelic face. "Well, Seb. I see I'm going to have to take charge here."

I had no time to respond. Tyler pounced into action. In one swift move he had stripped his own shirt of and thrown it across the room, then reached down and pushed me back onto the bed. He leapt on top of me, knees landing on either side of my hips and pressing in. His hands found mine and pulled them up over my head and pressed my wrists down firmly into the mattress on either side of my head. He bent down and planted those big pillowy lips on my mouth. His tongue darted out between my lips and filled me. I couldn't move my arms to grab him. He had me pinned in place. I could do nothing but accept his probing tongue and the grip of his knees and the weight of his shirtless body pressing down on mine. He started to grind against me, and I could tell he felt the bulge of my already hard cock against him. He shifted a little, so his own hardness pressed against mine. He made out with me passionately and kept at it, not letting me up, not letting me move.

He finally released his grip on my wrists to reach down and pull my shirt over my head. I bent upward to let him remove it. He traced a line around my chest to my neck and along my shoulders then up along my outstretched arms. He pushed his palms into mine and leaned down and took a nipple into his mouth. He sucked then nibbled a bit. I moaned loudly. "Oh, you like that, do you," he said, and moved to the other one. He nibbled a bit harder, and we both felt my cock pulse under his weight.

He let his hands up off mine and reached down to undo the button of my jeans. I reached up to caress his body, and he immediately stopped and grabbed my hands and pushed them back over my head. "No," he reprimanded me like he had authority over me. "My room. My rules. Put your hands over your head."

I obeyed.

He went back to work. Instead of going back to the button of my jeans, he reached down and pulled off my shoes and then my socks. Then standing over me he just looked at me. I didn't move my hands for fear he'd yell at me again. He had such a fucking grin on his face. His hands went back to my jeans and pulled the zipper down. Then he reached both hands into the waistband. He gripped both the jeans and my underwear and yanked them both down at once, leaving me naked. My cock snapped out of the elastic and smacked my stomach.

There I lay completely naked. Tyler still had his pants on. He turned around and faced away from me. "There. You want to look at my ass? There it is."

I watched from his bed as he peeled off his own jeans. Those two golden, round hairless orbs appeared. He bent over to pull the pants from around his ankles and stuck it out more than he needed to in my direction. As he pulled the jeans out from under himself, he spread his legs further, and I got a glimpse of his puckered hole. He turned back to face me, and his cock stood out at full mast in front of him. Mine was stretched out and up toward my belly button.

Tyler put a hand around his own cock then reached down and wrapped his other hand around mine. "Hmm," he said, "Yours is bigger." It was, but not that much. "And thicker," he added. Yeah, it definitely was. He looked at me before kneeling down beside the bed.

He bent over and opened his mouth. His lips parted and he slid down on my hard cock. This boy didn't waste any time. He pushed down all the way, so my stiff cock completely disappeared into his mouth, and there he stayed. I was buried in his throat. He continued to just stay down on it without moving. I could feel tiny little pulses of his moist warm tongue on me as I was buried in his throat. He came up for air and let out a gasp but immediately went right back down on my cock. This time he started bobbing his mouth up and down on it. I watched as my long cock appeared out of his mouth all

44

the way out to the tip of my head and then disappeared deep down into him. Again and again.

He looked up at me. I saw him look at my hands to make sure I hadn't moved them. He reached up with one hand and pinched one of my nipples. He pinched harder. And then harder until I let out a loud moan that anyone just outside his bedroom door definitely would have heard. He let up off my cock to look at me and say, "That's it. Moan for me."

He went back to work on my cock and kept squeezing my nipple. Hard. The pain was exquisite. This golden boy that looked like an angel had a bit of a bad boy edge to him. Finally he stood up. He reached into the nightstand by his bed and pulled out a tube. I saw it was lube. He squeezed it into his hand and bent over. Straddling my chest with his ass pointing toward my face, he gave me a show as he pushed a finger into his tiny little hole and slid inside himself. He held it inside before letting it out a little. He leaned in closer, his ass above my chest so I could really see the show. He was wiggling his finger inside himself and then pushed in with another finger. I heard him moan slightly as he stretched to let in two at once.

He tilted sideways to look me in the eyes. "Is this what you want," he asked.

"Yes!" I said with a gasp of air.

Still facing away from me, he positioned his ass over my cock. Pulling out his two fingers, he grabbed my cock and pointed it upward. He spread his legs further and bent down until it pressed against that warm, wet hole. "Don't move," he ordered.

I didn't move. He pushed and pushed until his hole opened up and allowed my cock to slide deep inside him.

45

It was his turn to let out the moan. He moaned so loud, I thought the whole house would come crashing through the door to find out what was wrong… or what was so very right.

"Oh fuck, it's so big," he whimpered. "Fuck." He breathed out loudly once, then twice. He pushed down, and his ass started to relax. Finally he opened fully, and my cock disappeared in that golden round ass.

He stayed there enjoying the full length of my cock completely lodged inside of him. And then he lifted himself up, allowing most of it to appear again before pushing himself back down on it. Again and again, he rose then dropped letting my cock in and out of his tight hole. I put my hands behind my head and enjoyed the view.

I was loving every moment of it. I was fucking the hottest ass I'd seen all year. But I was lying there, not allowed to move. He was doing all the work bouncing on my cock. I just lay there, watching his ass work over my cock. I was doing the penetrating, but I was definitely not in charge. Tyler was getting fucked by me, but he was in charge. He was calling the shots. For a moment I realized, I was getting used. I was being dominated by this hot little blond bottom. And I loved every minute of it.

After a while he turned himself around without letting my cock out of his ass. He turned, and we were face to face. He looked down at me and smiled. He put his hands down on my chest, but he didn't squeeze my nipples again. He had a look of ecstasy on his face, and he just kept bouncing on my cock, fucking himself with it. He leaned down as best he could and planted a kiss on my lips, darting his tongue into my mouth in the same rhythm as my cock sliding in and out of his ass.

I looked down at his hard cock. It wasn't really all

that much smaller than mine. I loved the look of it. It was such a beautiful cock, but it bounced there untouched. I could see dribbles of pre-cum on it. They had dripped down and were pooling on my stomach. A long string connected the head of his cock with my skin.

I wanted to stay like this forever. I wanted to live in this beautiful frat boy's round golden ass. But he started to squeeze around my cock every time he pushed down to let me deep inside. I wanted to last forever, but I couldn't. He was milking me toward an impending eruption. He started to sweat a little. I could feel his soaked cock rubbing against me. I could feel mine buried deep inside his ass. And I couldn't hold it back anymore. I started to moan in time with his thrusting pushes. My sounds became closer and closer to a crescendo, and with the loudest gasp yet, I felt the rush and pulse of my cock blasting to life inside him. And as I did he let out a howling moan, and I saw his cock let out a long stream of jizz that shot out across my chest. His cock completely untouched had erupted all over me. He shot again and again until I was covered in cum. Tyler looked spent and collapsed on top of me. He wrapped his arms around my neck and put his head down on my shoulder, breathing loudly. As my cock slid out of him, I finally felt the control subside, and I reached down and wrapped my arms around his warm, smooth body. I held him close to me, and we stayed there unmoving for a long, long time until I could sense Tyler was asleep on top of me.

The hours seemed to melt by. I'd dozed off and woke what could have been 15 minutes later or a few hours, or who knew maybe it was morning. The bliss of being wrapped in Tyler's body was all I needed, and I didn't care in the least about time or where I was or whether I should go home or not. After a moment, I realized Tyler had come awake as well. He turned his head and caressed his hands on my chest. "Who told you that you could move your arms?" he asked jokingly.

With every ounce of my body, I felt disappointment as he leaned up and separated from me. But I watched his naked body as he stepped across the room and opened a drawer. He pulled out a few towels and handed one to me.

"That was amazing," I said.

He sat on the bed next to me. "So, I have a confession," he said.

"What is that," I was at once very confused. What could he have to tell me?

"So I met Jill a few weeks ago, and she told me about you. I told her to bring you to the party tonight, and it was my plan all night long to make this happen."

That little bitch! Jill! Best friend ever. She set this up?

"Well," I said. "Then I hope those two rail her real good then."

Tyler smiled. "It would serve her right. But you know, if she got two, that would mean I owe you one more good fuck."

I could not agree with him more. "OK. But next time, I'm in charge."

* * *

After swapping phone numbers, I grabbed our empties and very reluctantly left Tyler alone in his room to get some rest. I put him down on his mattress completely naked and looked down at him. He offered to show me out, but I refused. I wanted to see him lying there in his bed naked with my last glimpse and then closed the door and found my way back upstairs.

I had to step oversleeping and passed-out bodies all over the living room. Music was still playing, but no one was dancing. It looked like people just passed out wherever they had been last standing. I quietly made my way to the kitchen with the two empty beer bottles and went to find a clean glass to get some water. As I was hydrating, I heard steps, looked over, and saw Jill coming down from the upstairs, her shoes dangling in her hand. She looked absolutely disheveled. Her hair was flying in every direction. Her clothes hung on her, clearly thrown back on quickly. I stepped out of the kitchen. She looked over at me, and we joined together to walk silently out the front door.

"So. Tyler, huh," she asked.

"Yes. Yeah. It was incredible." I looked over at her and said, "Thank you."

She didn't say a thing.

"So," I said as we walked out the front door of the frat house. "You spend the night in Paris, did you?"

Weekend Surprise, Part One

Weekends were so peaceful in the dorms. Most residents went home for the weekend, leaving less than half of us to enjoy the relative solitude of the empty hallways, lounges, and especially bathrooms. The worst thing about dorm living is communal bathrooms and showers.

The campus was full of old dorms, designed in the 1950s, that were completely devoid of style, charm, comfort, or amenities. Why did they think back then that students would enjoy living like convicts? The rooms were tiny and made of concrete block. A lot of guys referred to them not as rooms but as cells, because honestly, that's what it felt like sometimes.

The communal bathroom situation in my dorm was even worse. They didn't even have one on every floor. There was just one large one for all three floors of guys to share, and it was in the basement. Which meant when I needed to take a shower, or even just a dump, I had to trek downstairs and bring all my toiletries in a small, little, plastic bin. So dumb.

Weekday mornings, it would typically be full of dudes waiting to take showers before their classes. It was not uncommon to have to wait for a shower, but at least they were relatively private. Each shower stall had walls on each side, was curtained off, and each had a dry area with a little bench. It was nice to be able to toss on your robe or sweats after drying off and still have a little privacy behind a curtain.

And Saturdays it was pure bliss. There was almost never anyone there, especially early in the morning. So I loved getting up early and heading down and just spending as much time as I wanted to in the shower with no fear of running out of hot water or having to wait.

I mean it wasn't terrible. I'd already survived my freshman year, and if I'm being honest, the communal shower did provide a lot of eye candy. A lot of college dudes were not shy about walking around completely naked in the shower area, and I did not mind getting a full frontal visual of swinging cocks, even if they were always limp and soft. Heck, that just left more for the imagination.

It was the second weekend of November, 8 AM in the morning on a Saturday. You can imagine, even guys that were still around were still fast asleep after the typical hard-party Friday night of college life. So I got my toiletries pack ready, pulled on my fluffy white robe and slippers, and headed down to the showers. Before I did, I texted my friend Marco, asking him what time he wanted to go over to the cafeteria for breakfast together. It was our Saturday morning ritual.

Marco was one of my best friends, but I still hadn't really told him that I'm gay. I don't think he would have cared. I knew he came from a very liberal household, but for some reason, it just never came up, and I didn't really make a big deal of it back then. I wasn't getting any. I didn't know any other gay guys around campus after my first year there, though I was definitely hopeful that would change at some point, but I just didn't feel like announcing myself to everyone. Call it 'in the closet' if

51

you want to, but I would have never denied it if anyone ever cared to ask.

Anyway, there I was making my way down to the showers, and the dorm was a complete ghost town. Like I said, Saturday morning, 8 AM, nobody was up, and most guys were gone. I was looking forward to a nice private, unrushed shower. I made it through my dorm wing, down the stairs, and all the way to the bathroom without seeing a single person, but that changed as soon as I opened the door.

Swinging open the door and stepping into the front part of the communal showers, there at the line of sinks, I saw something I did not expect. A huge, muscular stud was standing at the mirror brushing his teeth. And I mean a fucking stud. His biceps were huge and flexed as he brushed back and forth. They just about pulsed. They were so incredibly thick, and a strong vein ran along the mountain of that upper arm.

My mouth dropped open. This guy looked like such a masculine dude. Not a dude. He looked like a man. He had a full and thick head of the blackest hair. And as he turned to notice me coming in the room, I got a glimpse of his huge, muscled chest, covered in a carpet of curly black hair that trailed down the middle of his six-pack stomach and disappeared into the top of a bright white towel that was loosely tied around the V of his hips.

I had frozen in the doorway, and I assumed this guy must know I had lost my breath looking at him. He was so hot, I couldn't breathe, but I finally got my legs to move on as he smiled through his tooth brushing. I saw the foam on his big lower lip, dribbling down into his beard hair. And then my eyes kept going down, looking him over, sizing him up, checking out his muscles, his amazingly hairy body, and then landed on a huge bulge in the towel.

There was no way he didn't know immediately that I was fucking him with my eyes. I had to control my instantaneous lust, so I kept walking closer and closer and took up a position at a sink three down from him. Turning away from him to look at myself in the mirror, I pulled out my own toothbrush and busied myself with my own oral care.

Finishing his, he spit into the sink and walked behind me and into the shower area. I watched him in the mirror, and I saw him looking directly at me, making eye contact with me in the mirror. Was that a smirk or a smile? Was he thinking, *yeah gay boy, I know you're looking at me.*

He was so hot and masculine. I'd never seen him before, and I figured he must be a senior, but I didn't think there were many upperclassmen still in this shittiest of dorms. I would have even thought he might be a grad student, but again I thought, there's no way they'd be in this dorm.

I heard a shower turn on and water starting to pour in one of the shower stalls. Fuck me, I thought, I want to see this. I have to see this. That towel is definitely off now, and he is naked in one of the shower stalls. But I also thought I better be subtle about it, because the last thing I wanted was to have the shit beaten out of me by a pissed off muscle stud.

I put everything back in my little tote and turned to the row of shower stalls. Only one was in use, which I was very grateful for. My hairy, bearded stud and I were alone. I stepped down passed the first two empty shower stalls and the next and the next. He had taken the very last stall on the right side. I threw caution to the wind. I walked all the way to the end and was determined to take the stall across from him. I know it was ballsy, but I was now committed to my mission.

I heard the water running and knew where he was. As I got to the end of the row, I went to turn into the stall to my left, and with a leap in my heart and stomach, I realized he had left the curtain to his stall completely open. Surprised I instinctively looked right over at him. He was lathering himself up, both his hands moving over his hairy torso slathered with soapy foam. I thought there was no way he wouldn't catch me staring at him, so I quickly turned into my stall.

My mind was rolling over a dozen filthy fantasies in a split second. I put a hand on my curtain and thought, I can't be that brazen and leave my curtain completely open, too. Can I? But he had. Why had he? Why was he there, showering, completely naked, alone with just me, putting on such a show? With only half a tug, I pulled my curtain but left it not even halfway closed.

I put my tote down on the bench, pulled off my slippers and pushed them into the corner. And then I reached down, undid the plush belt holding my robe closed, and with a nervous exhale swung it around and off my body. I hung it on the hook and stood there completely naked.

I mean, I'm no hairy, muscular stud god like the guy in the next stall, but hey, I'm a sophomore in college. Nineteen, barely any body hair anywhere on me, and I did get to the fitness center three or four times a week. Being so young, I could never seem to put much weight on, so I was skinny, smooth, and I had some nice bulges of my own, even if they were a lot more modest than the huge mountain of a man just 10 feet or so away from me.

I turned on my own water and let it warm up before leaning in underneath it to wash all over me, getting myself soaked. I turned and risked looking back out through my curtain. Sure enough, there he was in full view from where I stood. His hands were still traveling all over his body with soap. He had one hand on his massive chest, caressing himself almost erotically. I looked down and his other hand was twisted around, and from what I could tell, he was soaping up his big round ass with that hand.

He lifted his head and looked directly at me. Eye to eye, straight through me, his gaze was like a laser beam through my brain. Caught. He didn't pull his eyes away from me. He looked right at me and continued to soap and slather himself up, touching those huge muscles with both hands.

Finally, he turned sideways, but he kept his head facing me and did not look away. In profile I saw his other hand groping his ass. He gripped the huge mound of his glute and rubbed up and down on it. And he was still looking me right in the eyes.

I had no control of my own thoughts, and I could not look away even if I wanted to. I watched him. He watched me watching him. And then he turned back to face me directly. He reached down and grabbed his cock and started pulling.

Holy fuck. This was really happening.

His cock was long and fat while it was soft, but now it immediately rose and grew. In his hand was a huge, fat, thick, cock. It was a nice dark tan color, and he was stroking it and staring me down.

My hands were frozen to my side. I couldn't move a muscle, but I looked down to realize my own cock had already grown to its full hard length all on its own. While his was huge and thick and a swarthy deep color, my own looked pink and pale. But it was long even if it was a lot slenderer than his. I liked it. It was long enough and thick enough and stuck straight out. Fuck it all, if he was stroking himself, I could, too. I reached down and started jerking myself off.

I leaned back against the tile wall, pressed my shoulder blades into it, spread my legs a little, and started a nice slow stroking rhythm. When I looked back up, I almost jumped out of my own naked body. The hairy, bearded stud was standing in my shower stall. How had I not noticed when he came closer?

Not a word spoken, he approached me and stood right in front of me. He towered over me, probably 6'2 to my very average 5'9. He stepped closer, and our bodies almost touched. Without a word or gesture, not even a smile, he just reached over and took my cock into his hand. I pulled mine away, and he started stroking me while staring into my eyes. I let my hands fall to my side.

After enjoying the pull of his big meaty hand on my cock, I went to reach for his, but before I could get a hand on it, he was suddenly getting shorter. Lower and lower, first at my height, then he kept going lower. He was kneeling down in front of me.

This big muscular, masculine man was kneeling in front of me, and without any hesitation, he opened those big pillowy lips and slid all the way down on my cock until it disappeared down his throat. He went right to work, bobbing up and down, my cock sliding in and out of his mouth again and again. I could feel his beard tickle the length of my shaft as he let it all out except the head and then deep throated me to the hilt.

He reached up, and his two huge hands started fondling my body. He pressed one massive paw into my stomach then rubbed my smooth chest. Two fingers gripped one of my nipples and squeezed. I moaned loudly. If we hadn't been alone everyone would have heard as my moan filled the room and echoed off the tile walls.

I looked down to watch him suck my cock. The shower water was hitting him in the head, and he was covered in its spray as he sucked my cock. He did not stop sucking me. He just kept going and going. He was milking me like a pro. His hands reached around me and gripped my ass cheeks. He started kneading them like they were dough. He pulled them apart and rubbed a finger down the crack. I was in ecstasy already when a finger found its way to my tiny butthole. He rubbed on it, and I moaned again and again.

I was not going to be able to take it much longer. I had never imagined this was how my morning would go. Finally I couldn't take it anymore. Even though I wasn't very experienced, I knew enough to let out a grunt and whisper, "Oh fuck, I'm gonna cum."

But rather than pull my cock out of his mouth, he kept going and sucked harder in his wet mouth. He buried my cock in his throat, then let most of it out again, and started sliding harder and faster up and down on my shaft.

I repeated one more time, "I'm gonna cum," and then I did, blasting down his throat in what I could tell was a huge load of my boy cum. He moaned once slowly and long. Letting my cock fall out of his mouth, he looked up at me. With a smile, he pushed some of my cum out of his lips, and it oozed out to coat the beard hair of his chin.

He leaned back, placing one hand on the floor

behind him. The water from the shower was falling on his chest. And with the other hand, he jerked himself off. I watched his big, beefy hand pulling on his thick, fat cock, but it didn't take long before he erupted with a loud moan and huge jets of cum shot from rocketing from his cock into the thick forest of black, curly hair. He creamed himself again and again, breathing heavy and loud.

I looked down at him, white streaks all over his hairy torso, the black curls of his body hair filled with white spray. This big, hairy, muscular stud kneeling at my feet, I felt for that moment that I was the one towering over him. He was soaked in cum, and he had a huge grin on his face. I was feeling the power of my position.

I leaned down and said, "Good boy."

He moaned like he loved hearing that. He stood up, and I planted my mouth on his cum-salty lips. I pushed my tongue into his mouth, and I could taste my own jizz in him. I invaded his mouth for one more moment until we separated. He walked to the opening of my shower, closed my curtain with one pull, and I heard him re-enter his, this time closing his own curtain with a swish.

I showered for a longer time than I needed to. I let him finish up, and once I heard him pull his curtain open, and then the door to the shower room opened and closed, I knew he was gone. I put my robe and slippers back on and returned to my room completely and absolutely satisfied. It had been my first ever dorm sex, and I was never going to forget it.

Back in my room, I looked at my phone. Marco had texted me, *ready when you are come up to my room when you want to go*. I put on my sweatpants and a t-shirt, pulled on my sneakers, and headed upstairs to Marco's room on the third floor.

I bounded down the hallway with a massive grin on my face. I was so sexually satisfied at that moment; I knew it was going to be the most amazing day of my life. I got closer to his door and saw it open. As I turned in, I called out, "Knock Knock." I saw Marco sitting on his bed, pulling on his sneakers. And standing near him, I saw the beard first, then the hot, hairy muscular torso. It was him. It was my shower stud. He was in Marco's room pulling on a tight t-shirt. Marco looked up to see me.

"Hey, Kyle. This is my dad. He's visiting for the weekend."

My mind froze. My mouth remained wide open. My stomach lurched inside of me. Marco was smiling at me. Marco's father was smiling at me.

I stuttered, "Uh... uh... oh, your dad."

"Nice to meet you, Kyle," Marco's hairy, bearded Muscle Dad said to me.

"Hi," I managed.

"It's nice to put a name to the face," he added.

"Huh," Marco looked at him confused.

"Sorry, face to the name. Marco's told me a lot about you."

I managed to compose myself. He was obviously not mortified, not freaked out, or maybe he was just acting chill. No, he was really taking this in stride, like it didn't bother him at all.

"Nice to meet you, Mr. Russo."

"Oh, you can call me Leo."

Marco jumped off his bed. "Ready for breakfast? Dad said instead of the cafeteria, he's gonna take us to the diner. Sound good?"

I finally got my heart back out of my throat. "Yeah, sure. Sounds. Good."

"Cool," Marco said smiling. "Wait 'til you see his car." He pointed back out the door I had just come through, motioning for me to turn back out.

We made our way into the hallway. Marco led the way. His dad was behind me.

At the stairwell, Marco swung the door open and disappeared onto the stairwell, I felt Mr. Russo's, or Marco's dad's, Leo's hand on the small of my back. I looked back at him. He whispered to me, "It doesn't have to be weird unless we make it weird."

"No, no. It's cool. That was… it was hot," I admitted. Even though I was still in a bit of shock.

"I don't know about you guys, but I'm ready for some pancakes," he shouted into the stairwell.

Lock the Door

No one ever wanted to get up when the fire alarms went off. I could never understand who in their right mind would pull one at 3 AM in the morning, but it happened all the fucking time in the dorms. We were required to leave the building if the alarm sounded, no matter what time of day it was. Worse, as a Resident Assistant in the men's dorm, it was my job to make sure all the guys on my floor complied. I didn't want to get up myself, but there was definitely no way I could disobey the rule.

It was worse during exam week when it would happen several times a night. Yeah, not a week. Every night. Over and over. I thought it was probably the stress of all-night cram sessions or anxiety over tests that would make people pull the alarms. Regardless, whatever the stupid, fucked-up reason why someone did it, I had to lug my ass out of bed, grab my master key, and walk the entire floor, opening every door and ordering guys to get out of bed and leave the building. It did not make me popular.

Picture it. The third week of December. And I hadn't picked a university in a nice warm place like Florida. No. I chose a small college up north. So December? Yeah, cold. Fucking freezing. And at 1 AM, bone-chilling. Of course, that's when it would happen. CLANG. CLANG. CLANG. Fuck me. CLANG. CLANG. CLANG. Where

61

are my pants? CLANG CLANG CLANG. Get dressed. Grab the master key. CLANG. CLANG. CLANG. Fuck my life.

Starting at one end and working my way through the entire floor, I had to knock on every door and make sure every dude got out of bed, out of his room, and went outside. It was insanity. Most guys would stumble out voluntarily, put on robes or coats, and trudge down the halls to the stairwells. Yeah, can't use the elevators either. But if I knocked on a door, and no one answered, I had to use my master key and open the door to make sure everyone left. You can imagine how much guys loved that.

Now I know what you're wondering. Did I ever walk in on a guy jerking off? Did I get to see them jumping out of bed naked? Did I catch them in the act with their girlfriends? So first off, you're a pig. Second of all, so am I. Why do you think I'm telling you this story?

Anyway, don't rush me. I'm getting to it. Where was I? Third week of December. My senior year. My mind was fully focused on getting the fuck out of there, graduating, finding a job, getting an apartment, starting my life. But I had one more semester to go, and it was exam week for the fall semester. Tensions were high. Well, at least for guys who had been ignoring their courses for the last three months and now were facing finals.

So, there we were. Standing outside in the bitter cold at 1AM on a Tuesday, waiting for the alarms to stop and the all-clear to go back to bed. Resident Assistants were never popular during these moments, like it was our fault or something. Guys would look over at us with this 'what the fuck' look. Like we had any power to do something about it.

"Fuck this, it's too fucking cold for this shit,"

someone said right next to me. I turned to find Will, another R.A. from the floor above mine, shivering next to me wrapped in a blanket he'd obviously just pulled off his bed.

"Tell me about it," I said. But looking back at him, I added, "Dude, why didn't you put on a coat or something?"

Will just shrugged and then smiled at me. Oh and fuck, that smile. Dimples for days. I turned to look right at him. I have to admit. I'd had a crush on him for three years at that point. His piercing blue eyes were so striking, everyone commented on them. Even straight dudes. And even though he was wrapped tight under a heavy blanket, I knew that underneath it, he had a rock-hard body. I'd never even seen him shirtless or anything, but he wore tight tank tops constantly that accentuated his firm, round chest and tight waist very nicely. And in the last year, he'd chopped off most of his hair and now sported a very short military looking buzzcut. Added to his chiseled jawline, he looked like walking sex. And acted like it, too. He was such a cocky guy, but he was also so fucking hot, you kinda felt like, yeah of course he's cocky. If you were that hot, you'd be cocky, too. I imagined every girl on campus wanted to get fucked by him, and I assumed half of them probably had been. He was that hot and that sure of himself. I wish I had half his confidence. And looks.

"Can't we just go back in," he complained. "This is ridiculous. How long has it been? Like half an hour?"

I checked my watch. "Six minutes."

"Fuck you, Matty," he said to me with a laugh.

We waited and waited. Minutes went by. My feet were getting numb. Will mumbled and shivered and sighed. "Dude, seriously, why did you not put on a coat? That blanket's not gonna cut it."

Will turned to me. "Uh, yeah. It's worse than that, man." He nudged his shoulder against mine and nodded his chin toward me. Turning so he was facing me but away from everyone else, he opened the blanket. He was completely naked. And what a sight it was! Every inch of his rock-hard, muscular body stood before my eyes. He stood there, blanket spread open, like a streaker, showing me his entire naked body. In all its glory. It was better than I'd ever pictured in my fantasies. That chest, covered in brown hair trailing down a six-pack stomach. My eyes lingered on his belly button. Why was even that so fucking hot! And my eyes kept going down and landed on his cock. And what a cock. It hung between his legs like a club. Even in this freezing cold weather.

I don't know how long I stared at it, but I thought it might have been too long. I looked back up into his eyes. He was staring right into mine and smiling wide. He kept it open for me to look at him for an oddly long time, but he was letting the cold into his blanket, and he finally re-wrapped that glorious body up into it.

"Dude."

He nudged my shoulder again. "Yeah, I'm fucking freezing."

"Why the fuck didn't you get dressed?"

He hesitated, then admitted, "I wasn't in my room."

Oh, poor Will. He was getting some. Here I was complaining about this cold and having to get out of bed. He was interrupted in the middle of a hot fuck session. I was fully clothed with my coat on. He was buck naked under a blanket. Standing next to me. In all his fucking hotness. I wanted to bury myself into that blanket with him and keep him warm.

Finally, the alarms stopped. Will immediately said,

"Oh fuck me, finally," and started running back toward the building along with 100 other guys. He turned back at me and added, "See you for the next one. In an hour, I bet."

My mind was still busy picturing his incredible, naked body inches from me. He had peeled that blanket open just for me to see. I felt like we shared that special moment, and even though he did it jokingly and to show me why he was so cold, I still felt like it was a shared moment between us. He didn't know I was gay, and I figured if he had known, he probably wouldn't have done it.

I let most everyone ahead to get through the doors and lingered back with the vision still in my head before it finally dawned on me. Wait a second. He wasn't in his room. He was in someone else's room. Naked. Probably having sex. But... this was the men's dorm.

* * *

I didn't sleep a wink. My mind was still between the folds of that blanket. I laid in bed still in my clothes and coat with a boner picturing Will. Could it be true? Had he been having sex with another dude? We weren't the closest of friends, but I'd known him for the last three years. More than just in passing, but I wouldn't say we were like buds or anything. But now, my mind was fully focused on him and his muscular, hairy chest and those crazy hot abs and that deep belly button that I wanted to thrust my tongue into. And yeah, that huge thick cock. How was it so big in the freezing cold night air? Mine had probably been shriveled up trying to get back inside my body when we were outside. How big was that thing? And how big would it get when it's hard? Or in my hand. Or in my mouth. Or in... other places.

65

And then. CLANG CLANG CLANG. Why the fuck would someone. CLANG CLANG CLANG. This is the worst form of torture you can imagine. CLANG CLANG CLANG. 2 AM. Will was right, exactly one hour. CLANG CLANG CLANG. Oh, wait, maybe I'll get to see him again. CLANG CLANG... I leapt out of bed.

Never have I ever checked every door on my floor so quickly and gotten out of the building in the throngs of bodies walking like zombies down the stairs. Amazing how much zombies can curse. I made my way out onto the quad and stood in the exact same space I had been in before. Like I could somehow summon Will back to me. Maybe he'd been wrapped in just a blanket again.

But no luck. It was just me standing alone in the freezing cold night air while 100 pissed off guys paced around waiting to go back inside. No Will. No hot, naked, hairy chest. No big, fat cock. All I got was three guys from my floor coming over and complaining at me. "Come on, can't we go back in," Mitch lodged at me.

They were all bundled up and looking at me like I had something to do with it or that I could do something about it. Nick, Mitch, and Tim. They were all in the same fraternity, lived on the same floor—mine—and were basically inseparable. Mitch was a bit of a jerk. Of course he was the one complaining. Tim was annoying. But Nick was really nice. "Guys, I can't do anything about it," I said.

Mitch threw his hands in the air, "Man, this is so fucked up. Come on."

Tim added, "What the fuck? Who keeps pulling the fucking alarm?" Like we hadn't heard that question 100 times over. I just shrugged at him. "Can't they put a camera on it or something and catch the fucker?"

Nick tried to calm them down. "Chill, guys. Matty

can't do anything about it. He's out here just like us." The other two calmed down a bit, and the three of them just stood by me, I looked over at Nick and mouthed a *thank you*. He nodded and smiled at me without a word. Why hadn't I noticed how cute he was before? Probably 'cuz he was a frat boy so obviously straight, and we had nothing in common except we were on the same floor, and I was his R.A.

This one took a while. It was almost 15 minutes before the alarms stopped. I had spent every moment of that entire time scoping the crowd to see if I could find Will with no success. So I trudged back into the building with Nick, Mitch, and Tim. We made our way to our floor, and they each went to their doors. "Good night," I offered.

Mitch made some guttural sound in reply. Tim said nothing. But Nick at least said, "'Night, Matty." Mitch and Tim's door was already slammed and closed. I turned back around to see Nick still in his doorway looking my way. He had the room across from theirs that he shared with a guy who was always at his girlfriend's apartment, so he had it to himself almost all the time.

"'Night, Nick." My mind liked that moment of connection, too. Not as much as having Will's entire naked body thrust into my vision, but there was a moment there that I hoped meant something more. I walked to the end of the hallway to my door, my mind lingering on it, and when I got to my door, I wondered, if I looked back, would Nick still be standing there? I turned. He was still just standing there in the hallway, looking my way. I smiled but chickened out of any additional connection to the cute guy staring my way. I went in my room and closed the door. Damn. I was way too fucking horny. I chastised myself as I fell back into my cold bed. A naked

Will. A nice Nick. It didn't mean anything, I knew. They were straight boys. They didn't know I was gay, because I was too scared to come out. Even after three and a half years in college, I still wasn't open about myself. I didn't really think there was any reason to unless I came across other gay guys. I didn't want to risk being an outcast or being the token homo. Because I seriously figured there were no other gay guys in the entire school. I know, I know, I was stupid. But I'm getting to the story, trust me.

So thankfully that was the end of the alarms for that night, but I knew in the morning when I woke groggy and still tired that it wasn't the last of it. It was only Wednesday. We had at least two more nights of finals week to go.

* * *

By Thursday night everyone in the dorm was on edge as the night was coming to a close. No one would talk about anything other than exams and how many times we were going to get woken up during the night by fire alarms. Some guys said they didn't even bother changing out of their day clothes, which if we're being honest was usually just sweatpants anyway. And others joked about sleeping with their shoes on.

I was in the hallway coming back from the community bathroom where I had been brushing my teeth and ran into Mitch and Tim. "I bet it's someone trying to sneak some chick into the dorm," Mitch was saying.

"Or out," added Tim.

When they saw me coming down the hallway, Mitch said to me, "Dude, seriously, can't you just let us stay in our rooms? You know it's always a false alarm."

"Come on, man, you know I can't do that. I'm not the enemy here, dude. Whoever's pulling the fucking alarm is. Stop busting my balls." I was definitely on edge just like everyone else, because typically with a jerk like Mitch, I wouldn't usually give it back to him. I think I surprised him, and he at first didn't know how to respond.

"All right, all right, chill, dude," he finally said, putting his hands up in the air.

"You think I want to go outside in the freaking cold?" I was on a roll.

Tim nudged Mitch in the side, "Come on, man. Let's get as much sleep as we can before the damn thing goes off." As I left their doorway, I looked over at Nick's door across from theirs and wondered where he was. You would almost always see all three of them together.

And sure enough, they were right. Not long after midnight, it started. CLANG CLANG. Typical drill, I had to walk the hall, see that everyone left the building. I would knock on a door. If there was no answer I'd open it with my master key. When I found guys still in their beds, I had to yell at them to get out of bed, get dressed, and go outside.

So there it was a little after midnight. I made my way door to door, got all the guys out. I did note in my head that when I knocked on Nick's door then opened it to look inside, he wasn't home. I thought, he probably went home for the weekend already. A lot of guys left on Thursdays.

It was almost the last night of finals week, I thought. Almost free. But sure enough, CLANG CLANG. Another fire alarm not a half hour later. We'd barely gotten resettled back inside when we were again forced out of our beds. This was going to be a long night. Our record was six. I hoped to fucking hell we weren't going to get to that number again.

Midnight. Fire alarm. 12:30. Fire alarm. 1:20. Again, fire alarm. 2:30. Fire alarm. The guys were in a rage. Mitch and Tim banded a group of guys together to patrol the fire alarm on our floor. They vowed if they found the guy, they'd beat the shit out of him. But after 20 minutes or so, they lost interest and went back to their rooms. Besides, they weren't really thinking it through. There were at least three or four fire alarms on every floor.

I settled back into my bed. Maybe it was the memory of seeing Will completely buck ass naked at that fire drill earlier in the week, but I was horny. Lying in bed, I decided to start jerking off. I pulled off all my clothes, grabbed my handy bottle of lotion, and laid down on my back. I sized myself up, thinking about Will's big cock. I wondered how big his got. I was thinking definitely bigger than mine. I mean, I'm no shrimp. I like my cock. It's probably average, and it gets the job done, but my mind just kept thinking about Will and his body and his cock, his bright blue eyes and his dimples. How cocksure of himself he was to throw open that blanket and show off his hard, muscular, hairy body to me. My cock rose in my hand, and I smeared lotion all up and down the shaft.

I lost myself in picturing what I would let Will do to me, and I enjoyed the feel of my hand on my hard shaft. I kept it slow. I wanted it to last. When I got close, I stopped. I was edging myself without really knowing that was a thing. But hey, I was in college, and if I wasn't going to get any raging hot gay sex with other dudes, I could at least enjoy my wank session. But of course, that's when it happened again. A fifth time. CLANG CLANG CLANG. Fuck me. I had a raging hard on, smeared with lotion. CLANG CLANG CLANG. I heard the commotion of cursing and doors slamming in the hall.

CLANG CLANG CLANG. I had to get up. I had to make sure everyone left. I regretted the decision not to live off campus. CLANG CLANG CLANG. I stood up and looked down. My cock was sticking straight out. I grabbed my sweatpants. Fuck this is going to be obvious. How am I going to hide this? Underwear. I needed underwear. CLANG CLANG CLANG. I had to find some, because like most guys on campus, I didn't usually wear any. Especially when I wore sweatpants. It was one of my favorite things about college. Guys would just let it swing free in their sweats. CLANG CLANG CLANG. OK, OK, I swore to the room.

It took me a while, longer than ever, to get myself situated. I wiped my cock vigorously with tissues to get most of the lotion off. It would not be a good thing to go outside in front of everyone with lotion spotting my crotch. I couldn't find a pair of clean underwear, so I just pulled my sweatpants on. I went to my closet and found my coat, and by the time I got out into the hallway, it was already a ghost town.

I was almost proud of my guys. They got themselves out without me yelling and ordering them to go. Except for the constant alarm, it was as quiet as it had ever been. But before I went down myself, assuming I was the last to go, I did have to go door to door and use my master key. I opened a door, looked in, found the room empty, and went on to the next. I made my way down the hallway. I got to Mitch and Tim's door, unlocked it, looked in, found the room empty, and closed it back up again.

I turned around, and there in front of me was Nick's door. He hadn't been at any of the alarms so far that night, so I assumed he was gone for the weekend. But then I heard music playing in the room. I inserted the key into

71

his door. I turned the knob, opened the door a crack, and stuck my head through. My mouth dropped open wide.

There on the bed was a naked Nick. Well, I figured it was Nick. He was face down, ass sticking up in the air over his spread-out legs, knees pressed into the mattress. And in between those legs, facing me, pumping over and over and over again into his raised ass was a naked, glorious Will. With every athletic thrust, he was fucking hard into Nick's ass, and Nick was letting out a rough, muffled moan. He had his face buried in a pillow trying to muffle the sounds. Even with the music playing, I could hear his loud, vocal grunts as Will's very large cock pummeled his ass.

I stood there frozen, mouth open wide. The key in my hand was still in the door lock, and I couldn't move. I couldn't look away. I didn't want to. Will was covered in sweat. His hairy, muscular, rock-hard body was glistening in the dimly lit room. Nick had his legs spread wide and was offering his round, smooth ass up in the air for this god-like stud. My cock had settled down a slight bit when I had put my clothes on, but it was now a raging hard-on in my sweatpants.

Will looked up and saw me standing there. He looked me right in the eyes. Nick hadn't seen me; didn't know I was standing there. But he was still moaning loudly into the pillowcase, face covered. With every thrust of Will's cock deep into his ass, Nick moaned and grunted. It sounded like he couldn't take any more with every single thrust, but they kept going. Over and over and over, Will drove his cock in and out of Nick's smooth, pale, round ass. Will's blue eyes bore into mine, and then a giant smile erupted across his face. He didn't stop pummeling Nick's ass. If anything he added to the vigor and speed at which he was sliding his cock in and out of the frat boy's willing ass. All while staring into my eyes.

Will nodded at me and pointed at my hand. He was pointing at my hand that still held onto the key. I looked back into his eyes. Without pausing his relentless fucking, he mouthed words to me that somehow I understood immediately. *Lock. The. Door.*

Before Nick could look up, I realized this was intensely awkward. What would happen if Nick saw me? He would freak out. Will obviously didn't care. He was still grinning wildly. I think he was proud to be caught. I wanted to stay. I wanted to be next. I wanted to touch him. I wanted to touch them both. I wanted what each of them was getting. But I knew what I had to do.

I turned back out of the door, pulled it closed without a sound. And I locked the door. Like Will told me to do. I made my way outside, the vision of his incredible, naked body for a second time in a week bore into my brain. And this time I got to see it in action. Not just action. But fucking a guy. Fucking Nick. My nice neighbor. Nick, ass up, getting railed by that hairy, muscular stud. My view of the world seemed to shift right there in that moment. I didn't even realize I'd made it all the way outside.

I walked away from the building still dumbstruck. I didn't say a word to anyone as I walked through dozens and dozens of pissed-off guys waiting in the freezing cold to go back to bed. My mouth was still dropped open when I heard Mitch laugh loudly. I looked up to see him pointing at me. "Matt, dude, you got a fucking boner there, dude." Mitch was laughing. Tim was laughing. A few other guys were laughing. I looked down to see the visual outline of my hard cock tenting out inside my sweatpants. I'd never live that one down.

* * *

I went through the next day like a zombie. Tests were over, and the semester was done. Guys were packing up and heading home for the holidays, so it was a busy, raucous Friday in the dorms. Most were flying out or driving away that day. A very small number of us would still be there through the weekend, especially us resident assistants who would be the last ones to pack up and go by Monday morning. No one would be back until the second week of January, but mostly guys were just taking a suitcase with them and leaving most everything behind in their rooms.

Even though it was a busy, frantic day, my mind was stuck on one image. Nothing else lasted in my mind that entire day except the vision of Will's hot, hairy, naked body fucking Nick face down on his bed. I could still see the glistening sweat in his chest hair, the way his hands pressed down on each side of Nick while his hip pivoted in and out of Nick's willing, raised ass. I could still hear Nick's muffled grunts lost in his pillowcase and see the bright paleness of the round orbs of his ass as Will looked right through me with those incredible eyes as he piston-fucked that frat boy.

The only other thing that kept going through my head was what would I say to Will the next time I saw him? I mean, he had smiled so widely when I walked in on him. He'd seemed almost proud to have me catch them in the act. But Nick. Nick probably still did not know I saw. He had kept his head buried, never looked up, and I assumed Will probably didn't tell him. But Will knew. We had looked each other right in the eyes. He had smiled at me and mouthed those words, *lock the door.*

I wondered if he was worried that I would report them. He was so cocky in that moment. It made me hard thinking about how in charge he was and how unphased he seemed over being caught. He had smiled at me. Like we were sharing his great secret between us, not even with Nick. But still, he might be worried. I decided not to bring it up with him, though, if I did see him before we all left for the break.

Or maybe I should. Maybe I should let him know that not only did I have no intention of reporting him. I wanted him to do to me exactly what he did to Nick. That's why my mind was so obsessed with what I saw. That's why I was walking around all that day with a raging hard-on. I was more sexually frustrated than ever. And the idea that there were actually guys getting hot gay sex and I wasn't, that was freaking me out. Not just any guys either. Will. Hot piece of man meat Will. He had shown off his entire naked body to me at the fire drill, but someone else got to enjoy it. And it was with cute Nick. Right on my floor. Cute frat boy Nick. Another guy I finally admitted to myself that I lusted after. Fuck it all.

* * *

By Saturday night the dorm was a ghost town. Every guy on my floor was gone, including Nick, who I hadn't seen since he was getting plowed face down on his bed Thursday night. I went to the fitness center. I hoped maybe a workout would refocus my thoughts. The entire gym was completely empty, and even though I was all alone, I could still sense the level of college dude hormones and testosterone that usually pulsed through the air. I looked at myself in the mirror. I wasn't half bad.

I worked out regularly, but my mind immediately started picturing a naked Will again. With his incredible lean muscles, he must be in this room all the time.

I posed for myself in the mirror without any worry of self-consciousness being so completely alone. I lifted my shirt. Come on, I was definitely not half bad. I didn't have Will's manly tufts of hair leading from a full beautiful bloom across his chest and trailing down the middle of his washboard abs, but I looked at my stomach. It was smooth and flat. I didn't have the bulbous mounds of Will's six-pack, but I was lean. I didn't have his hair, but I was sleek and smooth, if you like that sort of thing.

I realized how much Will had woken up my mind to the deep lust I had for the male figure. I was checking myself out. That was something I really had not done much of before. I turned sideways with my shirt still lifted and gauged my slim waist. Yeah, fuck it, I could admit it. It looked good. Maybe a little boyish, which wasn't my own taste, but I thought if I ever do find another gay guy, he'd like it.

Then standing sideways, I checked out my own ass. Where my waist was tiny and slim, I realized my ass really stuck out. It was full and round despite my thinness. It was more prevalent than I really had ever thought. I dared a little further, only because I knew I was all alone. I pulled on the back of the waistband of my athletic shorts and slid them down, revealing my naked ass right there in the middle of the workout room. Yeah, round and pale, and damn it looked smooth as fuck. I caressed it, and it felt satiny smooth. Fuck my life, why couldn't I find a guy who would appreciate all this.

I yanked the shorts back up and tried to work out a little more. I was inspired by thinking about making myself, keeping myself desirable. I wondered if Will would ever agree to work me out and help me get bigger and more muscular. But I had to stop fantasizing about that, because I was beginning to sport a hard-on. Finally I gave up on working out, because my mind was still laser-focused on my hot friend. Maybe, I thought, I'd just go back to my room and jerk off.

* * *

My bags were packed and near my door. I wasn't heading home until Sunday afternoon. I tried watching some videos on my phone, listening to music, but my mind was still laser focused on picturing Will's hot naked body. I was so frustrated I couldn't do anything. I went to the community bathroom at the end of the hall and took a shower to try to get my mind off him.

Alone as I was, this was the perfect time to linger, soap myself up, enjoy the unending hot water. But of course I had a raging hard-on the entire time. I jerked off with a soapy hand picturing Will, wondering about how big that cock would get, how it would feel pushing into me. The frustration was so real in my mind, I lost track of how long I was in the shower, but I didn't even get to finish myself off when the hot water started to run out, and I was suddenly hit with the chill we all became accustomed to with these old pipes and insufficient water heaters. I quickly rinsed off the lather and dried myself off.

Walking back to my room, I was again struck at how empty the dorm was. A building always alive with dozens and dozens of college guys on every floor partying and screaming and causing all sorts of commotion. I liked the feel of the absolute solitude and even in a moment of carelessness let my robe fall wide open and walked back to my room with my entire body out for no one to see.

I got back into my room and was hanging my damp towel over the back of my desk chair and still in my open robe. I lay on my bed, let the robe fall open, and grabbed my cock. Just as I got it to full attention, I heard a single knock on my door. I leapt out of bed pulling the robe closed around me as the door opened. Who was even still here in the dorm? And who knocks and just walks in any way? Rude... I turned to the door while grabbing the edges of my robe to close it, and Will stepped into my room.

I had barely had a second to cover myself before our eyes locked on each other. I was frozen. Surprise, anxiety, eagerness, worry, wonder, so many emotions turned me into stone. Again I stood there, looking at Will mouth wide open, not speaking. He must have thought I was a complete buffoon.

"Hey," he said stoically.

"Hey," I repeated.

I didn't know what to say. It seemed neither did he. We just looked into each other's eyes without emotion.

"So. Are we good," he asked.

Every ounce of oxygen poured out of my lungs in one huge exhale. "Yeah, we're good."

Will smiled. "Cool."

We returned to a moment of silence, just looking at each other. I needed to let him know, though. To assure him, I said, "I'm not going to report you or anything. Or tell anybody."

Finally he smiled. Fuck me, those dimples. "Thanks." And then he added my name. "Matty." The way it sounded coming through his lips made my head spin. I wanted to hear him say my name again. I wanted to hear him repeat it over and over.

"Will," I said. "It's cool. I was just… surprised."

"Yeah," he said hesitantly. "I need to tell you something." I was suddenly confused. Need to tell me something? I mean, I already know. I saw. I watched.

"What do you mean," I asked.

"About the other night," he said, pushing his hands into the pockets of his jeans and looking down. "I..," he paused before finishing his thought. "I was on my way down here to see you."

"Oh," I said. I didn't know where he was going with this, what point he was trying to make. But whatever it was, he ended up fucking Nick, so I didn't know why it would matter that he was coming to my room.

"No. I mean, I was coming down here to tell you something. I mean, not tell you something. I was coming down here cuz I wanted to see you. I wanted to…" he trailed off.

"What?"

"I was coming down here to fuck you."

"What?" I stared at him absolutely frozen. He looked back up, and his eyes bore into me. I had no idea what to say, what to do, how to respond. It was everything I would want to hear, but I was so taken off guard, I couldn't contain my leaping heart inside my chest.

"I think I probably had a raging boner in my sweatpants thinking about you. Nick stopped me in the hall. He started chatting me up. I've never seen him without those other guys around, and he was, well I could tell, he was flirting with me. I was just so surprised, and then he just reached out and grabbed my cock, and he invited me in, and that was that, and you know what happened next. I mean, why not, right? That kid is so hot, I mean, yeah, I was all in. But I had forgotten what I had really meant to do. Why I was really down here. And I needed to tell you."

I processed what he had just lodged at me like it was data that didn't make sense to my brain. He was coming down here to fuck me? But why? What? How did he know I would want that? How did he know I wanted that? And now he was there in front of me in my room. We were alone. Mad hot Will is here in my room telling me he wanted to fuck me. I realized I still hadn't said anything back to him.

He broke the silence. I was grateful, because I still didn't know what to say. "I saw the way you looked at me when I flashed you. How you looked at my body. Your eyes got so wide. Your mouth opened. You stared at my body like you wanted to dive into that blanket with me."

Caught. That was everything that had gone through my mind.

"And then you looked at my cock," he said, and a grin spread across his face. "And I knew you wanted it. I knew you were gay. I've wondered that for so long. I... I've hoped for it for so long. I flashed you on purpose to see how you would react. And it worked. I saw the way you looked at me."

Every word that came out of his mouth was the absolute truth. He saw right through me. He saw me. He knew. He probably knew better than I did. Fuck, this hot fucking man standing in front of me. Lust and desire were bursting inside of me. He looked right into my eyes. He wouldn't look away. He didn't even blink.

Finally, I said simply, "Yes."

The grin on his face spread even wider, and his eyes widened as he looked at me with a sudden hunger, like he was about to pounce, to make me his prey. I realized my hands still gripped each edge of my robe, and as his gaze held me, I let go, and my robe eased open revealing a long, thin swath of my naked body from my neck down to my now-exposed, still-hard cock.

Will stood there another moment. I matched his grin. Finally I could admit it, and he was here, and we were alone, and this was everything I wanted right there in front of me. I nodded my head at his hand, the same way he had to me just the other night. "Lock the door," I commanded.

Will raised one eyebrow and a flat smile bloomed on his face. One side of his mouth furled up, almost in an evil look, like he wasn't happy, or like he was going to attack. I felt like his prey. Fuck, yes, if he was going to attack, I was going to surrender.

He reached back with his hands and felt for the doorknob. He turned it with a very soft click, and I was alone with him behind a locked door.

"There," he said. "Locked. Now. Drop the robe."

If he were a sorcerer, I would not be surprised. He spoke. I obeyed. My two hands took hold of the sides of my robe, pulled back until it fell of my shoulders, and I let go. It fell straight to the floor in a pile about my feet, and I stood in front of him, completely naked head to toe.

He stood there, still fully clothed. Shoes, jeans, a hoodie. I stood there completely vulnerable, completely exposed, with my hard-on sticking out at him. He just stared at me. He looked me up and down like I had when he opened that blanket just the other day. But where I saw a muscular, hard, hairy, ripped stud of a jock, his eyes were looking at my slim, smooth, waifish figure. Where my eyes on his incredible body probably felt like desperate, horny admiration, Will now standing in front of my naked body made me feel incredibly intimidated, controlled, helpless even.

He stepped forward and crossed the room with three firm paces to stand right in front of me. He eased closer still until his nose almost touch mine, and I could feel his breath on my face. He reached up and put a flattened palm directly in the middle of my torso and rubbed up then down.

He sighed, letting out so much tension, I felt it in my own body. "Oh, baby, so fucking smooth. Your skin is so soft. I knew you would have an incredible body under those clothes, but I didn't know just how hot. Fuck, not a single hair." His hand continued touring all over my chest, my stomach, and around the top of my hip. His other hand reached up and caressed my shoulder and then my neck. He was touching every inch of my body.

I reached up to put my hands on his still covered chest when he froze. He grabbed my hands in his and returned them to my side. "No. I'm not finished." I obeyed. His spell on me was complete. I would do nothing without him telling me to, without his approval.

He stepped around me, caressing and touching me all over. His fingers lingered up and down my back. A tickling sensation flowed through me, and I breathed out. He leaned in what I could tell was a smile close to my ear, and his tongue darted out and touched on my ear lobe. And then his hands made their way to the rounded orbs of my ass. He gripped each cheek very softly in each hand and rested his chin on my shoulder.

"Fuuuuuuuuck," he moaned. He was softly holding

my ass in both his hands, slowly shifting my flesh back and forth. Then a finger traced between them along the crack. One hand reached forward and pressed into my stomach. He pressed firmly against my back, and I was lost in his gripping arms. He held me firmly against his body and darted his tongue into my ear. The sensation erupted through my brain like wet lightning. How could such a thing feel so hot, so erotic. My body went limp in his arms.

He kept me there, caressing and groping my body with both his hands. I felt like his toy, his plaything, His hands moved all over my body, taking pleasure out of me. His mouth closed on the base of my neck, and he kissed me softly, his tongue on my skin. "Oh, baby," he moaned.

His hands started groping me a little harder. His rubs were deeper, engaging my muscles. He traced my stomach up and down with one hand while the other remained on my ass. Then he reached up and drew circles on one of my nipples. He took it between two fingers and squeezed. I breathed out with an audible moan, the pulse of the passionate touch coursed straight down my body to my cock, which twitched upward.

"Oh, you like that, don't you," he whispered in my ear. He squeezed harder, and I dropped my head back against his shoulder.

"Oh, fuck, yes," I could barely get words out, I felt so much desire flowing through my naked body. I felt the powerlessness of being wrapped in Will's arms, completely naked, being touched all over, not being allowed to touch him. He was still fully clothed. His hands used me for their pleasure. He was enjoying me, enjoying my body. It filled me with amazement to sense him taking such pleasure from me, from my body.

The one hand released my nipple and reached up and wrapped around the base of my neck. The hand behind me lifted off my ass, and then with a sudden shattering swing, it slapped hard against my ass letting out a cracking slap sound. I shrieked, but the pain while surprising and sudden, coursed through me like wildfire. Every nerve in my body wanted to explode with passion.

"Oh, that is a sweet ass. So round, so smooth. I bet nobody's ever touched you like this," he moaned right near my ear.

"No," I said.

"But you're letting me."

"Yes."

He turned me around in his arms, and when we were face to face, he planted his mouth on mine. His tongue immediately buried itself between my lips and invaded me. It sought out my tongue and pressed deep inside. His lips were against mine. His teeth grazed my lower lip, and I was being kissed passionately by my friend, by my hot, muscular friend. He was so in charge of me, I wondered how he knew what to do, how he could be so sure of his every move.

His hands were all over me. His mouth was pressed to mine. Finally I risked it, and without being told if I could I wrapped my arms around his shoulders and pulled him in even harder. He had one hand on the back of my neck and one hand on my bare ass. I felt like every inch of me was in his control. He had full ownership of my body.

He turned me until I felt my mattress against the backs of my legs. He urged me down, and I bent my legs until he sat me down upon my bed. Then he did something I didn't expect, and he kneeled down in front of me. My cock was hard and fully erect, sticking straight up, and now it was inches in front of his face. He leaned down and took the head between his lips. Fire erupted throughout my being as I felt the warmth of his mouth slide down my cock, and he let inch after inch of it in.

His arms wrapped around my hips, and he pulled me toward him with my cock buried in his throat. I've never felt so hard in my life. He let it slide out and back in again. I was breathing audibly and letting out gasping sighs. He reached up and again squeezed my nipple, the other one this time.

Electricity pulsed through me as the pinching pain on my nipple blended with the warm, wet silkiness of Will's mouth enveloping my cock. I threw myself backwards, and he kept going, working my body like it was his orchestra to conduct.

His hands disappeared from my body and slid into the pocket of his hoodie. Coming back out, I saw he held a white tube. Without letting my cock out of his mouth, I heard the plastic pop of a top opening. I looked down to see he was squeezing lube out on the fingers of one hand, and before I could think about what was happening, a slick finger landed right on my butthole and pressed.

There was a slight chill to the liquid, but that dissipated as his index finger urged my hole to open and let it in. It was so slicked with the lube, his finger pushed in easily. No one and nothing had ever been there before. Maybe my own finger a few times, but I didn't really think that counted.

Will continued to suck my cock as he eased his finger in and out of my ass. I was amazed by my own body, how it so willingly let him in. It knew how much I wanted this. The wet mouth sliding up and down my cock, the hard finger sliding in and out of my ass, I began to moan with sounds I never thought I would make.

Will pushed, and a second finger joined the first. Just one quick guttural sound came out of my lips, and then my body accepted the invasion. He pushed, and I moaned. He sucked, and I enjoyed it. Finally he let my cock pop out of his mouth with a suctioning sound and looked me right in the eyes with a huge smile. "You like that, baby?"

"Oh, fuck yes," I said. "Fuck yes."

He pushed a third finger against my hole. "I gotta get you nice and loose, Matty. Cuz I'm gonna fuck you."

I looked down into those insanely blue eyes. He had a massive grin on his face like he owned me, like he was in charge of my entire fucking universe. "Yes," I said. "Please."

"And I have a big cock, baby. Big and thick. And you're gonna take it all. No complaining."

I gave him a huge smile right back in complete agreement to his randy statement. "Just take it slow, please. I've never…"

He interrupted me, "Yeah, I didn't think you have."

He kept pushing his fingers into me. He added more lube. I could feel my muscle getting used to the onslaught. He started sucking my cock again for a few minutes, and then he stood up. He took one step back and peeled off the hoodie. He kicked off his sneakers and flung them across the room. They hit the back of my door with a thud and fell to the floor.

Turning back to me, he tore his t-shirt off over his head, and there it was—that incredible hairy, muscular torso. Fuck, he looked like such a man. I could only stare, even though all I wanted to do was touch him all over. I wanted his chest and his abs and that incredible deep belly button in my hands. I wanted to caress and touch him and lick him and enjoy his body.

But then he undid the button of his jeans, and my mind went right to that. The zipper went down, revealing the hair continuing south. I could see in the opening triangle of his jeans that he wore no underwear. He pulled down, and his huge cock popped out into full view. Fuck me, it was thick and hard and long. The head was full and round and made the whole thing look like a club or a baseball bat. Fuck, how was that whole thing gonna get pushed inside me?

His jeans off, Will finally stood over me also completely naked. I went to kneel on the floor with every intention of taking that massive cock into my mouth, but he pushed on my shoulder to urge me back down on my back onto the bed.

"I fucked that frat boy face down. Ass in the air. But not you, Matty. I have to look you in the eyes. This is what I want, and I have to see you for every single second of it." He reached down and turned me, so I was lengthwise along my bed on my back.

He squeezed the tube hard over his hand and let a huge gob of the slick stuff into his hand. He smeared his cock all over until it glistened brightly. Then he brought that hand between my legs and pushed it against my already-wet hole.

He pulled himself over me and kneeled between my legs. Then he pulled them up in the air, one in each hand, and rested them on his shoulders. I could see his massive, huge cock pointing right between them.

He reached down and took his cock in hand and found my wet hole. He pressed the head against me, and I

Matthew Cooper

breathed out. At first nothing happened, but he just kept the
pressure right on my button until finally my muscle obeyed
every screaming emotion as my brain begged it, *let him in
let him in*. With a firm, single push from Will, the head of
his cock finally pressed me in just the right spot and forced
its way into me. The feeling overwhelmed my brain. Will's
eyes bore into mine. His torso pressed my legs down. His
arms kept them placed on his shoulders, and they folded
until my knees practically touched my own shoulders. He
had me bent in half, and then his cock was sliding into me,
slowly, very slowly.

I breathed in and out, and Will took his time. He
knew that monster was a lot to take, and he followed the
pace of my breathing. As I inhaled, he relaxed. As I
exhaled, he pushed into me a little more. Until my ass
finally relaxed, and his hard, long, thick, cock
disappeared into me. All of it was inside me. I felt like a
champion. How did I do it? I impressed myself.

Will even looked surprised and smiled at me
admiringly. We said nothing, just stared at each other. I
could feel my ass becoming used to the invading cock. I
felt Will's hips press against my ass. He was completely
buried in me, but that didn't stop him from pressing
harder against my ass, his cock desperate to plow even
deeper into me. My mind was sent over the moon, and he
pushed and buried his cock so hard and so deep inside me,
I felt like it owned me.

He slowly pulled half of it back out of me but then
reversed and slid back down deeply to the hilt. I let out a
huge sigh and moan as my ass welcomed him in. "Fuck,
fuck, holy fuck, you're so big," I said.

"Oh, baby, you love it, don't you. Take all of it.
That's it. Give me that ass. I waited long enough." Will

started sliding in and out of me. The slick, wetness of the lube allowed it to ease in and out of me. My muscles were fully relaxed to his constant onslaught of fucking my virgin ass. Virgin no longer. He was taking me, and his cock was claiming me.

"Oh, Matty, I've wanted this for two years. I never thought it would happen. I was so sure you were straight," he admitted to me as he pounded my ass. "What took us so long to figure this out?"

His blue eyes were all I could look at. I put my arms around his upper torso and pulled him closer to me. "I thought I was the only one," I admitted. "I never thought you..," I trailed off.

He pressed his mouth against mine again and kissed me passionately while his fat cock opened me up. He started going faster. Not as fast as he was pounding Nick the other night, I could tell. It was slower and more erotic.

He was much stronger than I was, and with a quick grapple, he picked my body up off the mattress and sat me down on his cock as he rolled onto the bed. "I want to watch you ride it. That's it. Push down on it. Ride it, baby."

I put my hands on his shoulders and pulled my legs up. I was sitting down on his huge cock planted deep inside me. I lifted myself up so most of it slid out, then dropped myself down on it, faster than I had expected, and I impaled myself on it, letting out a huge shriek. "Fuck," I screamed. "Yes!"

Gripping his shoulders, I started bouncing on his cock. In and out of me. Deeper and deeper, faster and faster. My ass was milking him. Will looked at me with amazement in his eyes. "Oh baby, do it. Fuck yourself with my cock."

My hands were on his shoulders. His hands were gripping my back as I rode him like a desperate whore. I wanted his cock in me forever. I wanted to be owned, fucked, used. I was breathing heavy and sweating. I looked down at Will's body. He was so fucking hot, I couldn't take it anymore. I reached down and started stroking my own cock while riding his.

He watched as I jerked myself off. He was buried inside me over and over. He leaned in and took one of my nipples into his mouth and started to chew on it. I couldn't take anymore, but neither could Will. He was breathing heavier with every moment. And then I let out a moan that took me over the edge, and at the same moment, Will gasped. We looked into each other's eyes.

My cock exploded all over his hairy chest, and at the same exact moment, Will grunted loudly, and I felt his cock spasm inside me. Gush after gush erupted from my cock as I felt Will's cock pulse again and again inside me.

Sweat covered me. Sweat and my cum covered Will. I leaned over, and he gently held my body in his arms as I laid down beside him and collapsed onto the mattress. He wrapped me in his arms and kissed me hard.

We fell asleep in each other's arms. He held me in front of him, fully wrapped up in his arms with his firm, hairy chest pressed against my back. I'd never felt safer. I slept soundly blanketed by his body in the deeply silent dorm.

No fire alarms woke us, but at 2AM, I was still jarred out of my deep slumber. But this time it was to the feeling of his hard, fat, thick, long cock, rubbing down the middle of my ass. Will woke up, too, and started sliding it more and more. I grabbed the lube and handed it to him. "Round two," I suggested.

Will fucked me again that night, and when we woke in the morning, he pinned me facedown like he had Nick, and I told him to fuck me like he did that frat boy. My face buried in the pillowcase, Will pounded me good and hard. My round, smooth ass was more than happy to take it over and over.

When we looked at the clock, I remembered I had to get going to head home for the holidays. Will did, too, so he dressed and found his shoes near my door. "So," he said finally. "See you after the holidays, I guess."

"I sure hope so," I smiled.

Will came over to me and wrapped me in his arms one last time. "I waited two years to do this. We've got one semester left. When we get back from break, we're going to have to make up for a lot of lost time." He reached around and groped my ass firmly.

He finally let go and turned to the door. He smiled at me and touched my face with the back of his hand. "Ok, I should go," he whispered.

He grabbed the doorknob and turned. He pulled, but the door didn't budge. He pulled on it again. "It's locked," I said.

A Mouth Is a Mouth

Emily had just texted Jay. He looked at his phone, and he smiled. It was just what he was hoping for.

Billy asked if you want to come with us to the party. Say you'll come.

Was she serious? Say you'll come? Nothing would keep Jay away from attending the end of year party thrown by the wildest, musclehead fraternity on campus. Sure, there was the chance he'd have the crap beaten out of him or one of the senior members of the frat might tell Billy to get rid of the theater queen. He knew it wasn't his typical crowd, but ever since his best friend Emily started dating the hot, stud, frat boy Billy, he found himself a third wheel with them or going to parties or hanging out with a crowd he wouldn't typically be welcomed into.

And for the most part, even the meatheadiest of Billy's friends were always nothing but nice to him, but he'd never been invited into the belly of the beast—the frat house. Where he would be outnumbered about 30 to one.

While he deep down inside fantasized about all the crazy hot, frat jocks all living in a house together, he knew it wasn't a place where a gay, theater major was going to be welcomed with open arms. As hot as they all were, these guys were not known for their stimulating conversation, interest in the arts, or openness to gay guys like him.

But nothing was going to keep him away from being tossed into a shark tank full of hotness, even if he might get devoured.

Of course I'll come. Wouldn't miss it!

Emily and he were finishing their sophomore years. This end of year was special. When they returned in the fall, they would be upperclassmen. It sucked for Em, because Billy was a senior, and he was graduating, but he didn't think their relationship would really last anyway, though he would never say that to her.

Sure, he knew exactly what she saw in Billy. He was hot as fuck. His body was insane, bulging muscles, gorgeous face, and he got Emily into all the hottest and best parties, since he belonged to the most popular frat. So yeah, he knew what she saw in the guy, but still, he wasn't particularly the brightest bulb, and it was slightly painful trying to come up with conversation with him, but Jay still didn't mind having him around. While he knew he could never hook up with this hot, raging stud, he could at least fantasize about it when he jerked off. And that was good enough.

Promise me I'm not going to get beat up, he texted Emily.

After a very long pause, three dots finally appeared on his screen. *You'll be fine. They're really nice guys. And besides aren't all frats kinda gay?*

Not really! Most frats are testosterone filled houses where gays like me get beat up.

He knew he was being dramatic. And the truth was the idea of being cast into a frat house full of drinking frat boys partying and celebrating the end of the school year sounded more like a golden opportunity to find one willing to experiment or try something new. And he hoped that something new they'd want to do would be him.

* * *

Later that night Jay was trying on shirts in front of the mirror. He knew he was going to be the skinniest, scrawniest guy at the party, and no one was going to care about what he was wearing, but he still wanted to look good. Even if all the meathead frat boys were in sweatpants and sports jerseys, Jay was still gonna look good.

He finally landed on a gold button-down shirt with a shiny thread woven in. It glittered in the light, and he loved it. He opted for no shirt underneath and left four buttons undone, so the middle of his chest was fully visible. When he leaned over, almost his entire chest came into view. He turned sideways and looked at his own ass. Round and well-stuffed into his tight jeans, he thought to himself, *fuck I look good.*

And he did. The gold threads in the shirt brought out the shine of his soft, blond hair. He kept it a few inches longer than he used to so that it had a little movement to it. And it fell to the sides of his face, framing out his sparkling green eyes and the permanent rosiness in the pale skin of his cheeks.

My little angel, his mother used to say. Or as his geekier friend Eric would always say, "If you were in the Rings movies, you'd definitely be an elf." None of it, he knew, was something that a frat boy was going to notice, so he just shrugged at his reflection in the mirror as his phone dinged.

Ready to go? Meeting Billy there.

Yep. Meet you downstairs.

The dorms were co-ed, but full floors were one gender only, so Jay was on one floor, Emily on another. When he got down to the lobby, she was already there. She looked gorgeous in a short, white strapless dress. Jay always wondered how those dresses stayed up, but he didn't care enough to ever ask. He never really concerned himself much with women's fashion or, well, women for that matter.

"Wow, you look sexy as fuck, Em," he said. He knew she would appreciate that.

"Well, thank you. And look at you, Mr. Sparkly. Love the shirt."

"Too much," he asked. Mr. Sparkly was not exactly the right vibe for a frat house party.

"No," Emily shrieked. "You look amazing."

Jay just rolled his eyes. "Yeah, but I will stick out like a sore thumb in a sea of gray sweatpants I bet."

Emily nudged him, "You know I love gray sweatpants."

"Who doesn't?"

* * *

Jay and Emily walked off campus onto the streets of the surrounding neighborhood. It was a short five-minute walk to a side street tucked away behind the back gate where a long row of giant, old Victorians stood one after the other. The town called it Devon Drive, but decades ago, most of the houses were bought up by the various campus fraternities and sororities, and it was commonly referred to by the students as Frat Row.

Billy's frat was the third house down, but they could already hear music and voices and the general cacophony of a party in full swing. All the other frat houses stood dark and empty. Everyone, even other frat and sororities, must be at this one crazy party.

Stepping up on the porch, they were already pushing

their way through an enormous crowd of bodies. "Come, on," Emily said loudly leaning close to Jay's ear. "Let's find Billy."

"And a drink," he added. Emily nodded back to him.

They wound in through the living room, found the kitchen. It was packed with people all trying to get drinks. There was a keg with a huge ring of dudes all waiting their turn with an empty red, plastic cup in hand. There was an enormous punchbowl with a bright, red liquid in it. Jay knew from experience that would be a recipe for disastrous inebriation.

Emily was squeezing into the back of the kitchen where the counter was covered with bottles. Her hand appeared extended back toward him with a cup in it. He accepted it, but rather than join her in trying to put together a mixed drink with the vodkas and rums and other options on the counter, he decided to join the bustling ring of guys around the keg.

He was outmuscled by every single guy there, and as new ones joined the crush, he lost his place in any semblance of a turn based on how long each guy was waiting to pour himself a beer from the tap. He knew he had to be a little more forceful.

He pushed in a little more firmly in between two thick muscular shoulders. The guy to his left turned his head and looked down at Jay who was a good four, maybe five, inches shorter than most of the guys pushing toward the keg. For a minute Jay didn't know if he was gonna get pushed backward or punched.

Jay looked up at the guy. *Fuck, he's hot*, Jay thought in his mind. The muscles were one thing, but the big, round brown eyes looking down at him were warm and bright. The hair was buzzed to barely a scruff across the entire well-built head. He looked like he might be ROTC. His firm, strong, muscular arm wrapped around Jay's shoulder.

"Boys, boys, come on. My little buddy here has been waiting. Let him in. Here gimme," the hot muscle stud started shouting. He put his own red cup between his teeth and grabbed the tap from another guy. Turning to Jay he pointed the tap at him. Jay lifted his cup, and with his arm still wrapped around his shoulders, the guy poured Jay his beer right to the rim of the glass. He removed his arm from around Jay to pour himself some beer. Jay felt the loss of its weight on his body and missed it immediately.

"Thank you," Jay said and stepped back away from the feeding frenzy.

The guy turned, too. "Hey, no problem. Who are you?"

"Uh, thanks. Jay, I'm Jay. I came with Emily." The guy looked at him confused. "Billy's Emily."

"Oh no way. Em. She's here," he looked around the room to see Emily pouring her own drink. "Em!" He called. She turned her head and nodded at him. "Any friend of Em," he said and held his cup up for Jay to tap his against in a cheers.

"Dude, that shirt, though, that's kinda gay."

Jay was instantly offended by the comment. He knew this was the moment he would get tossed or pummeled, but he didn't care. "Well, I am gay, so," he snapped.

"Oh, nah, dude, I didn't mean it like that. I was just kidding," the guy objected. "But hey, you're gay, and you got style, so technically I was right then. It's a gay shirt, right?" Jay couldn't stay angry, because this guy's warm eyes were full of what seemed like a boyish innocence, and those big lips looked so inviting while he spoke.

Jay laughed, and the guy joined him. "It's cool," he said. "And yeah, I guess it is a little gay."

To Jay's utter surprise, the guy reached out and took a hold of the top of the shirt. He caressed the fabric up and down where the buttons lay open over Jay's bare chest before pressing it down against his skin and rubbing it into place. Jay felt the hand on the contour of his modest but still there chest muscles. "Nah, it's nice. It's really nice." With a pat of his hand on Jay's chest, he said, "I'm Nate. Nice to meet you." And before Jay could say anything in response, the hot, muscular frat boy had turned and stepped away into the crowd.

To himself, Jay said, "Yeah. Nice to meet you. Too."

He sipped his beer, which was surprisingly cold, and waited for Emily to rejoin him with a full drink in her hand. They ventured out into the crowd to find Billy.

* * *

The party raged on and on into the night. Jay was, as he had expected, pretty much ignored by the frat boys and the sorority girls. None of his friends were there. He recognized a few faces from campus and from random classes, but no one he was familiar enough with to strike up a casual conversation. And he was just shy enough that he wouldn't approach total strangers in a party situation. So he relegated himself to wandering around with Emily and Billy as a third wheel. He hated that, and as the hours wore on, he felt more and more like he didn't really belong there.

"Em," he called out to her over the loud music. "You need a refresh?"

She shook her head and pointed at her full glass.

"Billy, you good?" he asked.

Billy didn't hear him, so Emily answered for him. Looking in his cup, she said, "He's good."

Jay nodded his head in the direction of the kitchen and separated from them, making his way back to the keg. The party had been going for so long, there wasn't as many bodies cramming into the small space. Everyone seemed to still be drinking, and the party was still in full swing, but the refills were becoming more infrequent.

As he approached the keg, his body was hit from behind with another body, bigger and stronger. Arms reached across him from above his shoulders and got to the hose coming out of the top of the keg before he could grab it. He felt pushed forward by the bigger someone behind him, and then he heard, "Buddy. Buddy Boy. Jay the Gay!"

Turning around, he found Nate with a big grin on his face. He looked happy and a little tipsy. "Oh. Hey Nate."

"I got it, I got it," he protested to Jay and pointed the tap at the cup in Jay's hand. "Here. You need a freshie."

"Uh, yeah, thanks," Jay said as Nate pointed the tap into his cup. But they were met with a swooshing sound, and nothing came out.

"Fuck me," Nate said annoyed. "Come on."

He tried for several seconds before Jay said, "I think it's tapped out."

Nate threw it down, "Well, fuck that. I probably didn't need another beer any way."

Jay laughed and looked at Nate's face. Yeah, he seemed in a good mood and maybe a little tipsy, but not messy. "Probably a good time to stop."

Nate tossed the tap onto the top of the keg. "Ah, fuck it. Come on. Come on. You should meet the boys." He grabbed Jay's arm and pulled him toward the other room. He kept his hand wrapped around Jay's wrist as he led him through the room full of bodies.

Left and right, in between this group and that one,

Nate pulled Jay to a sliding glass door and out to a dark backyard. There on a patio were three or four other guys. Jay swallowed hard, worried about fitting in. He looked around. *Fuck me*, he thought, *one hotter than the next*.

There were two guys that could have been twins sitting on an outdoor wicker couch. They had taken their shirts off. Their muscular chests were completely hairless and bulging round and hard. Their abs were obvious even sitting down.

Another guy was standing beside the couch. Jay looked up to see a monster of a dude. He was around 6'2 and a mountain of muscle. Jay immediately thought he must be on the football team or something.

"Dudes, dudes," Nate announced.

"Nate the Eight," one of the two shirtless sitters shouted. "Where the fuck were you?"

"The fucking keg is completely tapped. Dudes. This fucking sucks. But hey, this is my boy Jay. Say hello."

The two half-naked frat boys on the couch both said, "Hey." The tall standing guy, though, actually turned to Jay and smiled. He extended a hand to shake, and Jay reached out to accept it.

"Hey Jay. Where'd you come from? I'm Alex."

"Nice to meet you. I, um, came with Emily."

Nate immediately added for him, "Billy's Emily."

"Oh yeah, cool," Alex said.

One of the two shirtless guys had stood up and came closer. "Nate, Nate, answer me this." Jay turned to take notice of this guy. He wasn't much taller than Jay, which surprised him. "Why are all these bitches so fucking stuck up, huh? Why?"

Nate had a hand pounding him in the chest. "Dude, I don't know. Fucked if I know."

The guy turned to Jay, "Dude, do you know? I mean, look at me." He flexed his arms, and when he did, he spilled a large splash of his beer on the ground. "Look at me. Dude."

Jay looked. The guy was so hot, Jay didn't know what to say or do. But he was told to look, so he looked. His skin was so smooth. His muscles were so incredibly well-rounded, Jay wanted nothing more than to reach out and grope the short guy in front of him.

"I'm hot, man. I'm fucking hot as fucking hot. I'm a fucking gymnast, man. So why won't any of these stuck-up bitches let me fuck them?" He was lodging all of his complaints at Jay now.

"I mean, I don't know, man," Jay managed.

"It's fucked, dude." The guy turned to go back to his seat.

But Nate interjected. "Fucking teases, dude. You know that."

Alex was shaking his head. Jay didn't know whether it was in agreement or in disgust at his friend's rather uncouth commentary. Jay figured it was probably in support of the complaint.

Nate was leaning in close to Jay's head. "Sorry about that. They're a little drunk."

"It's cool," Jay said. "It's kinda funny." Then he added to the group. "Wait, so you guys can't get laid? I mean you're all in frats. We common folk always assume frat guys are getting it all the time."

The two on the couch let out a whispering *pssh* sound and rolled their eyes. Alex looked forlorn but added, "Maybe Nate gets all the pussy he wants but not the rest of us."

Nate objected, "You know that's not true."

The other shirtless guy on the couch finally joined

the conversation, "Well maybe if you didn't rip every girl in half when you fuck them, you'd get more pussy."

Nate smiled at that, "What can I say? I'm blessed."

Jay's eyes widened. "Wait, is that why he called you Nate the Eight?"

Alex was nodding. The other two looked jealous. Nate just smiled and tilted his head with a smile on his face. Jay's mind leapt into the night sky. His thoughts just kept going through his mind over and over. *I want to see it. I want to see it. I want to see it.*

The two on the couch stood up. They looked more like twins than ever as Jay noticed they were both about the same height, same build, same completely hairless muscle bodies. He realized they were both probably gymnasts.

"Come on," one said to the other. "Let's see what else they got to drink if the beer's out." And they ventured back in the house. Alex followed them, leaving Nate and Jay alone together.

Jay hoped with every fiber in his being that Nate wouldn't walk away. Instead Nate spoke, "Dude, you're really gay?"

Jay was happy the conversation was going in that direction. "Uh, yeah. Why?"

"Just like, you don't like pussy at all, man? That's so crazy."

Jay laughed. "Uh, yeah, that pretty much comes with the territory, not liking pussy."

"Yeah, but I mean, you like dick, man?"

"Guilty as charged," Jay joked and immediately felt like a dork.

Nate was shaking his head, "Man, I just don't get it. Like how one dude can like pussy, and another dude just wants the D. Me I could never do that." Jay was crestfallen with that comment. He was hoping this would have gone a completely different direction.

"Well, what can I say? I didn't choose to be…"

"Oh, no, no, dude, no. I didn't mean that. Fuck no. Just it's funny. I mean, you don't like chicks at all? Like 100% full 'mo?"

"Yeah, pretty much," Jay said. He hesitated but then dared it. "How about you then? Full on hetero?"

Nate hesitated. Jay's mind immediately opened up with anticipation. No matter what the answer, the hesitation turned him on like crazy. "Well, I mean, yeah. I love chicks. And I mean, I love my boys, but not in that way. I just don't think I could ever, you know, do anything with another dude's dick."

Jay knew with every comment, he was risking a full-on gay bashing, but he couldn't help himself. This Nate guy was comfortable enough talking to him all alone here, he had to try, "Well, sure. Maybe you wouldn't want another dude's cock, but you know what they say, a mouth is a mouth, right?"

Nate stood there. Big, strong, muscle stud frat boy Nate suddenly froze right there in place. Jay couldn't breathe. What did he just do? Should he add something else to his comment? Should he burst out in a laugh to let Nate know he was kidding? He found himself frozen in place, too.

Nate was thinking. He could tell. "I don't know. You mean, like, let a dude suck me off? I don't think I could watch that."

Jay thought, well fuck it, I'm down the road already, I might as well, "Who said you'd have to watch?"

Nate froze all over again. Jay braced for a fist to the face, but it didn't come. "I think I need another drink," Nate said and disappeared back into the house.

103

"Fuck," Jay said, shaking his head. "What the fuck am I doing?" He went back in to find Emily. At least if he was gonna die, he could be standing next to his friend.

* * *

Jay found Emily in the living room. Billy was beside her but engaged in a heated argument about the beer situation.

Emily said, "You about ready? I kinda want to leave before it gets too messy."

"Yeah, I should probably go, too," Jay said.

Emily pecked Billy on the cheek who protested for a split second about her leaving *so early* before turning away into the crowd. The pair made their way out the front door and onto the porch. They stepped down to the front walk, and there leaning against a tree in the yard, Jay saw Nate.

Nate turned to look at them. "Hey Em," he said.

"Oh hey, Nate," she said walking up to him. "Do you know Jay?"

Nate stuttered, "Uh, yeah. We um…"

Jay finished the sentence for him, "We met inside."

"You walking back to campus?" the muscular guy asked.

"Yeah," Emily said.

"I'll walk you back," he offered.

"Oh, you don't have to," she said. "Don't you live here in the house? And I've got Jay here to protect me."

Nate said, "No, I live in the dorms. Come on, I'll walk with you. Never can be too safe, right?"

Emily smiled, "Well, sure. We're all going the same direction, right?"

The three took off through the front gate and down the street. Jay was speechless. He had no idea what to say. They made it to the rear gate of campus, walked through, and made their way down the sidewalk through the quadrangle that led to the dorm.

Emily filled the silence, "So Nate, you a sophomore, too?"

"Yeah, we'll be juniors next year. Kinda exciting," he said.

"What are you studying," Jay finally found something to ask.

"Finance," Nate answered. Then added, "You guys?"

Emily responded faster, "I'm an art major. Jay's in theater."

But Jay corrected her, "Speech and Communication with a minor in theater."

"That's a mouthful," Nate said.

* * *

They made it into the dorm building and into the elevator. Jay hit the '3' button for his floor, and Emily hit the '2' for hers. Nate didn't hit one. Jay took specific notice of that. When the elevator opened on the second floor, Emily kissed Jay's cheek and said, "Good night, Jay. Good night, Nate. Nice seeing you."

"Night, Em," Jay said. The door closed, and again he found himself alone with Nate. This time in the close confines of an elevator, they stood side by side silent. Jay's heart pounded so hard, he was surprised they couldn't hear it. When the door opened on the third floor, he took a step out, and Nate did, too.

He froze there in the elevator lobby of his dorm

floor. The elevator door closed behind them. Jay looked up at the taller guy. Nate shoved his hands into his pockets before saying animatedly, ignoring any tension that Jay was feeling, "You tired? I'm not tired, are you? You're not going to bed, are you?"

Jay stammered, "Uh, no not really."

"Cool, cool," Nate said then lowered his head and looked at the floor. In a tone that tried desperately to sound nonchalant, he added, "Why don't we hang in your room?"

Jay was exploding inside. "Yeah, sure, that's cool." Cool? It was fucking mind-blowingly awesome. He walked down the hall to his door and pulled out his key.

He turned his head back to see Nate following behind him, head still facing straight down at the floor, hands buried in his pockets. His shoulders were rounded down, and he looked like a shy. little boy suddenly.

Jay turned the key in the door and suddenly thought about his roommate. *Please don't be home, please don't be home, please for the love of all fucks please don't be home*. The door opened.

His roommate wasn't home.

Nate followed him into the room. Jay tossed his keys on the desk on his side of the room. "Have a seat," he gestured toward the chair at his desk. But Nate stepped past it and sat down on the small bed.

"You want a bottle of water," Jay asked, but Nate didn't answer. He was met with silence, so he bent down to open the small cube refrigerator anyway.

"So is it true," Nate finally said. Jay was confused.

"Is what true?"

"What you said? Is it true? That a mouth is just a mouth?" Jay almost fell over. He gasped and let out a joyous breath.

"Well, yeah. Feels the same no matter who's doing it. Right?"

Nate looked up. *Fuck*, Jay thought, *he's so fucking hot*. They stared right into each other's eyes for a brief minute, but Nate broke the link first, looking away. He turned to the side and grabbed Jay's pillow. He slunk back quickly and sharply. He pushed his legs out further into the room and spread his legs.

He slid all the way down, so he was lying back across the bed sideways. When his head hit the mattress, he pulled the pillow over his own head, covering it completely. From under the pillow, he mumbled, "Is it OK if I don't watch?"

Jay almost dropped the two water bottles in his hands. His cock leapt to full attention in his pants, and his breath poured out of him over and over. Oh my fucking fuck, his mind was leaping in somersaults. He didn't say a word.

He walked over to the frat dude lying on his bed, face covered. Standing between the spread legs, he knelt on the floor. He reached up and caressed Nate's crotch. His hand instantly felt the very large bulge of what lay hidden in the jeans. He rubbed and rubbed again. Nate let out a huge sigh.

Jay let his hands disappear under Nate's shirt and felt his washboard stomach. Just a small little tuft of hair lined the center of it. He reached up further and found the huge round orbs of Nate's pecs. He put his hands all over them, feeling the soft, smoothness of the muscular guy's flesh. He squeezed a nipple softly and heard Nate moan into his pillow.

Reaching back down, he undid the button of the jeans, then the zipper. Oh he was going to take care of this stud completely. He pulled the sides of the jeans along Nate's hips. Nate got the message and pulled his ass up off the mattress slightly so the jeans could slide down. Jay kept pulling until they were around his ankles and left them there. This was not going to be a get naked together cuddle fest, he knew that.

Nate wore red boxers. Jay put his hand back to Nate's crotch and felt a long, not a very long shaft. With his other hand, he reached under and palmed a sizable pair of balls. Cupping them and very softly moving them back and forth, his other hand sensed a rise. What was already a long cock came to life and started getting even longer.

He couldn't stand it any longer. He had to see it. He gripped the elastic and pulled the boxers down. Nate again obliged, lifting his weight. As Jay pushed them down the thighs, Nate's cock came into view. Mother fucker, Jay thought. Holy shit. A huge cock sat before his eyes. Thick, fat, long, a massive head, slightly browner than Nate's light beige body.

Jay gripped it in his hand to lift it up erect and straight up. His eyes widened. His mind started estimating. Fuck yeah, this is Nate the Eight. Maybe more. He leaned forward and took the big fat head between his lips.

When he darted his tongue out to lick it, Nate let out a moaning *ahhh*. Jay had to lift himself up a little to get the whole cock in position in front of his mouth and then opening wide, he pressed down, letting the cock slowly slide into his mouth. He had to open wide for the girth of it, and he loved every inch as he slid down on it.

He looked up. Nate's arms were pressed firmly on top of the pillow holding it against his face. He was not watching. Was he pretending Jay was a chick? No doubt.

No chick would do as good as I'm about to, he thought.

The cock between his lips began to disappear deeper into his mouth. It was huge, and he didn't know if he was going to be able to deep-throat it all the way, but he was going to try his hardest.

He gripped Nate's hips and pushed down. He felt the head of the massive cock hit the back of his throat, but he wanted more. There was still an inch or two to go. He pushed. He'd reached the back of his throat, but he pressed on, and finally his throat opened up, and the last two inches disappeared as he fought any gag reflex that may have come up. His nose hit the flesh above Nate's cock. It was buried to the hilt down his throat, and he was loving it. He kept it there.

After a moment, unable to breathe with the massive cock inside him, he finally had to lift off it. He coughed a little as it came out, and he took a moment to breathe, but he wanted it back inside. He immediately went right back down on it.

He slid it in and out, pressing all the way down each time. His mouth started getting wetter and wetter, and the cock shaft gleamed with his spit coating it. Slicked up, it eased in and out of his mouth. He started going a little faster, sucking a little more. His hands reached back up, and he caressed the amazing muscles of Nate's torso.

He saw Nate's arms relax. Yeah, he was loving it. Jay did not stop sucking the enormous cock, up and down, in and out, again and again. He rubbed Nate's abs and pecs. And then he reached over and squeezed a nipple again. Nate let out a huge moan. Yeah, he liked that.

Jay reached over with his other hand and squeezed both nipples at the same time. Nate almost screamed out a moan as Jay pushed down and deep-throated the huge cock. He tried to squeeze his throat a little more before pulling back off.

He kept sucking and sucking. He squeezed Nate's nipples. He reached down and cupped his balls. Pulling his lips off the cock, he put his tongue on the huge balls. He was surprised they were so smooth. So it was true. Straight guys were shaving their pubes, too. He wet them up with his tongue then let one slide into his mouth. He sucked very softly, then he went to the other one.

They were huge balls, but he tried and succeeded in drawing both of them into his mouth while he stroked Nate's enormous cock. He could not believe how big it was. What was wrong with these girls on campus? Why wouldn't they be dying to suck this cock, to get fucked by it? He knew he would love it if Nate would pound his ass. But he knew not to ask, and he loved sucking it.

He went back to the cock. Holding it in both hands, he kept it up straight and went back down on it with his mouth. He began to slide it in and out of his mouth again and again. His spit was flowing, and the cock was drenched. He didn't want to stop. He kept sucking it in and out of his mouth, milking it.

Nate was moaning like mad. It was a sound of pure ecstasy. Jay was delivering a world class professional cock sucking. Even as big as it was, he was so proud of himself for getting it planted deep into his throat again and again.

How did this night end up so wildly perfect? This was everything he could have fantasized about. He wanted it to last forever. Nate was still moaning. Jay was still sucking. He reached up to squeeze the nipples again. He could tell this straight boy loved that. They just don't know it. Straight girls never pay attention to a guy's nipples.

Nate stopped moaning. Jay looked up. Nate's arms came down off the pillow. Jay kept sucking, squeezing, servicing. He pulled up and held just the head in his mouth. Fuck, it was a big round head. He licked it while holding it in one hand.

He saw Nate's hands take a hold of the pillow, and then he pulled it to the side, revealing his face. Jay looked up. Nate's eyes were closed, but then he opened them and looked down at Jay.

Jay kept the cock in his mouth and slid halfway down on it. He met Nate's gaze, looked him right in the eyes. The straight boy was watching him suck his cock. What was he thinking? Jay's cock grew even harder in his pants. He could feel the precum all over dripping like crazy.

He pushed down on the cock again. He wanted Nate to see his entire giant cock disappear down his throat. He pushed fast and opened his throat, accepting the entire length deeply. Nate let out a huge sigh and then gasped, "Fuuuuuck."

Jay looked back up. Nate had a huge grin on his face. And the straight boy who a moment ago wouldn't even look at him, reached down with one hand and caressed his cheek. He pressed the back of his hand against Jay's face and then spread his fingers out and threaded them through his blond hair. With a little urge of that hand, he pushed Jay back down on his cock and let out another deep sign. Yeah, he liked it.

Jay kept sucking. *Man, can this boy last a long time*, he thought. He didn't mind at all. He was so happy about it. Jay was never happier than on his knees with a cock down his throat. And what a cock this was. And on a straight boy.

Then Nate leaned up. Jay didn't expect it. But with the bend of the torso beneath his head, he was pushed away from the cock. Nate leaned over and put both of his hands on Jay's sides. He gripped his shirt and pulled it up. Jay lifted his arms, and Nate pulled the shirt off his body.

Kneeling there now shirtless, Jay looked up at the muscular frat boy. Nate reached down and put his hands on Jay's chest. He rubbed. He gripped under his arms and squeezed his torso. He reached down along his sides, feeling the width of his slim waist. He reached up and put a hand on his neck. With his other hand, he returned the favor and squeezed Jay's nipple. The hand on his neck reached up, and a finger slid into Jay's mouth. He sucked it and closed his eyes.

"Stand up," Nate ordered. Jay was fully compliant. He knew he'd do anything Nate wanted. He stood.

Nate reached up and undid the button of Jay's jeans. He pulled the zipper down and then ordered, "Take them off." Jay was so surprised, he let out a gasp, but of course, he listened. He pushed his shoes off then peeled off the jeans.

Jay's cock was still hard as a rock. It was so hard it was almost sore. Nate just grabbed the small briefs Jay wore and yanked them down without a second thought. All the way to the floor he shoved them down in one fast motion. Jay's cock bounced up. Wet and hard, it dripped on the floor.

Nate looked at it. He was surprising even himself. He didn't touch it, but he reached up and gripped Jay's hips.

"Well, yours isn't that much smaller."

"Uh," Jay protested. "Yeah, it is."

Nate looked up at Jay as he stood and smiled, "True. But it's not small."

Jay didn't know what to say. Was Nate going to… no, he wouldn't *return the favor*, would he? Jay really didn't think so, but Nate was staring at his cock, and it was inches away from his face. It was almost like he was thinking about it. But then Jay saw a change in Nate's face. Yeah, maybe he had thought about it for a split second there.

"You want to finish your job," he asked.

Jay just nodded. Nate just leaned back on the bed.

Jay kneeled down and went back to work. Nate's cock was down his throat in one thrust. He started sliding it in and out of his mouth, slamming it with vigor deep into his throat.

Nate moaned and moaned. "Oh yeah, baby. Suck it."

Jay did. He put his hands on Nate's abs. He thought, if this is gonna be a one-time only thing, I'm gonna enjoy the feel of this body.

His spit was pouring out over the huge cock in his throat. His eyes began to water. He reached one hand down and started stroking himself.

Nate grabbed his head and started pulling him up and down on his cock. Nate was taking charge of it. Jay let him. And then he was being face-fucked. "Oh yeah, baby, that's it."

With both hands still gripping Jay's head, Nate stood up. He put one hand under Jay's chin, and the other pressed against the back of his skull. Nate started pistoning his cock in and out of Jay's mouth. Jay's other hand fell useless at his sides as he vigorously jerked himself off while his mouth was used by the hot frat boy.

113

Nate pulled his huge cock out of Jay's mouth and gripped it in his hands. "Look at me," he ordered.

Jay opened his eyes. Nate had his giant cock pointed right at his face, and he was jerking it hard and fast. Nate stared right into his eyes. A huge grin on his face. The cock was locked on target, and Jay knew what Nate wanted.

"You like that, don't you?" Nate rasped down at him.

"Yes."

"You want it?"

"Yes."

"Yeah, you're gonna be my cocksucker from now, aren't you?"

"Yes."

With that, Nate let out a huge moan. Jay closed his eyes just in time, and the giant cock let out blast after blast after blast of cum that exploded all over his face. White jizz coated him. It kept on, shot after shot. Jay couldn't believe how much cum was erupting all over him. Nate's cock was still convulsing and shooting out warm jizz as Jay felt it starting to pour down his neck.

Finally Nate stopped pulling, and his cock stopped erupting. Jay was absolutely drenched in cum. He had loved it so much, he realized his own cock had erupted untouched. His load of cum was shot out all over the floor between his legs.

There was cum all over his forehead. It was in his hair. His cheeks both had a stream flowing down. His neck was coated, and now it was reaching down all over his chest. He looked up at Nate who had a huge grin on his face.

"Fuck, that's so hot."

Jay smiled up at him. Nate reached down and smeared a hand through the cum dripping down Jay's face. He pushed his fingers into Jay's mouth, who opened up and sucked them in. Nate rubbed them around his mouth before pulling them out again.

Nate pulled his pants up. Jay was still kneeling at his feet, but Nate put a hand on his shoulder. "No, don't move. Stay right there." He then repeated himself, "Fuck, that's so hot."

Jay eased back so Nate could get a better look at his neck and chest.

"Fuck," Nate said. "You're right. No girl's ever gonna do that for me. Not like that." He pulled out his cellphone and added, "What's your number?"

Jay related his number, and Nate entered it into his phone.

"I lied to you, you know. I don't live in the dorm," Nate admitted.

Jay laughed. "Yeah, I figured that out."

"OK, I'm gonna go. You stay right there. OK?"

"OK."

"I'm gonna call you. OK?"

"OK."

Jay just nodded. Nate smiled and stepped out from in front of him. He went to the door. He opened it and was gone. Jay grabbed a towel and wiped up his cum from the floor. His face, neck, chest, he was still drenched in Nate's cum as it slowly dried on him, but he didn't want to wipe it off. Just then his phone dinged. On the screen he saw a text message from a new number that said simply, *Nate*.

Jay turned the light off and got into bed. He texted back, *Jay*. He fell asleep smelling of cum with a huge smile on his tired lips.

Truth or Dare

Ted sat on a couch in the living room of Rebecca and Olivia's off-campus apartment wondering where everyone was. They'd been talking up their party for weeks. Rebecca and he had been 'a thing' since the beginning of the semester, so he knew he had been expected to show up early to help them get ready for the party. They said the party would start at 9:00 and go all night, but as Ted looked down at his watch, he saw it was 9:45, and no one had shown up yet. He wondered if he should be feeling bad for the girls, but they didn't seem concerned.

"So," he finally ventured. "Didn't you tell everyone the party starts at 9:00?"

"Oh, Ted, chill out," Olivia immediately responded. "Nobody shows up to a party on time. They'll get here."

Ted didn't really care, except that he was incredibly bored. Rebecca didn't need his help at all. A keg of beer was delivered hours before. They had bags and bags of snacks on the kitchen table ready to be tossed into bowls once the partygoers arrived. Music was queued up. Coolers were filled with ice, and bottles of heavier alcohol and mixers were stacked on the counter along with piles of big, red plastic cups. There was vodka, rum, tequila, seltzer, cranberry juice, triple sec, a giant handle

116

of sour mix, even a giant bowl full of sliced lemons and limes, the girls had thought of everything.

He looked around at the huge two-bedroom apartment filled with nice furniture and décor. *Must be nice coming from money*, he thought. Rebecca's lawyer daddy and Olivia's dermatologist father ensured these girls lived in a level of luxury most students on campus would die for. Ted had survived the last three and a half years in the crappy cinderblock dormitories, sharing a claustrophobic room with another guy every year. He was so eager for the end of this, his senior year, so he could get a job and get on with his life.

Ted was a stellar student, and he knew he'd grab a great job in the city once he graduated. But college wasn't really the four years of debauchery and partying that he had always heard it would be. Every trip home, his overly eager father would grill him with 100 questions. What girls was he hooking up with? What amazing parties was he going to? Was he, as his father always put it, sewing his wild oats? He had no idea what that meant, but whatever it was, he figured he probably was not doing it.

While Ted was technically considered by everyone as 'Rebecca's boyfriend,' and they were 'seeing each other,' if he were really honest with himself, he just did not feel it. Sure, she was rich and hot and nice, but when they were alone and slouched on this very couch together on many an evening through the last semester, they would inevitably start making out and groping each other. And Ted would feel nothing. There would be no butterflies in his stomach, no desire and lust erupting in his mind, and definitely no stirring in his pants. He thought he knew why, but he just couldn't seem to admit it, not even to himself.

He sat back down on the couch alone while the girls went to their bedrooms, probably to reapply makeup for the third or fourth time or look at themselves in the mirror again. And sure enough, Olivia called out, "Bec, do you think I should wear a dress? How about my red one? It's so hot."

"Oh my gahd, no," Rebecca called from her room to the other. "It's a party not a prom. No dresses. That tank is perfect. Your tits look amazing. Don't they, Ted?"

Ted was mortified to be added into their girl talk. He didn't know what to say and knew he didn't want to anyway. Both girls appeared in their respective bedroom doorways and stared at him.

"Well, Ted," Olivia said. "Bec asked you a question."

Ted shrugged and said simply, "Um…"

"Ted!" His girlfriend was glaring at him. "Tell Olivia her tits look amazing."

"Your tits look amazing." There, he thought. I said it.

Olivia smiled and thrust them in front of herself and bounced her shoulders back and forth. Then both girls looked over at him again.

Olivia's smile disappeared and she made a flailing gesture with both her arms waving them in the air. "And what about your girlfriend? Ted?"

Rebecca was looking at him with a blank stare.

"Your tits look amazing, too."

Both girls looked at him then each other. "Men," they both whined at the same time and disappeared back into their rooms. *When oh when would other people get here*, he wondered.

"Liv! Is Scott coming? I know you guys broke up, but he's coming, right?" Rebecca's voice carried across the apartment.

"Oh yeah," Olivia responded from her room. "And I think he said he's bringing most of the team." Ted perked up at that. Olivia inviting the guy she had been seeing but broke up with was surprising, but he was just mostly excited that Scott would be coming.

He had missed their months of double dates since Olivia announced that she and Scott were no longer *together-together*. She had adamantly proclaimed that they were just friends and still the best of friends just not boyfriend-girlfriend. But Ted had known it would be the end of their foursome dinners and movie nights. He felt more alone than he should with his girlfriend, just the two of them, on Saturday nights, but that was all he'd let his mind think on that.

"Wait," he called to the girls. "He's bringing his teammates?" Ted immediately felt unnerved. Scott was on the wrestling team, and they were known to be insane party animals. They drank like fish and made every party a wild rampage. Ted never fit in with them. He was a nerd, too smart to fit in with athletes and jocks and frat boys. Being around a room full of Division 1 wrestlers was not what he had been expecting for the night.

"Are you sure about this? They'll probably trash your apartment. They're a bunch of animals," he added.

The girls finally came back out of their bedrooms, both completely changed into new, different outfits. Both somehow looked sluttier than they had before. He knew it was a weird thing to think about his own girlfriend, but he couldn't unsee her pushed-up breasts and the belly under her crop top. How short were those shorts? In the moment he wondered if he should feel jealous. Because he didn't.

"Oh Ted, you're such a stick in the mud. Put your

books down for one weekend and just have some fun, will you?" Rebecca chastised him. "It'll do you good to be in a room full of testosterone. Maybe you should learn a thing or two about having a good time."

"Hey, I know how to have a good time," he objected.

Olivia laughed, and Rebecca joined her. Both girls looked at him like he was a charity case or something. Olivia walked behind the couch toward the kitchen and patted him on the head, "All we're saying is, Ted, you should lighten up a little, have some fun, go wild, get drunk. Promise me you won't just sit on the couch all night long. I will not have a party-pooper shit on my party."

"I know how to have fun," he protested. Rebecca leaned over the back of the couch and planted a kiss on his cheek then ruffled his hair with a waving hand.

"Is that what you're wearing," she asked before walking off to the kitchen following her roommate. Ted looked down at his clothes. A yellow, button-down shirt, freshly ironed, was tucked neatly into his jeans with a pretty nice leather belt. He felt the white collar of his undershirt above the one undone button at his neck. He had on a nice pair of loafers.

"What's wrong with what I'm wearing," he asked.

* * *

Around 10 PM, four of Olivia's female friends from her art classes showed up. They made their way straight to the kitchen and started opening bags of snacks and dumping them into bowls like they were the hosts. They attacked the bottles of vodka and mixers like a feeding frenzy.

Ted stood up from the couch, so he didn't seem rude.

120

He knew that's how Rebeca would put it. But the girls mostly ignored him. One that he had met before, Stacey, smiled at him with a quick nod before she ripped open a bag of potato chips like she hadn't eaten in days.

Ted looked around the room. Four newcomers, Rebecca, Olivia. He was in a sea of women and felt immediately uncomfortable, like he was the lone white iris in a sea of blue ones. He noticed one of the art girls trying to open a jar of salsa having a hard time. He put his hand out in a gesture that he could help, but she gave him a smirk and tried harder to open the jar. With a huff, she handed it over to Ted. With one twist, he easily opened the jar and handed it back to her. She rolled her eyes and turned away from him.

"My big strong man," Rebecca said from behind him while twisting an arm around his waist. "Get a drink. It's a party."

"I'm good for now," he said.

"Please don't be a fuddy duddy at my party."

"Why would you say that? Am I too boring for you or something?" Ted was a little surprised at her tone. And this whole thing with both Rebecca and Olivia. Stick in the mud. Lighten up. Fuddy duddy.

"I'm just saying I wish you would just go crazy or something for once. Loosen up. Why can't you be more like Scott and his crew?"

Ted was taken by surprise by the comment. "What, wild, out of control jocks? Is that what you want, Bec?"

She immediately tilted he head and patted him condescendingly. "No. Baby. I love you. You're gonna be so successful. I just, you know, sometimes I wish you'd just, I don't know, get drunk, go crazy, tear your shirt off and dance on the ceiling. We're in college. Have a little fun."

"I have fun," Ted countered, but Rebecca had already turned her attention to the girls pouring drinks.

"Pour one for me, ladies," she shrieked. And then they all shrieked together.

Give me strength, thought Ted.

* * *

By the time Ted planted himself back on the couch, the front door burst open to a loud cheering from the new arrivals. "Let the party begin," shouted the leader as he burst through the door. Ted turned his head to see Scott at the head of a pack of four, maybe five, no six counting Scott. It was Scott and his friends, some of them his teammates from the wrestling team. Ted felt a wash of relief flow through his body. He thought to himself, *at last I'm not the only guy here.*

He looked at Scott who was in the middle of hugging Olivia and lifting her off the ground in his muscular, bare arms. Bare arms, Ted noticed. As he brought her back down to the floor, Ted realized Scott wore a tight tank top and immediately felt overdressed.

Scott had a massive smile on his face, and he beamed like he'd just won an award or passed his finals. Ted could tell Scott loved a party. Maybe this is what Rebecca wanted him to act like. He didn't know if he could.

As the rest of Scott's crew flowed into the room, Ted felt more and more overdressed. Tank tops, athletic shorts, tight t-shirts, facial stubble that made them look like they hadn't shaved for two days. They probably hadn't. One guy wore sunglasses. It was 10:30 at night, Ted thought. What the fuck do you need those for?

Ted got up from the couch. He figured he should greet these guys. It was his girlfriend's apartment after all. He was kinda like a pseudo-host, he felt. But before he could make the greeting, Scott had turned his head and noticed him first.

"Teddy," he shouted. "Teddy! My man! I haven't seen you in weeks. Come here!"

Ted found himself wrapped in the strong arms of the wrestler who gripped him right around and enveloped him in his arms. Ted felt his feet lifted off the ground in the bear hug. He laughed in surprise and put his own arms around Scott's shoulders.

Feet back on the ground, he was face to face with Scott. He immediately missed their double dates with the girls. How they would sit together in a booth in a restaurant, just the two of them while the girls disappeared for the ladies' room together constantly. Or how they would be yapping away about some minor campus gossip, leaving Scott and him to lean against each other and quietly make fun of them.

"Teddy, man, I've missed you! Boys, boys, this is Ted. Bec's man. He's the best of the best." Scott had released Ted and was pointing at him square in the chest. All the other guys looked over. They all smiled at him quickly before disappearing into the kitchen to surround the keg and grab at red plastic cups in an urgent need for beer.

One lingered for an extra second and extended a hand to Ted. "Mikey. Any friend of Scott," he trailed off. Ted took note of Mikey's bright, brown eyes, full of warmth. In a split second he felt like he had a new friend. Ted shook the extended hand, and Mikey then gripped his shoulder and rocked him back and forth with a big smile and direct eye contact before joining the other guys who were pouring beer after beer.

"Dude, come on," Scott was saying at his side. "Looks like you need a beer, too." Ted felt Scott's arm on his back pushing him toward the kitchen. Urged forward, he didn't defend and found himself pushed into the midst of the pack of muscular jocks. Mikey was already handing him a beer and then Scott.

The guy with the keg hose in his hand dropped it down on top of the aluminum cylinder and raised his cup in the air. "Party," he shouted. All the guys whooped loudly, so Ted joined them.

"Party," they all replied. Ted chugged a mouthful of beer and fought off his throat's reaction to the wash of alcohol. Turning around, he saw Rebecca watching him and smiling wide. He nodded to her.

* * *

More and more people poured into the apartment. Ted tried to count heads, but he stopped bothering when he got to 80. The music blared. The drinks were flowing. But Rebecca had thought it through soundly. Rather than worry about the neighbors complaining, she had invited them. And they were lined up on the sofa, drunk and still doing shots.

Ted made himself useful and kept the kitchen clean, throwing away empty bottles into the recycling bin, picking up dropped chips, and wiping up spills. Rebecca appeared and grabbed his arm. "Enough. I told you. No boring shit," she whined at him. She pulled him into the living room through the bodies and into a group of three girls he hadn't met.

"Guys. This is Ted. My boyfriend. Ted. This is Amanda, Molly, and Sabine." The three girls smiled at him.

"Oh, so this is the famous Ted," Amanda said with a sing-song tone.

"Hi."

Molly extended her hand for a shake. "Molly."

"Ted."

Rebecca pointed at the third girl, "And this is Sabine."

"Sabine. Nice name. French?" Ted asked.

"Originally, yes," the girl said with a smile and a beautiful accent. "But I have lived here for eight years."

Ted moved his hand from Molly to Sabine who just placed her hand on top of his without gripping. Ted thought, *oh is that some type of French thing*, but didn't ask. She smiled at him and turned her attention across the room surveying the mass of people.

"So, Ted," Sabine asked nodding at the cluster of Scott and his wrestling friends. "Which of these boys are single?"

Ted blushed. "Oh, I don't know. They're not my… I mean, I don't really hang with them much. But I guess Scott is."

Rebecca almost spit her drink out in shock. "Ted! You know he just broke up with Olivia."

Ted looked sufficiently chastised. "Well, yeah. That's why I know he's single." Ted saw Sabine look back over at Scott with a certain kind of engaging look in her eyes. She was sizing him up, and he immediately regretted pointing him out to her. Rebecca's elbow found Ted's side.

"So, Ted," Molly tried to change the conversation. "Becs said you're a finance major?"

125

Ted was happy to switch gears. "Yeah, I graduate this May. Hoping to get a job in the city."

"Nice," Molly said. She seemed very friendly and nice. "That sounds awesome. I'm accounting. But I'm only a junior. Once you get your job, next year you can help me out."

Ted smiled. "With any luck," he said.

Becs chimed in, "Yeah, Ted's gonna be rich."

Ted looked at her sideways. "Sorry?"

Amanda raised her glass. "Snag a good one!"

Becs laughed and pushed her glass against Amanda's. Molly rolled her eyes but then also put her glass up against the others. Ted watched them and felt like he hadn't heard this type of thing from Rebecca before.

"Is that why you're with me," he blurted out without thinking. "Cuz you think I'm gonna make a lot of money?" He regretted it before he even finished the words.

Rebecca tried to laugh it off, but it came out a little fake. "Pssh, what? No. Ted. Teddy. Why would you think that?"

Molly looked back and forth between the two. Amanda had lost interest. Sabine was still staring over at Scott barely aware of them. Ted let the awkward silence sit there for a moment. He didn't think he should continue, but he did. "Well, you said I was boring. Why would you be with a boring guy if you can have some jock stud like one of Scott's friends over there?"

"True," Sabine said instinctively. She then looked at the others. "Oh, no offense, Ted. I don't mean you are boring. But yes, it is true. Why would you stay with someone you think is boring, no?" She returned her gaze to the group of guys. *Was she staring at Scott's ass*, Ted thought. *Why would she think she could get Scott?* He downed his entire drink in one gulp.

"I just said I wanted you to have a little fun tonight, Ted. I didn't mean you're boring."

"That's what it felt like."

Molly interjected. "Any way... enough of this conversation. Ted, you're amazing. Becs loves you. She talks about you all the time. And she's right, let's have some fun. Who needs a refill?" And she turned toward the kitchen. Ted gave Rebecca one last glance and followed the other girl, empty cup in hand.

* * *

Ted had a great conversation with Molly about their business majors, classes, hopes for after graduation. Ted thought she was a really, great person and probably someone he should keep in touch with. They probably could really help each other out with job hunting in the next few years.

After they had exchanged phone numbers, Ted realized they'd been chatting for a really long time. Looking at his watch, he saw it was 2:00 AM. Coming out of the kitchen, he and Molly saw the party had dwindled down to just a handful of the closest friends of Olivia and Rebecca. Ted was there, of course. Amanda, Rebecca, and Olivia were in the corner. And Sabine was holding court in the middle of the room, surrounded by wrestlers. Ted looked around but couldn't find Scott in his survey of the room. The bathroom door opened, and Scott appeared. Ted felt relieved but then wondered to himself why. He shrugged it off. Scott was like his wingman. That's what they called it. Like his bro. *Yeah*, he thought, *he's my bro*.

The neighbors were leaving, barely able to stand or

walk. They were hugging Rebecca then Olivia and stumbled their way to the door. Olivia called after them, "We'll turn it down, promise!"

One of the neighbors turned his head back, "Oh don't worry about it," he slurred. "We're gonna pass out." They slammed the door so loudly everyone in the room fell silent. The wrestlers that were left made their way to the kitchen. Ted counted them, Mikey and Scott and two other guys whose names he hadn't gotten. Olivia and Rebecca. Sabine, Amanda, and Molly. The party had definitely started to wind down.

"OK," he called out. He had to show Rebecca he could be fun. "What now!"

"Music!" Olivia shouted. "Let's dance."

From the kitchen the boys had reappeared with freshly filled cups of beer. "No! Party game," Mikey blurted out. "Let's play a game!"

"Strip poker," one of the wrestling guys shouted out.

"Oh, don't be a neanderthal," Sabine giggled and slapped his beefy shoulder.

Ted looked over at Scott who matched his gaze for a long moment. Not breaking eye contact, Scott raised his arm in the air, the one not holding his beer. "I know, how about Truth or Dare?" He was still staring right into Ted's eyes. Ted's stomach turned over, and he thought his heart had stopped for a split second.

Rebecca, Olivia, and Amanda, and the two wrestler boys were all calling out in unison, "Yes! Yes!"

Ted broke the gaze with Scott and saw the bodies descending on the middle of the room around the couch. Chairs were being brought closer together in a ring. As bodies planted themselves on the couch and on chairs, Ted realized there wouldn't be enough spaces, so he sat down on the floor between the end of the couch and a cushy recliner that Sabine had angled toward the circle and sunk into.

The wrestlers had also sat down on the floor, letting the girls take spots on the furniture. Rebecca and Olivia were in the kitchen and came back drinks in hand.

"Wait, no, no, this isn't gonna work," Olivia objected. "No furniture. Everyone sits on the floor. In a circle, everybody."

The wrestlers went to work eager to show off their strength and muscles. The couch was relegated to the far wall. The chairs were pushed back. And the group of college students sat in a ring on the floor of the emptied room.

There was a wrestler on each side of Ted. They were so muscular, he felt like he could be squished at any minute. He turned to his right. "Ted," he said.

"Matty," the guy said in response. He had a mop of messy blond hair. He wore a bright blue tank top that was so skintight, Ted could see his tiny nipples pressing into the fabric.

Before Ted could fully turn back over to his left, the other dude said, "Benny." Ted took him in. Buzzcut that looked like it would be jet black if he let it grow. Another tight tank top over muscles, Ted noted. But this one was black, and a small tuft of black chest hair appeared above it.

Ted looked back at Matty who was still smiling at him. Ted noted the smooth, pale skin of Matty's neckline. Turning right, Benny's Italian looking complexion and chest hair was a stark contrast to the blondness and paleness of Matty.

"So do all wrestlers have names like Benny and

Matty and… Scotty, I guess?" He tried to joke. At first they didn't seem to get what he was asking.

"I don't know, maybe we do… Teddy?" Matty joked and leaned his smooth muscular shoulder against Ted. Rebecca walked back from having moved a chair and noted that Ted was sandwiched in already. Ted looked up at her standing behind him. He smiled. She shrugged then walked over to the other side of the circle and sat directly across from him, right next to Scott.

Sabine sat where the couch had been. "What is this Truth of Dare," she asked.

Olivia took charge sitting between Amanda and Molly. "OK, the rules are simple. One person calls out another's name. That person has to pick, truth or dare. And they have to either answer a question or do what they're told to do. Then they get to pick the next person."

"I think I understand," Sabine answered. "But what are these dares? Something sexual I imagine, no?" Ted did not like it that she looked right at Scott when she asked her question.

Olivia was more than excited to respond, "Oh they can be anything. And you have to do it," she said.

"Within reason," Rebecca warned.

Olivia shrugged, "Well, yeah, within reason." Mikey who was sitting next to Scott made some kind of comment in his ear.

"See," Rebecca called out. "That's what I was afraid of. Guys. Don't be gross. And a woman always has the right to say no."

"I didn't say anything," Mikey acted offended.

Sabine considered. "But what is to stop someone from always saying truth? This way you would never have to do anything, no?"

Olivia and Rebecca looked at each other like no one had ever thought of that before.

Ted suggested, "We can flip a coin."

"Good idea," Matty said.

"Yeah, good thinking," Benny offered.

"Hold on," Rebecca objected. *Who's being a fuddy duddy now*, Ted thought. "Let's not get crazy. That will be too many dares. Truths first. Let's do a few rounds of just truths first."

Molly offered, "How about a die? Yeah, roll a die. One through four you have to tell a truth. Five or six you have to do a dare."

Rebecca again didn't seem happy. "Just a six. One through five you have to tell a truth."

Olivia stood up and made her way over to the closet. "OK, that will work. One through five you have to tell a truth. Roll a six you have to do a dare. But once we get going, we're going to change it to five or six."

Everyone seemed to nod. Ted rolled his eyes, *this is getting overly complicated.*

Olivia had pulled an old Monopoly box from the top shelf the closet and dug out a six-sided die. Returning to the circle she sat down with it in her hand. She held it out.

"OK. Since I have the die, I will start." She turned and looked at Scott. "Scott," she called out and tossed him the die. He grabbed it out of mid-air and smiled back at her.

"Fine," he accepted and rolled the die onto the floor in the middle of the circle. It bounced a few times and landed to show a two. "Truth," he announced.

Olivia looked over at him. "OK, we'll start out tame. Truth. Do you miss me?"

Everyone kinda let out a little aw sound. He smiled over at her. "Sure I do."

Olivia returned the smile to him. *So self-serving*, Ted thought. But they were looking at each other with smiles. Ted realized they were both happy. Neither was heart-broken.

Maybe, he thought, *you can break up and remain friends with someone*. He looked over to Rebecca who was talking to Molly to her right.

"Ted," Scott had called out. Ted looked over surprised. Scott was calling him out as next.

"Dude," Matty blurted out. "Pick a chick, man. That's how you play the game."

Scott snapped back, "There are no rules, dude. Chill." Then he repeated himself, "Ted."

Ted leaned into the middle of the circle and grabbed the die and threw it out. It landed right in front of Rebecca's foot. A three.

"OK," Ted said, looking back over to Scott. "Truth."

Scott smiled, "Do you miss me?"

Ted had to laugh. "Yeah, man. I miss you."

Sabine looked confused. "What does this mean?"

Ted explained, nodding at Rebecca then Olivia. "We used to go on double dates all the time."

Benny on his right put his head down on Ted's shoulder in a mockingly romantic way, "Aw, that's so sweet."

Scott added his own statement. "I miss you too, buddy."

Rebecca was rolling her eyes, but she added, "I miss you, too, Scotty," and put an arm around him in a hug.

Molly kicked the die back to Ted, "OK, enough of your sick lovefest. Ted, who is next?"

Ted was torn. Should he pick Rebecca? Should he specifically not pick Rebecca? What are people gonna think if he does, if he doesn't? "Molly," he finally said.

"Smart man," Rebecca immediately said.

Ted tossed the die over Molly who rolled it. "One," she said. "Truth."

Ted had to think. If he was honest with himself, he didn't really want to know anything in particular about this girl, and he only picked her on a whim. He thought and thought.

"Come on," Matty said, chugging on his beer.

"OK, OK," Ted said. "How many guys in this room have you hooked up with?"

Rebecca looked mortified. "Oh my gawd, Ted."

Molly laughed and shrugged it off. "That's OK. No big deal," she offered. "Easy. None." She put out her hand and nodded at the die that had fallen close to Ted. He picked it up and slid it over to her. Matty leaned into his right ear and whispered, "Les-bi-an…"

"What," Ted whispered back, surprised. "Seriously?"

Matty just shrugged his shoulders. Molly pursed her lips and blurted out, "Fine. Matty." She threw the die at him, and it landed in between his crossed legs.

Matty threw it way too high in the air, and the die almost hit the ceiling. "Calm down, tiger," Molly mocked him. The die hit the floor and bounced several times. It landed near Sabine. She looked down and announced. "Six."

Everyone whooped and made various mocking noises. Matty didn't seem to mind. Ted could tell this guy seemed ready for anything.

"OK, then. Dare," Matty said almost proudly. "What you got, Mols?"

The attention then turned back to Molly. She had a conniving grin on her face. She thought and then announced, "OK, take off that shirt."

Matty did not mind in the least. He stood proudly and stepped into the middle of the circle. All eyes were on him, and Ted could tell he liked the attention. Reaching down, Matty gripped the bottom of his tank top and pulled it up. Inch by inch his completely hairless torso appeared, and once it was raised half-way, Ted could see the rippling abs one after the other. As Matty lifted it over his head, his smooth rounded chest was revealed. He tossed the shirt across the room and flexed in an overly dramatic way. All eyes, both guys and girls, were staring at his insanely buff body. Ted felt flustered and looked around the room.

Sabine had a big grin on her face. "Fuck me," she said. Ted could tell most of the girls were all thinking the same thing.

"That's my boy," Benny catcalled.

Matty sat himself back in his place beside Ted, die in hand.

"Sabine," Matty said quickly.

She accepted the die eagerly. "OK, let's see what this game is all about." She rolled the die and looked for the result. It landed near Benny who looked down at it. "Five."

"Oh, you're lucky I said only six," Olivia said. "That means truth."

"Yes, fine, truth," Sabine said.

Matty looked at her. Everyone looked at him waiting for what he would ask the French girl. Ted turned his head to him as well. He could not believe how muscular the guy next to him was. And his skin was so smooth, so hairless. Ted wondered what it would feel like it he touched it, like satin or porcelain. Looking away, he saw Scott staring at him.

"OK, momma," Matty said finally. "What's better about American guys than Frenchies?"

Olivia acted offended, "Oh Matty. That's rude."

"What," he said.

Sabine answered right away. "Well, just this," she said gesturing at Matty's shirtless torso. "Look at your muscles. You are a real man with this body. American men work out and look good. French men they are all so skinny. Twenty-eight inch waists and no muscle. They don't eat anything. They all look like… like…" she stuttered for a moment and then finished her thought. "Like Ted here."

Ted was surprised and offended. "Me? What about me?"

Sabine just snuffed. "You are too skinny. You need to work out, make yourself strong and hot. You should sweep Rebecca off her feet. I bet you couldn't even pick her up."

Ted was mortified. He looked at Rebecca who didn't seem to object to what Sabine was saying. Some faces looked like they felt sorry for him. Others were just shocked at what she'd said, probably thinking how rude she was being.

"That's not true," one voice objected loudly. "Ted looks great." But it wasn't Rebecca. It was Scott. All heads turned at once to look at him. "Sabine, maybe you just want to be crushed by some muscle head, but Ted's a good guy, smart and nice. Any girl would be lucky to have him."

Ted blushed from Scott's words. He could see some heads nod in agreement, but looking at Rebecca, she was as white as a sheet. Maybe Scott's words hit a little too close to home for her. She looked down at the floor and not at him.

Sabine just simply said, "I'm sorry, Ted. I did not mean to offend you."

"It's OK," Ted said. "I'm not a muscle hunk." He reached over and rubbed Matty's bare shoulder. "Like these wrestler dudes." *Fuck*, he thought. *His skin is smooth. Shit.*

"I knew you wanted to cop a feel, you perv," Matty grabbed Ted's hand and moved it onto his own pec. Ted pulled it back, and Matty reached over and groped Ted. Ted was caught by surprise as Matty's hands explored the front of his torso. "And you're wrong, Sabine. You should feel this chest. He may be skinny, but he's in good shape."

Ted blushed a bright pink and finally pushed Matty's hand away. "Stop it. Who's the perv now?"

Rebecca stood. "You know what, maybe we should take a break." She strode to the kitchen.

Sabine objected. "No, no. Let's keep going. I like this game. Truth is good. Ted, again, I am sorry."

"It's OK, it's OK," he said. "Go ahead. Pick."

"Olivia," Sabine said immediately. "You are our hostess. So I call on you."

Olivia took the die from her. "OK, come on lady luck." She threw the die.

It landed in the middle of the circle, and everyone saw it at the same time, and everyone called out in unison. "Six! Dare!" Laughs and eager catcalls rang out.

When quiet came over the group, Olivia offered, "All right, Sabine. Do your worst."

Sabine considered a moment. "Very well. Olivia." She paused dramatically. "Make out. With. Rebecca."

The group shrieked. Matty called out, "Yeah, baby. Sabine, I knew I liked you."

Benny looked like he was about to explode. "Yeah, boy, it's on now. Come on!"

Olivia looked at her roommate. Rebecca shrugged like it was no big deal. Olivia pushed in between Rebecca and Scott. Ted watched as she leaned in and planted her lips on his girlfriend. Their hands reached up for each other's shoulders and necks. They leaned into each other. Ted could see their tongues intertwine. The boys were all silent with gaping, wide-open mouths. He thought Benny would start drooling. He heard Matty moan in overt excitement. The other girls were pretending to be uncomfortable. It went on too long.

Finally they stopped. Rebecca looked over at Ted, and he knew she wanted him to be mad or offended or jealous to have some strong reaction. But he didn't really feel anything. He was filled with a feeling of, he didn't know what to make of it. Indifference?

Rebecca seemed more uncomfortable looking over at him than she had with her roommate's tongue down her throat. What did she want from him? It was just a game. These kinda things happened in this game.

Olivia got back to her place. The boys calmed down from their moment of getting to watch two girls make out. Matty joked, "I think I need to adjust myself."

"All right, monsters. Remember, payback is a bitch," Olivia said. And added, "Scott!"

He turned to her and smiled, "Of course you'd call on me." He grabbed the die and tossed it. It skittered across the floor, hit Ted's foot and bounced to a stop.

Ted looked down at the white cube by his foot and announced, "Six."

"Dare! Yeah, boy!" Matty almost screamed.

"Oh shit it's on now," Benny added.

All eyes turned to Olivia. She smiled widely. Ted could tell she knew what she was going to do. Scott had a half smile on his face. Ted wondered if his friend was going to have to take his clothes off or do something embarrassing. Was she going to make him kiss a guy? Would it be him? *Wait*, he thought, *why am I thinking about that?*

Olivia raised her head up and announced, "Seven minutes in heaven!"

The boys on either side of Ted both started bobbing back and forth and making ooh and ahh sounds. They pointed at Scott and laughed.

Sabine looked confused. "What is this, what does that mean?"

Olivia explained. "It means that Scott has to get in the closet and stay in there for seven minutes."

Sabine asked, "Alone?"

"No," Olivia said. "With the person of my choosing."

Sabine understood. "Ah, now I understand. So who?"

Olivia waited. Everyone looked at her, anxious and wide-eyed.

"Ted."

Ted froze in his place. Scott's face dropped. Ted thought he looked mortified. Ted didn't know how he felt. Scott looked him in the eyes, his face unmoving, mouth hung open. He didn't say anything. He didn't move.

Matty was the first to jump up followed by Benny. Matty grabbed Ted under his arms and hoisted him up with one swift move. His muscles were too strong for Ted to be any resistance. Benny leapt over and pulled Scott to his feet. Both found themselves dragged across the room to the hall closet. Benny opened the door, and Ted saw it was crammed full of hanging coats and a vacuum cleaner, and ironing board, a few boxes. There was no room in there for two bodies, but he found himself being pushed into the coats, and then he felt Scott being pressed in beside him.

As he half fell into the tiniest space, and Scott was shoved in beside him, the door was slammed shut to the sound of laughter. He didn't have control of his balance, but there wasn't even room to fall. Scott, who was about three inches shorter than him, was pressed against the front of his body. Scott was at least able to stand straight up since he was shorter than the coat bar, but Ted had to lean his head down. He could feel his cheek press against the side of Scott's head. He felt his soft hair against his skin.

"Fuck," Scott said. "Are you OK?"

"Yeah, yeah, I just need to get my footing." Ted reached to grab the bar the coats hung from. A vacuum cleaner pressed into his back. He couldn't move back, so he had to lean into Scott. "I can't make any room though."

"It's OK, it's OK," Scott moaned as he tried to move his arm. With nowhere else to put it, Ted felt it reach around his waist, and they were forced to hug together while they got their feet settled.

"Wait, there's a light. Let me get it," Ted said. He reached up and pulled the chain, and they were at least able to see. Ted looked down at his shorter friend. He was glad that he was so skinny, as Sabine had pointed out. But Scott's muscular thick body along with his meant there was no room to spread out, and they remained pressed against each other.

Scott had already put the one arm around Ted. Ted thought that was a good idea, that it was making a little more room, so he reached around and put his arms around Scott as well. Their bodies pressed together, arms around each other, Ted breathed a moment and let his mind settle on their predicament.

Scott looked up at him. Their eyes locked. Ted gave him a smile. Scott smiled back, and Ted felt his hand open up against the small of his back. He felt a deep convulsion in his stomach, like 1,000 birds taking flight. The silence stood between them as the laughter and catcalls in the room outside subsided. Ted thought maybe they'd been forgotten.

"We have to stay like this for seven minutes," he asked.

"Yeah," Scott answered. "I… um…"

Ted looked at Scott and saw some type of worry or concern in them. "What's the matter?"

Scott pressed his head against Ted's chest. He stayed like that for a moment, breathing in and out. He wrapped his arm a little tighter around Ted. Ted felt himself being hugged. He returned the gesture, and the two of them hugged each other warmly and firmly.

Finally Scott looked back up at him. "Ted. I know this is my dare. But I want to tell you my truth."

Ted was a little confused. "What?"

Scott breathed out with every bit of air in his lungs. "Teddy. I'm gay."

Ted was completely and utterly shocked by the admission. He didn't know what to say, what to do. He was struck dumb and mute. He could not believe the words Scott spoke. His thoughts started swirling. *How could Scott be? He's such a stud. He's an athlete. He's a jock, a dude. I'm the nerd. I'm the…*

"Ted, please say something."

"Scott. You're… you're… gay? I had. I had no idea. But you were with Olivia."

"I know, I know. That was a mistake. And I knew it.

And she knew it. I just, I was confused. And. Please tell me you don't hate me."

Ted was mortified by the question. "Scott. No. No. How could I hate you. I'm not a homophobe. No, I'm just. I'm just shocked. I never thought you were…" He trailed off not having to finish the sentence.

Silence stood between them, but Ted kept his hands around Scott and did not let go. His mind was racing 1,000 miles an hour. He felt the floor fall out from under him. Maybe the entire earth. Everything he'd been hiding inside himself, and here was Scott able to just say it out loud and admit it.

"Ted." Scott hesitated. "Teddy. That's not everything. Please. I have to tell you this. Teddy. I love you. I have loved you for a long time. I think that's why I stayed with Olivia so long. Because I wanted to be with you. Every minute, every date we went on together. I wanted it to be just us. And I know, I know. You're with Rebecca. I know, you're straight. And I don't want anything from you. It's just, it's just I had to tell you. You're just so amazing, and Rebecca is a fucking idiot, and I just, I just hope someday I meet a guy as so fucking awesome as you."

Ted couldn't breathe. He couldn't move. He couldn't take his eyes away from Scott's. He couldn't speak. What was he doing? How could he have been so deep in denial? How could everything he had ever wanted, ever dreamed of, be right there in front of him all this time, and he didn't know? How could Scott be saying he loves him when it was the other way around all along? He was so desperately, so madly, so passionately in love with Scott. He was the dork, the nerd, the smart student, the boring one. He was the boring dude. Scott was the stud, the jock, the athlete.

He had to say it. He was ready to burst with a raging

passion. He was crazy, insanely, wildly in love with Scott, too. "Scott, I…"

But before he could get another word out, the closet door was flung open, and they were dragged out in a cacophony of whoops and cheers. "Yeah, buddy, you did it! You survived," Benny was calling out as he dragged Scott away and out of Ted's arms.

Ted turned and found himself staring into Matty's face. Not Scott's. The half-naked blond wrestler reached in and pulled Ted out from between the coats. "You didn't ruin our boy's virtue in there, did you, stud?"

Ted looked confusedly out into the room, "What?"

* * *

With the two of them being stuck in the closet on the last dare, the circle had separated around the apartment. Sabine was on the couch with Benny next to her, his arm wrapped around her neck. Ted looked around. He couldn't see Scott. He turned to Molly who was near him. "Molly, where did Scott go?"

"He left."

"He what?"

Molly put a hand on his arm. "He took off. As soon as you guys came out of the closet. What happened in there?" She seemed genuinely concerned.

Ted didn't know what to say. "Nothing. We were just. Talking." He looked around and didn't see Rebecca either. He turned for the kitchen.

He didn't know what to think or what to say. He moved in a fog of confusion but also of expanding clarity. He knew what he was. He knew what he wanted. How did he ever not know?

As he got to the kitchen, he saw Rebecca with her back to him, talking to Amanda. She was talking on and on, and Amanda's eyes went wide open when she saw him. He caught the tail end of what his girlfriend was saying, "...so yeah, I know he's boring as fuck, but he's going into finance. He's gonna be so rich."

She turned to see Ted standing there. All the color washed out of her face. Amanda stood mortified. Rebecca squirmed, but Ted didn't give her a chance to say anything more. "We're breaking up," he said simply.

Walking back out to the living room, Sabine was now straddling a shirtless Benny on the couch, her face planted on his, kissing wetly and loudly. Matty was watching over them, still shirtless and still hot. Ted thought, yeah, he's insanely, stupidly, crazy hot. But he's... he's not Scott. He bolted out of the apartment.

* * *

At first he marched in a speed walk back to campus. His mind firmly set on his destination. For a block he strode one foot after the other, but then his determination took over him, and he took off in a mad sprint. Block after block, closer and closer. Through the gate onto campus, he did not make his way back to his dorm but to another one.

He burst through the front door, and the security guard said, "You have to sign in." He scribbled his name madly, furiously. He didn't even bother with the elevator but instead went right to the stairs. He opened the door and bounded up, skipping more than half the steps. Up one floor then the next, he knew exactly where he was going.

He marched down the hall and stood in front of the door. He didn't knock. He didn't hesitate. He grabbed the

143

knob. It was unlocked. He flung the door open, stepped inside, and slammed it shut behind him.

Scott stood in front of the window, looking out. He turned to see Ted standing there, panting heavily. His hands were dropped straight down on either side of him, hands clenched in fists. Sweat began to pour down his forehead.

They stared at each other. Ted gathered his breath. Scott looked sad or worried.

"Teddy."

"My truth," Ted said forcefully. "You want my truth? I broke with Rebecca. I love you. I fucking love. I have always loved you. I didn't understand it. I pretended to myself I didn't understand it. But I knew it. Deep down inside I knew it." He trailed off. Scott's face warmed. His shoulders eased, and he looked like he was about to collapse. "Oh, and I'm gay, too. Or bi. Maybe I'm bi. I don't know. Fuck. All I know is, I want you."

In one swift step, Ted was across the room and wrapped his arms around Scott's muscular body. Ted gripped him in an embrace that took his breath away. He leaned down to the shorter wrestler and pressed his lips firmly on his mouth. Scott opened his lips, and Ted's tongue invaded his mouth. Scott reached up and wrapped his arms around the taller man's shoulders. He let his head fall backwards and Ted pressed hard into him.

Ted's arms wrapped around Scott's hips. He gripped him hard, and grabbing onto his round, firm ass, he lifted him clean off the ground. Scott wrapped his legs around Ted's waist, and they continued their passionate kiss.

Ted turned toward the bed and rested Scott down upon it. Scott looked up at the taller man looming above him. Ted looked in charge, masculine, commanding. Everything Rebecca said he wasn't, he was. In this moment with Scott laid out on the bed before him, Ted was in control.

He pulled his own shirt off so hard, a button popped off and fell to the floor. He pulled the undershirt off over his head. Then he reached down and pulled Scott up into a sitting position. He gripped his shirt, and rather than lift if off, he squeezed his fingers roughly and ripped it. He pulled, and the fabric submitted to his will. It ripped and frayed. Scott gasped under Ted's forcefulness and pulled off his own shorts.

Ted looked down at the muscular, short man laid out on the bed in front of him. Still in his own pants, he felt the power of being in charge, of still being clothed while Scott lay there naked and exposed.

Finally, Scott said, "I dare you to fuck me." But he didn't wait. He reached up and grabbed at Ted's belt, undid it, and flung it away. He undid the button and the zipper on his jeans and yanked them down to his knees. Ted pulled back to get them off as quickly as he could.

Scott's eyes went wide when he saw the throbbing bulge in Ted's underwear and wasted no time in yanking them clear down to the floor. Ted's enormous cock bounced out in front of his face.

"Oh fuck," Scott shrieked. "Why is it always you skinny fuckers?"

Ted laughed a devilish chortle and put his hand to the back of Scott's head. The wrestler needed no urging, opening his mouth, and letting Ted's huge cock into his mouth. Scott let out a sigh and a whimper as he tried his hardest to get as much of it inside him. "Exactly how many skinny fuckers have you been with," he asked.

But Scott couldn't answer with his mouth full of a huge cock.

He bobbed up and down on the thick, erect shaft. Again and again, he went as far down as he could. Ted's mind reeled. Here he was, in this bed with the hottest man he could ever dream of.

Scott pulled off Ted's cock, letting it flop out of his mouth, and leaned to his nightstand. He had a tube in his hand. Opening it, he slathered a huge gob of lubed into his hand and stroked it onto Ted's cock. "We're going to need a lot of this," he sighed.

Ted pushed on both of Scott's shoulders, forcing him onto his back on the bed. He brought his leg up and over the smaller but muscular guy. He lifted both of Scott's legs into the air and leaned in between them. With one hand he directed his cock right at the small, tight hole of Scott's ass.

"Fuck, baby, you gotta go slow with that monster."

Ted pressed the head of his cock against it. It didn't respond. He pushed a little more, and he felt the opening respond. Just the huge head of his cock finally slipped inside.

"Oh my god, Teddy. I've wanted this for so long. Fuck me, please fuck me. Go slow, go slow."

Ted felt more in charge with Scott's pleading. "Sshh," he commanded. He pushed a little more, and Scott let out a moan that shot passion through his every fiber. He looked down at Scott whose eyes were wide open, a smile beaming across his face despite the effort of opening up to him.

"Oh Teddy, give it to me. Gentle. I'm a little guy. I'm little. You're so big."

Ted just kept pushing ever so much more with every passing second. "Let. Me. In," he commanded. And finally he felt Scott's muscles relax, and his cock slid firmly and softly deep into his friend.

"Ahhhh," Ted let out such a sigh of relief and

longing and finality. His huge cock planted in Scott's ass, he had exactly what he had always wanted. Scott looked up at him, moaning and breathing heavy. "That's my boy," Ted smiled down at him.

Scott reached up and put his arms around Ted's shoulders. Ted pushed further in even though he was planted deep and to the hilt inside Scott, but he wanted more. He pushed and then he finally let his cock slide back out halfway. Scott moaned so loud, Ted thought everyone in the state would hear their passion.

He leaned down and planted his mouth on Scott's, and then he started fucking. His massive cock slid in and out of Scott's tight, warm hole. He could feel how firmly it gripped his cock, and he loved it. He pumped again and again while Scott moaned into his mouth.

Again and again, he fucked his newfound lover. He was the skinny nerd, but he was fucking the muscular, stud athlete. He was so obsessed with fucking, he hadn't even touched or looked at Scott's cock. Finally he reached down and stroked it. He was surprised at the first touch. He looked down and saw Scott's long, fat uncut cock in his hands. He lifted his mouth from their kiss to say, "Baby, you're not that much smaller than me."

Scott's eyes opened, and he laughed, "Uh, you're currently splitting me in half with that monster, so trust me, yeah, you're a lot bigger." Ted took that comment to heart and shoved his cock deep into his ass in response. Scott let out a huge moan.

"Teddy. I don't want this to just be a quick fuck. I want you."

"I want you, too, Scott. This is not just a fuck. I've wanted this for so long. I can't believe I didn't tell you. I didn't tell myself."

"Oh, Teddy. Keep fucking me. Don't stop."

Ted did what he was told. He lifted Scott's legs even further and really began to piston in and out of his ass. Pushing and sliding back out and planting his cock deep into Scott, he started to sweat from the relentless passion. Scott was moaning and whimpering, breathing heavy. He was riding a crest of being used and being loved at the same time. Ted felt how in charge he was, and he loved it. He pushed on and kept going, fuck thrust after fuck thrust, he knew he owned this hot little ass now. He would have it whenever and however he wanted.

"Fuck me, baby. Fuck me."

"From now on," Ted moaned. He felt the wave of euphoria spread over him, and with one final deep thrust, he exploded like never before deep and hard into Scott who knew it and felt it. And a moment later, with a loud sigh, Scott's cock erupted and splashed warm cum all over his own torso.

Spent and drained, Ted slid out of Scott's ass and collapsed on top of him. Holding him wrapped in his arm and pressed firmly together, Ted kissed him again passionately.

"I can't believe we finally figured this out," Ted said.

"Me too," Scott whispered.

They fell asleep in each other arms, and from that day on, that was their truth.

Help a Bro Out

Andrew could not get the sound coming from the other side of the dorm room out of his brain. As much as he tried to concentrate on the novel he was reading under the light of his tiny lamp, all his mind could register was the wet smacking sounds of his roommate and his girlfriend making out on the other bed just feet away from him.

Under the light of his reading lamp, he desperately tried to block out the sounds. They were bad enough, but every now and then Pamela, the most recent girlfriend, would let out a whispered moan. *By far this one was the most brazen and the most gross*, he thought. His room-mate's name was Bruce, but everyone called him Meat. He was a meathead, and while that was probably where the nickname came from, he would always brag that it was because the size of his cock. Andrew was his roommate, though, and he knew that was absolutely definitely not where the nickname came from.

Andrew had to wonder how disappointed this Pamela was going to be if they went any further, and he made his own stomach lurch even more thinking about it. She was pretty damn skanky, but he wondered if she was slutty enough to go all the way while he was right there in the room with them.

He also wondered if she knew she was at least the

sixth girl to be in Bruce's bed just that semester. As a particularly loud slurp sound came from the other side of the room, he dreamed of the end of the school year so he could submit the application for a new roommate for his senior year.

As he lay there with his book, completely grossed out by the two in the other bed, he also couldn't help but wonder what was wrong with him. His third year of college was just about over, and he had barely had any hookups at all. He briefly dated one girl who sang in the university chorus, but after two months of going out, he realized he just wasn't into her. She probably figured it out, too, and broke up with him rather abruptly.

He wished there were some way to advertise his more personal attributes. Because while Bruce had the moniker of Meat, he knew he was the one who really deserved it. The sounds of the intense makeout session were not doing it for him at all; in fact, they were really grossing him out to the point of almost feeling sick to his stomach. But he knew if a girl like Pamela could see his cock, not that he would ever want a girl like her, she would be begging him for a fuck. It lay completely soft in his pants, and he knew he was what you call a grower, but if it got hard, it would rise like the giant mast it was to its full eight and a half inches of thick cock meat. *Yeah, I got your Meat right here, buddy*, he thought to himself.

When the fuck were they going to give up this make out session, he wondered. It was after all 1AM on a Tuesday, and he knew Meat had an early class the next day. He was just glad that he had most of the morning free since his first class wasn't until 11:15. Nonetheless he put his book down on the floor next to his bed, turned off his light, rolled on his side facing the wall, and tried to fall asleep. That's when he heard the start of the whispering. At first he couldn't make it out, but after several sentences, it was clear Pamela was a little perturbed.

"Can't you get rid of him? It's fucking creepy," she whispered a little too loudly.

"It's cool. Look, he's sleeping."

"What if he wakes up? Tell him to give us some privacy."

"What do you want him to do, babe?"

"I'm going to the bathroom. Get rid of him. Can't he go sleep in a friend's room or something?"

Meat was usually not a demanding roommate, but Andrew knew what was coming. Fuck, he thought in his head, so strongly he thought it probably resonated through the room. Meat was gonna ask him to give them some privacy. Where the fuck was he gonna go?

Pamela got up out of the bed and announced loudly, "I'm going to the bathroom, babe. I'll be right back. OK?" The *OK* was louder than the rest. She obviously intended to wake Andrew up if he were in fact asleep, which he wasn't. Andrew heard the door open. The room was awash in light from the hallway. He turned his head toward the door and saw Pamela's round body backlit in the beams that were coming through into the room. For one brief instant, he saw her bare stomach as she pulled her shirt down to cover herself, and then the room was back in darkness as she closed the door and left.

Bruce turned on the lamp on his desk by his bed, and Andrew heard his feet hit the floor. "Dude, you up? Dude."

Andrew made a moaning sound, pretending that he was being woken up. "Huh? What?"

"Dude, I hate to ask you this. But can you give us some privacy?"

"What do you want me to do, Bruce?"

Bruce hesitated. Andrew rolled over and looked at him. He still had on his jeans but had lost his shirt. His muscular but doughy upper body was naked to the waist. Andrew wondered if he worked out so much, how did he keep such a significant layer of fat? He looked like that tire company's mascot, what was it called, he couldn't remember.

"Can't you go sleep in Pete's room? Or Rick's? I think she's gonna let me fuck her. But not with you here."

"Dude, please. Do not make me picture that. What do you see in this one anyway? You really want to hit that?"

Bruce let out a sound like he was sucking air out through his teeth, "Dude, why not? I'd fuck her. It's not fucking marriage or anything. You really oughta get out there yourself and get some. Your mind is going soft. But come on, seriously, can't you go somewhere? Quick while she's gone."

Andrew sighed loudly. Fuck this shit. Where was he supposed to go? The cafeteria was closed. It was February, so it was cold as fuck outside. He thought he could knock on a few different doors and see if anyone was still up. "Dude, it's fucking 1:00 in the morning. Don't you have an early class tomorrow?"

"Just for a bit. I'll be quick. I can text you when she's gone."

Andrew rolled out of bed and grabbed his phone. He looked at what he was wearing, just a pair of sweatpants, no underwear, and a ratty old t-shirt—which was what he wore to bed. Oh well, people wander the halls in worse, he thought. He got up, put his phone and room key in the pocket of his pants, pulled on his Adidas flip-flops, and went for the door. "Fine. But you fucking owe me, dude."

Bruce's face bloomed with a huge grin. "Buddy, you're the best. If you ever get a girl to go out with you, the room will be all yours."

"Fuck you," Andrew said.

* * *

Andrew walked down the hallway. The dorm was insanely quiet. Everyone was obviously already asleep. He looked at the base of the doors, and none of them had a shaft of light coming out. He walked by his friend Pete's door and listened. He heard nothing. He thought he would knock and explain the situation. Pete would definitely let him hang there for a bit, but he didn't want to bother him.

Walking further down the hallway, he came to the lounge. It wasn't really a lounge. It was just a wider section of the hallway where a couch and two cushioned chairs were set out. There were three large unpainted rectangles on the corner of the wall where years ago, there used to be pay phones. He thought about that; all those years, and these walls had never been repainted. He couldn't imagine what it must have been like being in the dorms with no cellphones and just three community payphones on each floor.

He walked over to the couch and plopped down on it with an annoyed sigh. He put his head on the armrest at one end and lay out across the three cushions, bringing his feet up to spread his body down the length. Fuck, he thought, he should have brought his book, but there was no going back now. What if Pamela had returned? He did not want to see her naked body, and he definitely did not want to see Meat's fleshiness nor his tiny dick.

He pulled out his phone and started scrolling

through Insta. It was taking forever for pictures to load. He looked up at the corner of his screen and saw just one bar. Fuck this fucking lounge, he thought. He was in the middle of a giant six story concrete bunker of a dormitory, and the service sucked. He tossed the phone down on his stomach and put an arm over his forehead, trying to block out the bright overhead lights.

Five minutes went by, 10,15. He was getting more and more pissed off, wondering how long Bruce and Pamela were gonna take. The image of two, so incredibly not-hot people fucking in his dorm room was stuck in his mind. He tried desperately to think of something else.

"Andrew," he heard a voice call out in a questioning tone. He looked up. His Resident Assistant was standing over him. Every floor had one student who was in charge of managing all the guys that lived on it, enforcing the rules, reporting anyone who violated them. "What are you doing out here?"

"Oh," he responded. "Hey, Jeremy. Um, I'm just giving my roommate a little… privacy."

Jeremy understood immediately and nodded, "Ah, yeah. Meat's getting some, is he?"

"Oh, ew. Please don't remind me, but yeah."

Jeremy came over and sat on the arm of the couch closer to Andrew's feet. "That girl Pamela, right?"

Andrew just nodded.

"Gross," Jeremy said. "What does he see in her?"

"I asked him the same thing. But really, what does she see in him?"

Jeremy shrugged. "Well, I guess she wants the big D."

Andrew scoffed. "Well, she ain't gonna find it there."

Jeremy looked over at Andrew intrigued. "No? With a nick name like Meat? And he's always bragging about it."

Andrew then sat up and looked over at Jeremy who was smiling widely at him. His bright blue eyes were focused on him fully. He wondered in the moment why he wasn't more friendly with the guy. "Dude, seriously," he said and held up his hand with two fingers presenting a space of about three inches in between them.

"No," Jeremy's faced widened in shock and amusement.

"I don't know how he gets so many girls, Jer. It's insane."

"Maybe that's why he can't keep them, though," Jeremy suggested.

Andrew sighed in frustration, "Meat. Yeah, meathead maybe. But not meat where it counts. If anybody should have that nickname, it should be me."

Jeremy seemed to freeze. He let out a gasp of air that had some sort of sound on it that wasn't words. "Whuzzuuhuhhh… whuh… what's that now?"

Andrew realized what he had just said and turned beat red. He could feel the warmth rise up in his face and in his ears. "Uh, I, uh, sorry, dude, I didn't mean to say..," he trailed off. But after a minute, he looked over at Jeremy who didn't seem to be offended by the comment, so Andrew smiled. "I guess I'm just frustrated. But, what can I say, I guess."

Jeremy was still silent, just looking at Andrew for some additional clarification or commentary. He looked like he was thinking about what he should say next. Andrew looked back and thought Jeremy had the kindest, warmest eyes he'd ever seen. I should hang out with him more often, he decided.

Jeremy finally responded. "So what are you gonna do, just stay out here all night?"

Andrew shrugged. "Well, he said he'd text me when they're done."

Jeremy crinkled his nose. "Dude, gross. I don't want to picture it."

"You and me both," Andrew said.

"Come to my room," Jeremy offered. "You can crash at my place. Perks of being an R.A, I don't have to worry about that shit. Got my own room," he bragged.

Andrew felt a wash of relief spread through him. That would sure beat being stranded out in the hallway lounge. And if he thought about it, the couch was really gross. "Yeah, that'd be great. Thanks."

Jeremy leapt up, "Come on. Slumber party!"

Andrew followed him to the end of the hallway. Jeremy's door was the end unit. Opening the door, Jeremy bent over beside it and extended his arm like a butler or doorman, "My lord," He mocked.

Andrew rolled his eyes and stepped into the room. Jeremy followed, turning on the lights and closing the door behind him. "Make yourself at home. It's not much, but it's twice the size when you think I don't have to share it."

Andrew looked around. Same as every other room, but he did take note that there was only one bed, the typical dorm room twin. He pulled the chair out from the desk and sat down. "Thanks for this, Jeremy. I owe you."

Jeremy opened the small cube fridge and pulled out two bottles of an energy drink and tossed one to Andrew. "Not a problem. Any time," he said with a smile and sat down on the edge of his tiny bed.

Andrew checked his phone. No text from Bruce. He looked over at Jeremy. He'd never been alone with his R.A. before. It struck him how handsome the guy was.

He noticed again how warm his eyes were. They had a glow about them. He saw streaks of green or gold in them. Hazel, he thought. His body was slender and sleek. He looked long and athletic, not overly built. Slim but not too slim. His mind paused for a second, surprised at its own thoughts. Why was he checking out Jeremy?

He had at times reconciled in his mind that while he was definitely straight, he wasn't like totally, 100%, absolutely, totally straight. He had, just like now, sometimes looked at a guy and thought, *damn he's a hot guy*. But he did wonder sometimes if he could ever really do anything with a guy. He knew he'd never pursue it, but he also wondered what he would do if the situation presented itself. And as his mind went over those thoughts, he suddenly became very self-conscious.

"So, how long do you think it'll be," Jeremy asked. "You can always just crash here if you want."

Andrew made note of the fact there was only one bed, and it was a twin. "Oh, knowing Meat, it won't be that long. I'm kinda surprised he's lasting this long," he mocked his roommate openly.

Jeremy laughed. "Can you even imagine having sex with him? He's so gross."

Andrew held his breath, shocked at Jeremy's question. Did he read his mind, that he was just taking in how hot HE was? Fuck, he wondered, does Jeremy think I'm gay? He shrugged and shook his head. "Oh, no, I do not want to picture that. Please don't put that vision in my head. And that Pamela chick. Can you picture the two of them together?"

Jeremy leaned back on his bed on his two elbows. Andrew across from him took note of how his stomach flattened out, how his shoulders bulged up. "Well, you don't have to worry about skanks like that. You're a really hot guy. You could get anybody you wanted."

Andrew's self-esteem blasted into orbit. He was so flattered by the comment from Jeremy. *He thinks I'm hot,* his mind overflowed with the compliment. But then his thoughts plummeted back to Earth, and he was back to his own awkward self in a split second. What was he supposed to say in response? "Um, uh, thanks," he stuttered.

"And you're a good-looking guy, too, Jeremy," Jeremy said.

Andrew blushed. "I, uh, no, yeah, sorry," he had to laugh, then pulled himself together. "You're a really hot guy, too, Jeremy."

Jeremy acted like he was surprised, "Well, thank you, Andy. That's really nice of you to say."

"Oh, fuck you," Andrew joked. They both laughed and chugged on their drink.

"But seriously, why don't you just crash here," Jeremy suggested again. He stood and put his bottle on the desk, kicked off his sneakers, and then with Andrew's eyes watching him from the chair, he peeled his jeans off and then his shirt. He stood there in just a tiny, low-rise pair of tight, blue briefs. Was he doing a strip tease right there in front of him? Was this show on purpose, just for him?

Andrew couldn't believe he was focusing so hard on another guy's body. Jeremy was slim and sleek, sinewy was the word he'd been looking for. Just a small tuft of hair in the center of his chest, and otherwise, he seemed smooth and soft all over. Andrew saw the rounded, firm butt facing him, and then Jeremy turned, and he saw a nice ample bulge in the blue briefs. And he was caught.

Looking up, he saw Jeremy's eyes looking at him before he had a chance to stop ogling his crotch bulge. Yeah, he was definitely caught before he was able to look up at Jeremy's face.

"Yeah, yeah," Andrew said stuttering and uncomfortable. He waved his arms down pointing at himself. "I mean, I'm already in my pajamas. Well, what I wear to bed. I guess, they're not really pajamas. Sweats," he rambled on.

Jeremy let him. He didn't let his guest off the hook from his awkwardness. "Me, I usually don't wear anything to bed, but I guess I should keep these on, yeah?"

Andrew's mind blew up again. Fuck, why did he want to shout out, *no take them off*? Instead he just slid off the chair and laid himself out on the floor. "Uh, yeah, cool, cool. I'm sorry, I don't mean to put you out. I really appreciate it."

Jeremy looked at the guy spread out at his feet. "You gonna sleep on the floor?"

"Uh yeah, I mean, where else, right? I don't want to be a hassle, I mean, we can't both fit in that bed. You got an extra pillow or something, though?" Andrew lay down on his back and put his hands behind his head. Jeremy's eyes immediately bolted down to the gray sweatpants he was wearing. And in that instant, Jeremy realized he was half hard. More than half hard.

Was Jeremy smiling? Jeremy loomed over him. He felt uncomfortable and adjusted himself, then rolled onto his side, trying to ignore the feeling he was feeling. He was trying to ignore the fact that he liked Jeremy's eyes on him. He liked that Jeremy saw and now knew about his significant size. He wanted people to know. Maybe Jeremy would tell everyone. Maybe he'd finally find

159

willing partners who would want to see his big cock. Maybe Jeremy wanted it. *What was he thinking?*

Jeremy reached onto his bed and pulled off the top blanket and tossed it down onto Andrew's top half. "Here, you can ball up the end of this and use it as a pillow. If you want."

"Cool," said Andrew accepting it. He used it to cover his body, relieved that his cock was hidden from Jeremy. "Thanks. So, good night."

Jeremy stood for one more minute in silence. Andrew thought it seemed like he was going to say something else, but then Jeremy went over to the wall, turned off the light, then slid down into his bed and got under the sheet. There was some light coming in the small window and under the door, and Andrew looked over and could see Jeremy lying on his side, still looking down on him on the floor. "Good night," he said.

The minutes went by. Andrew's mind kept racing a mile a minute. What was he thinking? He knew he was open to things. He always thought, if the opportunity came up, he would definitely be up for fooling around with another dude. And Jeremy was hot. Yeah, Jeremy was hot. He pictured his slim body again and that pair of blue underwear. How tiny it was, how the elastic hugged his cute round butt, how that bulge looked. He was so happy for the comforter covering him, because he was now sporting a full hard-on that was pressing up inside his sweatpants. He squirmed and rolled, not knowing what to do with the feelings that were washing over him. He let out a sigh of discomfort.

"Come on, dude," Jeremy said. "You can't stay on the floor. Come up. We can share."

Andrew freaked out silently. His mind wild with

fear and anxiety, or was it eagerness and anticipation and lust? Fuck yes, he thought. I want to be pressed against him. But his mouth ignored his thoughts. It was afraid of being found out. What if Jeremy was just being nice? What if he went too far and he freaked out on him? "Oh, no, that's OK. I don't want to inconvenience you."

Jeremy would not take no for an answer. "Dude, get up here. Come on. We'll make it work."

Not one cell in Andrew's body could say no a second time. He rolled up and dragged the comforter off the floor with him. "Fine," he said. "But if you are at all uncomfortable, I can get back on the floor."

Jeremy laughed. "Stop, come on, there's room. But we might have to spoon a little."

Andrew didn't think his cock could get any harder, but it did. It leapt in his pants. He didn't know how he was going to hide it, but he also wondered if he really wanted to. He wondered if the light coming in was enough for Jeremy to see it. It was huge, so he didn't think there was any way it wasn't completely obvious. He put his butt down on the edge of the bed. "How do you want me," he asked and immediately thought it sounded stupid as fuck.

Jeremy's hand was on his shoulder urging him down. "Come on, lie down. Here."

Jeremy pushed himself back against the wall to make more room in the tiny bed. He was on his side facing forward, and Andrew laid himself out facing the same way. He was hanging off the incredibly small, twin bed. He knew he had to pull back away from the edge, but he knew he'd be pressing into Jeremy if he did. He didn't have a chance to make the decision himself, though, because Jeremy's arm reached over him and wrapped around his waist. He felt himself hugged, and it felt so fucking good.

"Come on, you'll fall off," Jeremy said. His hand flattened against Andrew's stomach. He could feel its warmth through his shirt. And then Jeremy shifted, and his other arm came through under Andrew's neck. He was completely wrapped up in both of Jeremy's arms. And then those arms tugged him backwards, and he felt the length of Jeremy's body press into him. His back pressed into the front of Jeremy, and he loved it. But he knew he could not admit it. He was so freaked out that he had no idea how to react. Should he fight off the feeling? Should he object to the obvious embrace?

"OK," he said. "You're not being crushed?"

"No, it's OK. This is nice, isn't it," Jeremy asked.

"Uh, I, uh," Andrew was at a loss for words. He had no idea what to say. "Yeah, this is nice." He repeated Jeremy's words. He felt himself hugged more firmly.

"Hey, I gotta help out my bro, right?"

Andrew felt awash in warmth and friendship. Why was he such an idiot? This awesome guy was offering to share his bed with him. He was being hugged. He felt warm and liked, and it didn't hurt that Jeremy was hot. Those fantasies of trying things with a guy were alive in his head, and he thought to himself, *this is going to make the best spank bank vision to jerk off to tomorrow*. He put his hand down on Jeremy's arm that was resting in front of him and settled into the hug. "Yeah, this is great. Thank you."

"Any time," Jeremy said. And then repeated more slowly and deliberately, "Any time."

Andrew tried to fall asleep, but he realized he was lying on his phone. He reached into his pocket to pull it out. As he put it on the table, he saw the text message on his home screen. *Dude coast clear she's gone.*

He put the phone down on the table face down. Fuck that, he was not going anywhere.

* * *

He fell asleep, but after a while, with the body pressed against his back, the comforter that covered them, his t-shirt and sweatpants, and the arms wrapping around him, he felt hot as fuck. Every inch of him felt the heat. He felt sweat all along his back and knew Jeremy must feel it, too.

He thought about the fact that Jeremy was only wearing a tiny pair of underwear. He directed his mind to focus on his back. He focused on the skin of Jeremy's torso pressed against him. He let his mind shift focus lower. He felt Jeremy's thighs bent at the same angle as his, barely any space between them. And he dared focus on a more central point. His mind reached out to communicate with the nerve endings in the roundness of his own butt. *Do I feel anything against me? Yes, yes, there is something making contact. I can feel something pressing into my butt. It bulges. It is there, it is definitely there.* His mind reeled with the idea. Jeremy's cock was pressing against his butt.

The heat intensified. He sighed loudly. Jeremy shifted. He knew he couldn't turn around. There was no room to even move. He put his hand around Jeremy's arm that was around the top of him and urged it backwards and off of him. He sat up. "Are you hot?"

Jeremy answered immediately, "Yeah, it's hot. You must be hotter with those sweatpants on."

Andrew didn't know if he could do what he knew he should. He knew he wanted to, but he also realized an important issue.

Jeremy made it worse. "Why don't you take them off?"

Andrew stuttered, "I'm, uh, I'm not wearing... anything underneath."

"Oh," Jeremy said. "Well, that's OK. I'm cool with it. If you are."

Andrew couldn't control the thoughts swirling in his head. He reached down and pulled on the drawstring, untying it. Can he do this? Can he really do this? He pushed his thumbs into the top of the pants on each of his hips. His mind was still uncertain, but his hands were more than eager. They pulled the pants down quickly all the way to his ankles. His feet obliged and pulled up free of them. His hands then reached back up and pulled the t-shirt off as well.

Jeremy was leaning up behind him. He felt watched, looked at. He put the t-shirt down on the floor with the sweatpants. He was naked. He was completely naked in another dude's bed. With the other dude. His cock was so hard, it hurt.

"If it makes you feel less self-conscious, I'll take these off, too." Jeremy was reaching down and pulling his own underwear off. "There, now we're even."

Andrew put his feet back up on the bed and slid them in under the sheet. He pushed the comforter off the end of the bed. With a resigned sigh, he took the lead and pressed himself back against Jeremy. He wiggled in closer. He knew he wanted to. He knew he liked it. He was not going to hold back. This was it. His mind gave up any reservations it had. He wanted this more than he was allowing himself to think. His cock was so fucking hard. How did it know so clearly what it had taken his brain so long to admit?

Jeremy's arms were around him instantly. He was pulled back down into the embrace like before, but it felt more personal. He felt Jeremy's head press into the side of his neck. He felt his hand open up wide on his now naked stomach. The fingers caressed his flesh. The arm his head rested on top of folded around his chest.

Jeremy let out a sigh, and Andrew's mind went back to a survey of what it was feeling. Arms wrapped around him. A hand spread out on his stomach holding him back pressed against Jeremy's warm slender body. His thighs came in tighter now and hugged in closer to him. And then Andrew let his mind go right where it wanted to. He could feel Jeremy's cock against his ass. He kept his focus there, and he realized just what he was hoping. It was hard.

Andrew let out a huge whispering moan. Jeremy ever so slightly rotated his hip forward, pressing his cock against Andrew's ass with just a tiny bit more pressure. Andrew wanted it to happen. He wanted more. He put his hand on Andrew's and moaned again, and then he pushed his ass back against Jeremy's cock. It was on.

Jeremy slid his hand down Andrew's stomach, caressing and fondling the whole way. He pressed a finger into his belly button. Andrew had no idea how erotic that could be. The hand kept going south, and in a few seconds, it wrapped around Andrew's huge, hard cock. "Oh my," Jeremy whispered. "What do we have here?"

Andrew was so happy, he could barely respond. "Told you," he said.

Jeremy began stroking it. He twisted slightly so his

own cock managed to slide right in between the cheeks of Andrew's ass, in the crack where it burrowed in. He started rubbing it up and down.

"Fuck, how big is this thing," he whispered into Andrew's ear. "I know you've measure."

"Eight," Andrew admitted. "And a little more."

Jeremy took his hand off of it. He pulled his arm out from under Andrew's head. Andrew felt Jeremy lift himself up, and then he felt hands pushing him backwards on the bed. Jeremy straddled above him, and Andrew let his body roll until he was flat on his back.

Jeremy was towering over him again. His legs pressed into each side of his hips. He felt Jeremy's cock drop down on top of his own. He looked up at his R.A. He was so hot. How did he not ever notice this before? His lean athletic body, those warm eyes, the jawline. And then he looked at those lips, so round and full. It's like Jeremy knew what he was concentrating on.

"I have to suck your cock," he said. "I just have to. Can I?"

Andrew let a smile explode across his face. "Sure," he said happily.

Jeremy slid down, his knees came up and over Andrew's legs, and he pressed them in between, urging Andrew to spread them wider. Jeremy's entire body bent down between them until his head came down over his cock. One hand holding him up, the other picked up Andrew's hefty cock and held it straight up.

"Fuck me," Jeremy moaned. "What a fucking cock." His head dropped down, and with open lips, he descended on Andrew's huge cock. With a moan, he went down as far as he could, which was almost the entire way. Andrew was impressed.

With just barely an inch still outside his mouth, Jeremy pulled back up and then immediately slid right back down, letting the cock open his throat up to its girth and length. One hand at its hilt, he kept it sticking straight up and let it slide in and out of his willing mouth and throat.

He pushed on further and got almost the entire length down his throat. He kept it there, buried inside him, and he didn't move. He wasn't letting it back out. Andrew could feel the warm, wet pressure along the entire shaft until finally Jeremy relented and pulled off. With a gasp and a choking sound, Jeremy again exclaimed passionately, "Fuck."

But he went right back at it. Andrew could feel his new buddy's throat open more and more accepting the huge cock deeply. Jeremy stayed down on it for longer and longer. His grip on the hilt squeezed a little more. As he lifted his mouth off it, he began to slide his hand up and down the length of it.

Andrew couldn't take it very long. He was lying in a state of erotic euphoria. He never knew a mouth could be this talented. He looked down at Jeremy who was absolutely loving every minute of sucking his fat cock. *Yeah*, he thought, *you love that, don't you buddy*.

It was all too much. He felt the convulsions deep inside himself. He had to throw his head back. He was so close. Jeremy was stroking him and sucking him. Up and down the wet mouth soaked his fat cock. He wasn't going to be able to hold back much longer.

Jeremy looked up at him. They locked eyes. Andrew was breathing heavy and hard. Jeremy's hand started moving faster, gripped around him.

"I want to see it, buddy. I want to watch you shoot. Will you cum for me?"

"Yeah," Andrew gasped. "Yeah."

"That's it, bro. Shoot that load."

Andrew couldn't hold off. His cock was pulsing in Jeremy's grip, and then it exploded. A blast of cum shot up in the air and landed in his own face. Jeremy watched, and Andrew looked right at him, too. Another shot splashed across his lips from his own cock. And then shot after shot drenched his torso. His chest, his stomach. He felt it pool in his belly button, where Jeremy had caressed him with a finger.

He couldn't catch his breath. His cock kept dumping jizz all over him until he was a wet, white mess. Jeremy finally let go of his cock and laid himself out on top of him. He could feel the cum pressed between the two of them as Jeremy let it get all over him, too.

Face to face, he laid on top of him. Andrew was still catching his breath when Jeremy asked in a whispered tone. "Can I kiss you?"

Andrew didn't answer. He just reached up and put a hand on the back of Jeremy's head and pulled him down for a passionate open-mouth kiss. Jeremy's tongue impaled his mouth. He could taste the saltiness immediately. He accepted the invasion and wrapped both his arms around the slim, slender guy on top of him. He spread his legs further and then lifted them up and wrapped them around Jeremy.

They kissed for what felt like hours. Andrew thought he had only wanted to fool around mildly with another dude, but this was more than he'd ever thought he would do. His cum was smeared all over both of them. His arms held Jeremy tight against him and would not let go. He accepted a wet, salty kiss from this guy. He let his tongue invade his mouth. And he felt Jeremy rubbing his cock up and down on top of his spent but still huge one.

Jeremy didn't stop kissing him. He kept his tongue in Andrew's mouth, invading and exploring the warm, wet, inside. And then Jeremy's breathing started getting faster and faster. Until Andrew accepted a loud moan deep into his own mouth. And he felt the jets of warm, wet jizz blasting all over his stomach. Jeremy was shooting his load all over him, joining with his own.

Jeremy dropped his head down beside Andrew's. Their arms stayed wrapped around each other. Jeremy nuzzled into his neck and started kissing it over and over. Andrew couldn't believe this really happened.

"Holy fuck," he said. "That was so hot. I can't believe we did that."

"You're OK?"

"OK? Fuck yeah. That was incredible. I mean, thank you? Should I say thank you?"

Jeremy laughed. "I think it would be polite."

"Well, then, thank you."

Jeremy rolled off him and back to his original position. Andrew rolled, too, and pressed back in to be spooned again. Jeremy's hands caressed him all over his soaked torso, rubbing cum into his skin. They were both drenched in cum. The sheets were wet, but neither of them cared.

"So you'll stay the night, won't you," he asked.

"I'd really like that," Andrew answered.

"So can we do this again some time," Jeremy asked.

"Yeah," Andrew said and reached behind him to grip Jeremy's cock. "I mean, I have to pay you back some time."

Jeremy was a bit surprised. "Really? You would?"

"Yeah, I mean it's only fair."

Jeremy admitted. "Fuck yeah, any time. I mean, I assumed you were straight."

"Oh, I am," Andrew admitted. "But I'm not *that* straight. Not so straight that I can't help a bro out."

Through a wide smile, Jeremy said, "Well, straight boy, you can suck my cock any time you want."

Andrew planned in his head that in the morning when he woke up, Jeremy would not have to wait long for the favor to be returned. "All I know is, I hope Meat gets lucky all the time."

Weekend Surprise, Part Two

"So, Marco tells me you're a year behind him. A sophomore, is that right?" Leo, his father, asked me as he poured maple syrup on his short stack of pancakes.

"Yeah," I said. "We've been friends since I got here. Marco was my orientation peer last year, and we've been friends ever since." I looked over at my friend and then back to his dad again. They were both happily chewing down their breakfast. Marco had a giant omelet that hung off the plate on both ends. His dad Leo, who might still have the taste of my cum in his mouth from our morning rendezvous in the shower, was slicing into his pancakes. Our three coffee mugs stood intermingled in the middle of the small table.

"You guys must be having the time of your lives. I'll never forget college. Man, did I let loose. Wild times."

"Dad," Marco objected. "When was there ever a time you did not let loose?"

Leo shrugged and nudged his son. "All I'm saying is you boys must be sowing your wild oats, partying every night, getting wild. Nothing like living in the dorms, am I right?"

Marco looked over at me, like he was apologizing for his father with just a glance over at me. "You'll have to forgive my father. He's a free spirit. Isn't that what you call it, dad?"

Leo looked like he was enjoying my slight discomfort. But if I could have admitted to myself in that moment, I was insanely turned on by the reality of the situation. There I was out to breakfast with my best friend and his hot, muscular dad who had just sucked my cock in the shower barely an hour before.

Marco continued. "My dad thinks he's still young and hot. And fuckable."

I almost spit out my eggs. Leo was staring at me with a huge grin on his face. I picked up my coffee and took a swig. It was way too hot, and I had to drop it back down on the table and take a swig of water. "How old are you, Mr. Russo, if you don't mind me asking. You do look really young. You know, for a dad."

"No worries," he said, still grinning at me. "I'm 39. Had this one while I was still in college. Well, actually when I was his age exactly."

Marco took over the story. "College sweethearts. Love at first sight. Soul mates. It's all very disgusting."

"That sounds nice," I offered.

Marco shrugged.

Leo kept the conversation going without hesitation, though. "And how about you, Kyle? Sophomore, a year behind Marco here, so what does that make you then, 20, yeah?"

"Um," I stuttered. "Will be. In a few months."

Leo for once looked a little surprised and took a moment to respond. "So, 19."

Marco interjected, "That reminds me. We have to do something big for your birthday in December. A big party. Invite everyone."

"Can I come?" Leo asked.

"No," Marco stated firmly. Leo smiled at me and shrugged.

172

We continued eating. The server came over and refilled our coffee, which completely ruined my very detailed and exacting balance of coffee, sugar, and creamer. I hate when they do that.

As I added sugar to my mug, Leo continued his grilling. He obviously wanted to know more about me. "So, you don't go home on the weekends either, Kyle? I swear I would only see my boy here over the summer if I didn't come visit him."

"No," I explained. "I'm from California. My family is all still out there. So, it's a little far to go for weekends."

"What brought you to a New England college then," Leo asked.

"I don't know. It just seemed the right fit. I always wanted to go to a well-known liberal arts school like this one. My parents are originally from the Boston area." I explained, not sure if it was too much information or not enough. Were the questions just gonna keep coming all through breakfast? Did Marco think it was weird his dad seemed so interested in me?

As we finished breakfast, Leo took the check off the table with a flourish. "I got this. Kyle, I'm just so glad Marco has good friends. Now I know why he never wants to come home."

"Dad," Marco rolled his eyes.

Leo went off to pay the bill at the front counter. Marco was finishing up the last bits of home fries on his plate. "I'm sorry about my dad. He's not usually such an interrogator."

"It's OK," I said. "He seems really... cool."

Marco put his fork down. "My parents are, well, they call themselves free spirits. I don't really know what it means, but they had me really young, and they're... you know, not your typical parents."

173

I was intrigued. "How so?"

Marco lowered his voice to make sure his dad didn't hear. "Well, they're not really that much older than me, you know? They're very open about everything, which is both good and bad when you're growing up. We were always going to nudist resorts. And you know, things like, they smoke weed."

"Oh, damn, that's so cool. My parents don't even drink," I said, feeling a little jealous but also getting a better understanding of how what happened in the shower this morning could have happened.

Marco shrugged. "Yeah, they're really, really cool. I wouldn't trade them for the world."

Leo waved at us from the front counter signaling us to get up so we could leave. We made our way out of the diner and back to his car. I crawled into the backseat in front of Marco who took the passenger seat next to his dad.

As we drove back to campus, Leo asked me, "So what are you doing for Thanksgiving weekend, Kyle? Flying home to California?"

"No," I admitted. "I'm just gonna stick around campus. They have a big dinner for the students who don't go home. It's mostly the foreign students and those of us from far away."

"Oh, no no no," Leo protested. "You can't do that."

Marco looked over at his father. "Why don't you come home with me," he happily suggested. "Dad, would that be OK?"

Leo looked at me in the rearview mirror. His warm, smiling eyes bore right through me. "Absolutely. Kyle, we can't leave you stranded all alone for Thanksgiving. You'll come to our place."

"Oh really, I don't want to intrude," I objected.

Leo's eyes staring right at me forced my heart into my throat while butterflies reeled in my stomach. But at the same time, my cock stirred in my pants.

Marco was the first to say anything, though. "Kyle, you have to come. It'll be so fun. You gotta see where I grew up. You're gonna love our house. And we have a pool table. And my mom is an amazing cook!"

"Your mom."

* * *

Thanksgiving morning Marco and I were seated across from each other on a commuter train out to his parents' town. His dad, he had explained, would pick us up at the train station. So, we had a good hour together on the train.

"So, what's your mom like," I decided to ask.

Marco was more than happy to talk about his family. "Dude, you're gonna love her. She is totally a free spirit. Like what they used to call hippies, you know? She smokes weed and talks about her feelings. My parents both come from money, so please don't get freaked out about it, and like, they're not pretentious at all. It's not a big deal to them."

I didn't know how to delve without delving, how to find out more without letting on why I was a bit apprehensive about the weekend. I thought, *what's it going to be like meeting this woman? Hi, it's very nice to meet you. Your husband is an amazing cocksucker.*

Marco added, "Oh and don't get freaked out if you end up seeing her tits. Like I said, they're kinda like nudists. I'm just really glad you're coming. It'll be nice to have a buffer from their constant attention."

"They sound awesome," I said. "It must be cool to have parents who are so young."

"It is and it isn't," Marco said. "They're like friends sometimes, but they can be strict, too. They're not push-overs, but they're super loving. I mean, you met my dad. He's awesome, right?"

"Yeah, he's… he seems really cool."

"And he really likes you," Marco added. I almost choked on my own spit.

* * *

As we pulled into the small train station, I looked out the window and saw trees in every direction. The train was slowing down in front of a cute, little red brick building. Behind it was a tiny parking lot, and there I saw Marco's dad leaning on the hood of his car in a tight, white tank top. He was waving at the train. "There's your dad," I pointed out.

"Oh, my gawd," Marco rolled his eyes. "Would you look at him? It's not even that warm out."

"I don't know," I said without thinking. "If I looked like that…"

Marco nodded. "Yeah, my dad is a hunk, isn't he?"

I wanted so desperately to agree, but I still had never told Marco that I'm gay, and after what happened with his dad, I didn't know how to respond and decided on humor. "Yeah, total stud. So, I guess you take after your mother?"

Marco laughed loudly and reached over and slugged me in the arm, "Fuck you. And I will have you know, my mom is hot, too. Wait 'til you see her."

"Ew, Marco!" But he was already up out of his chair

and grabbing his duffle bag from the overhead rack. I followed him out of the train and onto the platform.

Leo already had the trunk of the car open, and we both tossed our bags in. Marco gave his father a huge hug. They both looked so happy to see each other. It was really amazing. My dad would never greet me like that. Leo wrapped his big arms around his son, and I saw him plant a kiss on the side of his head. Extracting himself from the embrace, Marco sang out, "You remember Kyle."

"Hello, Mr. Rus…" I began, but he gave me a very stern look. "Sorry, Leo. Hi Leo."

"That's better," he said and offered me an extended hand. I reached out to grab it, but instead of a handshake, I found myself pulled into a similar grappling hug. My head was practically crushed between two massive, mounded pec muscles, and I could feel the chest hair that stuck out from his tank top against my forehead. I returned as much of the hug as I could in my surprise.

"Dad," Marco said, while punching his father's huge upper arm. "Seriously, a tank top? It's barely 50 degrees out, and you're almost 40."

"*Almost* I will remind you, you little shit. Come on, get in."

Marco and I made our way to the passenger side as Leo got in to drive. Marco pulled the door open and didn't stop, "I'll get in back. You sit up front with my dad."

"Uh, OK."

We sped through the countryside. I hadn't really seen much of New England country in the last year and a half, and I was really taking in the beauty of it. Most of the trees were already bare, but it was still a gorgeous countryside. I rolled the window down and looked back at Marco. "Is this OK?" He just nodded at me.

After about a 20-minute drive, we pulled into a long drive with a giant stone sign at the end naming the development or whatever it was, something Estates or something like that. "Here we are," Leo said.

"This is where you live," I asked. What a stupid question. I immediately felt like an idiot.

"This is it. Paradise on earth," Leo joked.

"It's basically like a pretentious country club," Marco said. "Bougey bitches. And one hippy couple."

"We are not hippies. And you know that," Leo said. "Your grandparents are the hippies."

"True," Marco agreed.

"Kyle, don't let him corrupt you," Leo said to me, and he reached over and squeezed my thigh. "It's a really nice place. You're gonna love it." He left his hand on my thigh a little too long, and it caused my cock to start getting hard. I couldn't look back, wondering if Marco had noticed the gesture. But as he had to make a sharp turn into a smaller drive, Leo had to take his hand back. I could still feel its grip on my leg as if it were still there.

We pulled up to a monster house. I mean, it looked like a movie set. There was a huge door in the middle of a circular drive, and two rows of windows spread out in either direction from that center point.

"Holy fuck," I said without thinking. "Your house is so huge. It has like wings and shit."

"Oh," Leo objected. "It's not that big. But you'll be comfortable. Even though the wait staff has the weekend off." I looked over at him wide-eyed. "I'm kidding," he added.

A woman appeared in the front door. She had long blonde hair and was wearing a flowy dress. Getting a closer look, she looked like an angel. She was downright beautiful. She waved at the car as we pulled to a halt in front of her.

I opened the door, and she bent down to see her son in the backseat. I rose up, and she immediately grabbed me, "Oh, you must be Kyle. Hello." Again, I found myself in a warm embrace.

"It's really nice to meet you, Mrs. Russo."

She pushed her hands against my chest. "Oh, we will have none of that. And besides I don't go by that name. What woman has to take her husband's name? I'm Mary. Mary Hamill. It's so nice to meet you. Welcome to our home."

"It's nice to be here. Thank you. Mary," I added on. She smiled at me, obviously happy I used her name. Marco had popped out of the backseat and was himself pulled in for a big hug by his mom. Leo had grabbed both bags and was carrying them both to the open front door.

"Well, my big, strong husband has things under control. Come in, come in," she pushed us to the door, and we entered a foyer that I thought could have been the front room of a museum. It wasn't so much a foyer as it was a rotunda. A double circular staircase led up to a second floor, and doors opened to the left, the right, and in front of us.

"Damn, how do you not get lost in here," I gasped.

Leo was beside me, and his arm was wrapped around my shoulders. "Oh, you'll be fine. You're not afraid of ghosts, are you?" I turned my head to look at all three of them. And then they all laughed at me.

"Marco, your room is all ready for you. Let me show Kyle where he'll be," Leo offered.

Mary had already started back to the doorway to the rear of the room under the double stairs, and Marco was already halfway up one side of the stairs.

Mary shouted back at us as she disappeared through the open doorway, to what I assumed was the kitchen. "You boys get settled. I'm working on dinner. It'll be ready soon. Hope you like turkey, Kyle."

"Who doesn't," I said.

"Come on, Kyle. Let me show you to your room," Leo said as he put his hand on my lower back. I looked up at him. Why did he have to be so incredibly hot? His hand was pushing me toward the same stairs Marco had just gone up. As I turned to them, Leo left his hand on my back. I loved it, I wanted more, but I also felt a pang of guilt, so I bounded up two steps at a time to separate from him a little. At the top, though, I had to wait for him, because I had no idea where I was going.

In that moment I realized the fact that Leo was leading me to a bedroom. Just the two of us. I was instantly half hard even though I was incredibly flustered at the same time. But Marco saved me from whatever it was I was feeling by reappearing from a bedroom. "Which room we gonna put him in, Dad?"

"Your mom set up the one at the end there." He answered his son, then addressed me. "You'll be comfortable. It's the biggest one."

"How many guest bedrooms do you have," I wondered outloud.

Leo just laughed, and thankfully all three of us made our way down a long hallway walking by door after door until one at the end lay open. It was a huge room with a vast bed in the middle. It must be a king, I assumed. There was a small couch and a table, a tall chest of drawers and a short one, and even a small desk. It looked like a fancy hotel room suite or something.

Marco was pointing to the corner where there was

another door. "You have your own bathroom down here. You'll be really comfortable."

"Thank you," I said, truly amazed by the room. It was so well decorated. "This is amazing."

"You're our guest," Leo said. "Anything you need, you just ask." He bowed in a grand but silly way. "Your wish is my command."

"Good," Marco chimed in. "Then leave us alone, Dad."

As Leo stepped out, I got a quick glimpse in his eyes that looked like… regret over being told to leave the room or maybe eagerness over my presence in a bedroom in his home? Had he wanted to get me naked and suck my cock again? Fuck, I hoped so. But could I really do anything with this father and husband? My best friend's father at that? I mean, yeah, I already had, but at that time, I didn't know who he was.

Marco threw himself into the middle of the giant bed. "You're gonna love this room. It's so quiet. And this bed is amazing."

"This is insane," I said. "Really, I can't thank you enough. But I don't want to be a bother to your parents or anything. I just, you sure, it's OK that I'm crashing your family Thanksgiving?"

"Dude," Marco said. "It's totally cool. My parents already love you."

* * *

Marco left me alone to get settled in. I still didn't feel entirely comfortable with the situation, due mostly to the fact that Leo was my best friend's dad. No matter how open and free-spirited the Russos were, I still felt like

Marco would not be entirely comfortable knowing his best friend had fooled around with his dad. I decided that while I didn't have to feel as guilty as I had been feeling about it, I still didn't really want Marco finding out. Did that make me a horrible person? Or was it some type of gray area here?

I took a shower and stayed secluded in this amazing room for a little bit before dinner. I stripped off all my clothes and left them on the bed and went into my en suite bathroom. The shower was one of those rainfall showerheads. I turned it on and was immediately hit by the warm, strong jets of water.

My mind returned to that morning just barely a week ago. The basement shower in the dorms. Leo completely naked. That huge, fat cock of his. I hadn't even gotten to touch it, I remembered. Leo had gone right to his knees and sucked my cock.

I stroked myself with the memory of it. The way his lips felt on my shaft, the expert way he slid up and down on it. Just the idea of this older, muscular, hairy stud of a man on his knees servicing me, worshipping my cock. I felt so in charge, so powerful. How did I make that big, strong man want to fall to my feet and take my cock into his mouth? The way he didn't stop when I warned him. How he just kept sucking me, and I blasted my jizz down his throat.

I looked down at my cock now, stroking it in the warm water. It looked so long and so hard. I pulled on my pale, pink shaft and pictured Leo on his knees sucking me again. The vision was so real, so recent, it didn't take long before I blasted a load across the shower stall. I let out a huge sigh, feeling so relieved. The pressure had been building inside of me that whole day, it was good to release it. Though, I had the feeling it wouldn't last too long with Leo walking around as he does.

* * *

Marco's mother Mary was calling out from downstairs. "Marco, Leo, Kyle. Come, come, it's time to eat!" I got up out of the most comfortable bed I'd ever been in and made my way downstairs.

The table was spread like something out of a movie scene. I could not believe the spread. It looked like the perfect Thanksgiving table. Breads and vegetables. I saw cranberry sauce—the real kind not the can-shaped crap—and carrots and a giant bowl full of steaming hot stuffing. But in the middle of the table was a large empty space.

Leo came in from a sliding door out to a backyard veranda, and Marco had appeared behind me. The three of us men came together around the table, and Mary called out from the kitchen. "Well, they're finally here! I've been calling for you men! I will be right out. Take your seats!"

There was a seat at each end, which I assumed would be for Marco's parents, and one on either side of the table. I took one of those. Marco took the other, across from me.

Leo was making his way toward the kitchen door. I thought I should help, but he pointed back at me and said, "Take your seat, Kyle. You're a guest. Marco, keep him company."

"Are you sure I can't help?"

"Sit," he said. "Sit, we've got it covered."

Left alone, I looked at the chairs. So, I took my place at the table, but I didn't want to touch anything yet. I thought that might be rude, but everything looked so delicious, and I was hungry as fuck.

The Russos all came in together. Mary had a bottle of wine and what looked like a pitcher of iced tea. Leo carried an enormous platter stacked high with turkey parts and turkey meat, steam rising from it in front of his face. Mary took the end seat closer to the kitchen. Leo came round to the side of the table and placed the giant platter in the empty spot in the middle of the enormous spread, then came around and sat at the other end.

Everyone chowed down voraciously until we couldn't eat another bite. I tried not to be a total glutton, but everything was so incredibly delicious. Marco's mom was an amazing cook. We all settled back into our chairs completely sated.

* * *

After a round of coffee and an amazing apple pie for dessert, Marco's parents started clearing the table. Marco and I rose to help, but they shushed us back into our seats. They would not let us do anything.

I tried again to stand and pick things up, but I was immediately ordered back into my chair. I felt so bad, because I hadn't helped in prep, and now I wasn't helping clean. But Mary made the final proclamation on the matter, "You boys are home on break. No kitchen duty this weekend. Marco, why don't you take Kyle downstairs and shoot some pool? We've got everything under control."

Marco looked very happy being off the hook for kitchen duty. "Oh, great idea," he said eagerly. "Come on, Kyle. You any good at billiards?"

"As a matter of fact, I am," I said. I actually was really good at pool. My father owned a bar, and I had been playing for years.

"I'll join you boys in a minute," Leo said. And Marco led me through the kitchen where Mary and Leo were busy cleaning up the dishes and storing leftovers.

Through the kitchen, he led me to a door that he opened. It led down into a large, wide rec room basement. There was a full bar along one wall. Behind it were all sorts of liquors in full bottles. There were swiveling bar stools along it. It looked like a real bar. There was a massive television on the far wall with two recliner chairs in front of it. One faced the television, and one swung around toward us facing what lay in the middle of the room—a giant billiards table under a hanging green-glass lamp that lit it up brightly. On the wall was a wooden rack of pool cues and various movie and beer posters and signs.

"What the fuck," I said. "This looks like a full-service pub down here."

"This," Marco announced proudly, "is our man cave. My dad and I spend hours and hours down here. Isn't it awesome?"

"Yeah," I admitted while walking around to the other end of the pool table. I found the rack and the balls and pulled them out to prepare a game. I started putting the balls in order in the rack while Marco turned the television to a satellite radio station.

As current upbeat music started playing, he came back over and watched me placing the balls in order solid and striped in sequence. "Oh, you do know what you're doing," he commented.

"Care to make it interesting?" I suggested.

"No," he said with a laugh. "I don't think I do."

"Well, I racked them, so you should break," I offered.

We both went over to the rack of pool cues. I can't believe they had so many. I tried the feel of one then selected another. He looked at me surprised, like it made a difference. He grabbed one, too, and said, "No, why don't you break? Show me what you got."

"OK," I said and made my way to the end of the table. With a quick thrust, I sent the cue ball sailing down the table. It struck the pyramid of balls with a loud cracking sound. Balls flew all over the table. One went in.

"Fuck me," Marco said, impressed.

We got into the game, taking turns. After a few rounds, I was clearly way ahead. My friend was awed by my play.

"I didn't know you could play pool so well," he said.

I just shrugged. "My dad owned a bar. I grew up playing."

He watched as I sunk another one of my balls. One more to go, then the eight ball, and I would have the first game in the bag.

"So, Kyle, can I ask you something?" Marco said.

'Yeah," I said not thinking.

"You're gay, right?

I froze in place. I stood up straight and looked over at him. "Well, yeah."

I didn't have to wait long for his response. Which was good, because my heart had stopped. "That's cool," he said. "I mean, I thought you were. Just we never really talked about it."

"Oh, OK. Yeah, I'm sorry. I should have said so at some point."

Marco immediately contradicted me. "No, dude. Why? It doesn't matter. It's all good. But I didn't tell you this—my mom thought we were together."

"No way," I had to laugh.

"Yeah, I had to tell her you're just a friend. And then she asked me if you were gay, and I had to say I didn't know. So, I just thought I would ask."

I sunk my last ball and was lining up a shot at the eight ball that I knew I was going to make. I pointed my cue at a corner pocket, and as I made contact with the cue ball and sent the eight ball straight into that pocket, I asked, "So are you gay?"

Marco hesitated a moment. "Well, no. I'm straight. You know, I mean, mostly straight. Like I wouldn't be freaked out to, you know, experiment, or make out with a guy or do a threesome or stuff like that. But yeah, I like girls."

I wanted to ask him more, but as he went to the far end of the table and started re-racking the balls, Leo came bounding down the stairs. "Who's ready to lose?"

"Oh, don't be so sure, Daddy-O. I think we've got a pool shark here. He already beat me, so why don't you two play each other," Marco said nodding in my direction.

"Well, I can take anything you've got, Kyle," Leo said reaching for a pool cue. "Rack 'em, up."

* * *

Leo was a pretty good player, but I still beat him. He seemed pretty surprised by my skill. So next I let them play each other, and the game went on for a lot longer than the previous ones. Leo cursed when he accidentally scratched while going for the eight ball and lost the game.

"You know, if you boys want a beer, I can't offer it to you, Kyle. But Marco you know where they are," he said.

"Oh, that's OK," I said. "I don't really drink that much."

Marco did go behind the bar and get himself a beer. "You sure you don't want one?" he asked me. But I shook my head. He came back around and handed me a cola, which I gladly accepted.

We played game after game. At some point, Leo turned the television over to a sports channel and a rugby game came on the screen. As we started the next game of pool, I was constantly distracted by the incredibly hot guys going at each other on TV. Their massive legs were all exposed in their short shorts. I had no idea what the rules of the game were, but I didn't care. It was just beefy men grabbing and tackling each other and falling all over each other. I hoped my companions didn't notice how mesmerized I was by the bodies and hoped they just thought I was a fan of the game.

* * *

We played game after game of pool, and I won every single one against each of them. It felt like hours had gone by.

Marco was incredibly impressed by my skills. "OK, so I didn't know you're a pool shark. I didn't know you're gay. How many secrets do you have," he mocked me.

Leo turned his head quickly in surprise. He didn't say anything, but Marco noticed his silent reaction to what he had said. "I never asked Kyle, you know about his preferences. So, after dinner, we talked about it."

"Oh," Leo said. Was it relief I saw in his face? "So, you boys are like best friends, but you didn't know…"

Marco rolled his eyes at his father. "No, dad, we just never talked about it. 'Cuz it doesn't matter. It's all cool. Hey, at least we know we'll never fight over the same… person."

"True," I agreed.

We played game after game for hours. Leo nursed his beers, so I don't think he even had two. Marco had three at least, or there might have been one I missed counting. He was looking a little tipsy but not drunk. Just happy I would say.

"What time is it," he asked.

Leo looked at his watch. "It's early. Nine."

"Yeah, but after all that food, I'm so sleepy," Marco said.

"Oh, you're not going to bed so early," I protested.

"I think I might," he said.

"One more game," Leo suggested.

"Fine. But all three of us play. Cut-throat," Marco said. "And if I win, I get to go to bed. Rack 'em, Kyle."

I went around to the end of the table and got to work setting up the balls for the next game.

"You sure you're not a little drunk, sonny boy," Leo was making fun of him.

"No, just sleepy. What's that shit in turkey called?"

"Tryptophan," I answered.

"Well, we've had a long day," Leo said. "I might not be far behind you."

"Where's Mom," Marco asked.

"She probably went to bed already. She worked hard."

Leo squared up his shot and let loose. It was not a great break.

Marco went second and missed.

It was my turn, and I thought about Marco's comment. *If I win, I get to go to bed.* I thought about that. And I missed a very easy shot. Leo looked at me and tilted his head. Marco didn't notice. Across the table from me, Leo bent over and leaned his head into the shot. He closed one eye, and at the last second, the other one left the ball and glanced up at me. Leo almost missed the cue ball completely, and it skittered sideways.

"Dad, you suck," Marco made fun of him. Leo just shrugged.

Round after round, shot after shot, slowly Marco's balls disappeared from the table in succession as Leo and I suddenly became very bad at pool. Finally with a flourish, Marco sealed the victory.

"Woo hoo! I finally beat you, Kyle! Is that the first time all night you lost a game," he did a little victory dance.

I smiled and put my hands together in a silent clap toward him. "You won, fair and square."

"Good, now can I go to bed?" he sighed and put his cue stick in the rack.

"All right. Tomorrow, can we hit the golf course?"

"Oh, I've never golfed," I admitted.

"Well, then we'll have a chance to beat you then," Leo said. "I can teach you, Kyle."

Marco made his way around the table. Reaching up a hand to his father's shoulder, he pulled it down and planted a kiss on his father's cheek. "Night, Daddy-O."

"Night, Marco."

He then came around to me and flung his arms around me and planted a kiss on my cheek as well. "Night, Buddy. I'm so glad you're here. Love you."

"Love you, too, drunky."

Marco acted offended. "I'm not drunk! I'm just tired. You'll pay for that on the golf course tomorrow. It'll be fun. My dad's a great teacher."

And with that I was alone with Leo in the basement. He looked at me. I looked at him.

He walked to the pool table and reached down. "One more game," he asked.

"You're on," I said with a smile.

"Winner takes all." His words made me freeze in place. What did he mean? Did he mean what it sounded like? He was busy racking balls. So, I went to the opposite side of the table and added some chalk to my cue.

Leo pulled the triangle off the balls and stepped back. He grabbed his cue from where he had leaned it against the wall. I swung my cue and commenced the game. Balls flew in every direction on the table.

He didn't stand a chance. My half-hard cock directed my every move. I sunk ball after ball. Leo did, too, but it didn't matter. My mind was focused on what he had said. Even though I didn't know what it meant. *Winner takes all.* All I knew was I wanted to be that winner. And after finishing off all my balls, I buried the eight ball in the side pocket and nodded in satisfaction.

I looked up to see Leo smiling at me. "Fuck you're a good pool player. You win."

"Thanks," I said with a nod.

Leo sighed. "So, dessert then. Another slice of apple pie?"

Oh, is that what he meant? Fuck. That's not what I had in mind. But then I thought, could I really fool around with this married man, the father of my best friend, in his very home, while his wife was asleep upstairs?

191

Leo turned and went up the stairs without a word. I was left alone. I looked around. I guessed he would be coming back down, so I waited, but after a long while, I was still alone, and Leo hadn't returned. With every passing moment, I felt more awkward and uncomfortable. So, after another few minutes, I went upstairs. In the kitchen, I found no one. One single light over the counter was on, and the room was otherwise dark. Looking through the doorways to the dining room and to the front of the house, all the lights were off. I heard no sound from a television or anything. I stood there in the kitchen not knowing what to do.

I heard steps coming down the stairs, and Leo reappeared from the front. His hair was wet. He had obviously showered, and he had changed into a pair of athletic shorts made out of sweatpants material and a loose-fitting t-shirt. I don't think he expected to find me in the kitchen.

I checked him out from head to toe, but what really caught my eye was the bulge of his huge cock bobbing around in the loose-fitting shorts. It looked enormous, and he was clearly not wearing underwear.

"Oh, there you are. Did you want pie or ice cream or anything?"

"No," I answered slowly. "I'm not… hungry."

He went around to the refrigerator and looked inside for a minute. He looked like he was thinking. "Yeah. I guess I'm not really hungry either."

I walked around to the sink and found a glass and poured myself a glass of water. That brought me a lot closer to him. We were both on the same side of the long, impressive island counter in the center of their kitchen. I turned with my glass of water to find Leo leaning against the end of it. We were face to face, steps from each other.

He looked me in the eyes. "I'm really glad you're here," he said.

"Me too," I said. "Better than being alone in the dorms." I smiled but didn't know what else to say. Leo didn't say anything. We stood there in the dim-lit room, staring at each other.

"Everyone's in bed already. Passed out," he said in a really low tone. "Looks like they left us all alone." He threw that out there. Were we really going to do this? It's all I wanted and everything I worried about.

I looked right into his eyes. This man twice my age. His head of black hair was wet and messy, but his dark beard looked as well-groomed as ever. He stared right through me with his eyes so dark, they seemed almost black. I allowed myself to continue looking him up and down even this much closer to me, knowing full well he would know what I was doing. I looked at his rounded muscular chest under his shirt. His flat stomach and his rounded hip muscles gave him an incredibly impressive, sexy physique. His arms resting at his side, his biceps and forearms were still looking huge even relaxed. His thighs reminded me of the rugby players on the television. He was so tall, so muscular, he loomed over me.

I made my decision and went for it. "I won."

Leo lifted one eyebrow and the side of his lip curled. "You did." He reached out and put a hand on my bulge, which had already grown a little. At his first touch, it leapt up, eager for what might happen. I felt my cock grow longer and harder under the pressure of his hand.

I went to work. I urged his hand away from my cock. I gripped the bottom of his t-shirt and yanked it upward. I wedged it into his armpits and pulled it up over his rounded chest. Fuck, his body was amazing. He looked at me with a yearning look, but he left his hands at his side. I was in charge.

I put my hands on his shoulder and pressed in opposite directions. He got my message, and he turned around. He faced the counter behind him, and I got a glimpse of his glorious, huge, round ass, so beefy. He was just like those rugby players. He was so much bigger than I was, so much more muscular, but when I had touched his shoulders, he did exactly what I had urged him to do. Oh, this was on.

With one motion, I moved both my hands to the waistband of his shorts and yanked them down, and they dropped to the floor around his ankles. Oh, that incredible ass shone brightly in the dim light. Brighter and paler than the rest of his swarthy skin, he had a very distinct tan line, and his ass was like a beacon of light in the room. I had to grip it with both hands. I caressed it and squeezed and rubbed.

I pushed on the inside of his knees with mine, and he spread his legs further. I undid my jeans as quickly as I could. I pulled them down halfway down my thighs along with my underwear. My cock bounced in front of me like it could see Leo bent over the counter, and it knew what it wanted.

I saw a bottle of olive oil on the counter. I grabbed it and poured it out into my hand. I pressed my hand between his cheeks deep into the crack and found his warm hole. Leo was shocked and surprised I could tell. I think he thought he'd just be on his knees sucking me off again.

I put the bottle back down and pushed on his back between his shoulder blades. He bent over, putting his arms and head down on the counter. His ass stuck out even more.

With my oily hand, I stroked myself. I looked at this manly stud in front of me, bent over a kitchen counter, legs spread, sticking his ass out at me. All at my direction. My cock was raging hard. I stepped in closer.

I went right for it. I pressed the head of my cock against his warm, oily hole. I heard him moan. I took the bottle and drizzled more oil on my cock. I put it back down and pressed against him a little harder. I heard him moan again.

I reached my arm around as best I could around this big man, and I was just able to reach up to his face. I placed my hand firmly over his mouth, and again I pushed against him. He opened for me, and the head of my cock slid into his warm ass.

I could feel the moan in his mouth against my hand. He was breathing in and out, in and out. And I pushed forward. Inch by inch my cock disappeared into his ass. His moans of hesitation turned into sighs of pleasure. I was fully planted deep in Leo's ass.

He spread his arms out further on the kitchen counter. I felt his ass muscles fully relax, letting me in completely. I took my hand off his mouth and brought both down on his beautiful round ass. Gripping it I slid my cock half out of his ass. He was trying so hard not to make any sound at all. I had such an urge to slap his ass, but I knew it would be too loud.

I pushed my cock forward and buried it in his ass again. He breathed out deeply and fully. He was submitting to me completely and silently. I pushed a little more to see if I could get any deeper inside him, and when I knew I was as far as I could go, I slid all the way out until just the head of my cock teased his hole.

And then I went to work. In and out, fast then slow.

I got into a steady rhythm, then broke it when he wasn't expecting. I would slide all the way in, then I would just tease the last inch or two in and out, and then I would plant it with one thrust all the way deep inside his ass.

I remembered that big, fat, thick cock of his. He hadn't even reached down to touch it. He just stayed bent over, taking my cock. So, I reached around and gripped it. He was as hard as a rock. I touched the tip, and he was dripping like mad. It was so hot. My hand was coated in his dripping pre-cum. I brought it up and put my hands to his lips. I pushed my fingers into his mouth, and he sucked on them eagerly.

I couldn't take it much longer. I started slamming in and out of him so vigorously, I couldn't believe we were able to stay as quiet as we did. His breath was erratic and deep. With every thrust deep into him, he exhaled strongly.

Leo risked speaking and finally whispered back at me, "Oh, fuck me, Kyle. Fuck me." That put me over the edge, and I exploded deep inside him. Reaching around and gripping his cock again I stroked it to the rhythm of the dying pulses of my erupting cock inside him, and I heard him let out a silent sigh. His cock erupted in my hand. I couldn't see, but I imagined it splashed all over the side of the counter and pooled on the floor at his feet.

Pulling out of him, I stepped back and looked at him bent over. Leo, this big hairy muscle stud looked amazing ass up, legs spread, and freshly fucked in his kitchen. I couldn't believe this really happened. I already wanted to do it again, but we shouldn't risk it.

He finally let himself up and pulled up his shorts. He turned to me with a smile that looked like pure satisfaction and relief.

"Wow," he sighed. "That was incredible. I didn't expect that."

He leaned down and planted a big kiss on my mouth. His big, soft lips felt so good on mine.

"I can't believe that happened. That was such a surprise," he added.

"I'm here all weekend," I said.

Leo looked down at me, a smile blooming on his face. Yeah, it was gonna happen again.

The Cum Wall of Senton Hall

Senton Hall was a building full of classrooms way at the back of campus. There were no offices, no departments, just a boring building full of classrooms. Walking through its halls felt more like high school than college, except that if it were a high school, at least the corridors would be full of lockers.

There was no reason to go to Senton Hall unless you had a class there. And once class was over, everyone tore out of there to more interesting parts of campus where things were happening, even the professors. I mean, there was nothing really wrong with the building. It served its purpose. If there's one thing a college campus needs, it's classrooms, right? It's just that it was a sad, concrete-block, square building with no character. Maybe if one of the academic departments had their offices in there or something, there would be more of a spark of life in the darn place.

You don't get through four years without having a bunch of classes in Senton. By the time I was a second semester junior, I'd had at least one class in the building every semester. Now, I'm not complaining, because let me tell you about Senton Hall's little secret. I was lucky enough to find it my very first semester as a freshman. Well, I call it a secret, because no one ever talks about it, but evidence suggests that a whole lot of guys knew about it.

So, like I said, as soon as your class is over, you jet out of that building back to the dorms or the student center or another class. There is nothing at all to linger over in its hallways, so it can get real quiet real fast. Even when classes are going on, the doors are all closed usually, so even if there are hundreds of students in lectures, there's never anyone just hanging out there. Which brings me to the building's not-so-secret secret.

Up on the third floor, there is a men's room that is ridiculously enormous. I think it was probably originally a classroom that got converted into a john. It sat on a corner where two corridors come together, and it was a full-sized square room. It had two entrances, one out to each corridor. And this is the freaky thing. I've never seen anything like it before. Lining one entire wall was a row of urinals—I kid you not—there must have been like 30 in a row. Another wall was nothing but sinks. A dirty dozen. I know. I've counted them. And the other two walls were all stalls from one door, down to a corner and along the other wall all the way to the other door. How many dudes did they think would have to take a piss at the same time? And the really stupid part about it is, there was never anyone in there.

So, like I said, I stumbled across it my first semester. There was such an odd vibe about the room. I probably laughed at how ridiculous it is. But it was the absolute silence and solitude that struck me, and one dirty thought seeped into my mind. This would be the perfect place to rub one out.

I'd been sneaking into this bathroom to wank my wand for the last two and a half years. At some point after a few such trips, I noticed that the stall in the corner of the room seemed awfully big. Made sense, I mean, how do you make two rows of stalls come together at a corner? What do you do with the extra space? This one stall was stupid big. I think some of my professors had smaller offices. At least the adjuncts did. But I digress.

This huge corner stall was the secret I wanted to tell you about. I mean, if you were in there yanking your chain, nobody would know. And there was enough room that you could put your backpack down, take your coat off, and best part, there was even a sink right there in the stall. Fucking gold mine for the horny college dude who shares a tiny dorm room and usually has zero privacy.

But like I said, this stall was not my personal secret garden. The toilet and sink were along the one cinder block wall, and the other wall had nothing on it at all, except for… lots and lots of stains. The entire wall was covered in splash stains from end to end, from about four feet up all the way down to the floor. And someone in the past, who knows how long ago, fuck maybe this has been going on for years or decades, well any way, someone at some point painted on this wall just above head level in really neat letters, 'The Cum Wall of Senton Hall.' Yeah, those stains? Jizz. Cum. Sperm. Cock juice. Spooge. Whatever you want to call it. Dried splash stains covered this entire fucking wall. And for two and a half years, I'd been adding to the impressionistic painting that had more artists collaborating on it than anyone could ever imagine.

Some days and some evenings, I would head back to Senton Hall even if I didn't have a class. You remember those nights, when your dormmate would be hanging in the room all night long, and all you really needed to do was shoot one off. I got into a habit of going for a walk around campus, which always led me to my favorite quiet and private bathroom stall to yank my own chain.

My college wasn't particularly 'gay friendly,' and I honestly didn't have any outlets. Despite being in a dorm full of horny, college-aged guys semester after semester, I hadn't gotten lucky in those first few years. So, you can imagine how often I was shooting a load on that dank stall wall. I even got into a routine. I studied the comings and goings in Senton Hall. I figured out when the classes would start, how long it usually took students to leave afterward and when I could be assured no one would interrupt my wanks.

There was a sweet spot basically every evening for several hours. There were evening classes that only met once a week, so they were long classes that went on for hours. They started at 5:45 PM and didn't end until after 8:00 PM. The last shorter class let out at 6:00, and it took students about 10 minutes to clear out. By 6:15 almost every night, the halls of Senton were a ghost town. There were classes going on in the building, so it wasn't completely freaky for me to wander in, but with the exception of anyone who was there for their night class, evenings in Senton were blissfully devoid of anyone to catch me in my solo act. That is, until that one crazy night.

* * *

So there was this one Tuesday night in my second semester of junior year, I was sporting a crazy case of the hornies. My roommate was sitting at his desk studying, and it didn't look like he was going to leave the room at all that night. I had to cum, somehow, somewhere. I threw on a pair of shorts and off I went with one destination in mind. My private sanctuary. The Cum Wall of Senton Hall.

Now I do have to say, for all the cumming that obviously happened on that wall, I was a bit surprised that I never in those years bumped into anyone else intent on using its surface. Even though I could tell there were additions to it made all the time. Trust me, I studied those stains. I saw their patterns. I even planned where to add my new touches most of the time. There were a few times that someone else's artistic strokes were still fresh and wet. But for all the times I visited, I never bumped into another dude.

To be honest, even though I was gay, I had a feeling that my fellow wall blasters were just straight dudes getting their rocks off. There was no evidence that the wall offered any chance of meeting a guy who'd want to suck or fuck or have a gay old time with me. To most guys it was probably just a great place to jerk one out.

Anyway, sorry. Tuesday night, junior year. I made my way into Senton around 6:30 PM. It was absolutely silent. The halls were completely empty. I could see through the small glass windows in the doors that there were a handful of classrooms in mid-lecture. I practically ran up the two flights of stairs to the third floor and straight into the huge men's room.

My cock had started throbbing halfway across campus, knowing it was about to get attention, so by the time I got to the bathroom, I was at full mast. Sorry, something else I didn't tell you about me. I don't mean to brag. It's just the truth. I have a huge cock. Believe me, though, it's as much a curse as it is a blessing. I mean, it's big. And fat. You may think it's the best thing ever, but trust me, if you had to lug this thing around in your pants all the time, you'd understand.

So yeah, I've measured it. Of course I have. It's just

over nine inches. It looks even bigger on me, 'cuz I'm only like 5'7". I use two hands to whack off, and the head still pops out from my top hand. So yeah, when I'm hard and jerking, I love my big, fat cock, but it's a fucking pain in the ass otherwise. Imagine how awkward it is when everyone notices it bulging in your pants, even when you don't really want the attention. I have to wear underwear all the time or else it flops around or trails down my leg and makes a huge, long bulge. It's honestly more hassle than it's worth.

Sorry. I suck at storytelling. Where was I? Oh yeah, that Tuesday night, junior year. As soon as I opened one door to the men's room, I took a few fast steps toward my favorite stall in the corner. But when I was halfway across the room, the other door suddenly opened. I thought, fuck, who could possibly be here now? The classes started 45 minutes ago. There's no reason for anyone to be here. So, I took those last few steps to the stall, closed the door, turned the lock, and sat down on the toilet with my shorts still on, expecting to wait it out until the other guy took his piss and then fucked off to wherever he came from. Probably some dude who had to leave class to pee.

I sat there, not sure where he was or what he was doing. After a while, I heard him sigh. I didn't want to wank while he was in the room, and he didn't seem to be in a rush. Fuck there were like dozens of urinals and stalls for this dude to do his business in, whether it was a piss or a shit, he should be in and out. I peered through the crack in the door. I saw him for a quick second in the middle of the room. He moved one direction, then I saw him move back in the other direction. He sighed again. This dude was pacing. My cock was getting mad as fuck. It wanted attention, and it had already grown to its full length in my shorts. All I wanted was to jerk off. I needed that blissful release. Fuck, why would he not leave!

Five minutes I sat there. Five minutes he paced the room. Finally, I heard him let out a huge, frustrated sigh, and his feet appeared beneath the door. Oh, my fucking god he was standing right outside my stall.

"Dude," he whispered, even though we were obviously alone. "How long you gonna be?"

I'm not gonna lie. I was scared to fucking death. What did this guy want? It honestly did not dawn on me right away.

"What the fuck, man," I replied. "There are like a dozen fucking stalls in here."

His tone changed. It's like it suddenly got friendly. "Yeah, dude, but I need the wall."

"Oh." I mean, duh, of course he did.

"I gotta get back to class man. Hurry it up."

I was a little surprised, but I really shouldn't have been. I mean, I knew I wasn't the only one who took advantage of this awesome little oasis of wanking. He stood there. I sat there. I didn't know what to say. Finally, I stammered, "I was kinda waiting for you to leave."

"Dude," he called out, almost at full voice. "You haven't even started yet?"

What he did next scared the fuck out of me. I saw his hand appear on the top of the door. His other hand braced the metal wall of the stall, and he pulled them apart slightly. That spread the gap just enough so the tiny metal button that fit into the latch popped out of its little hole, and the door swung open. He stood there in the open door and looked down at me just sitting on the toilet, my shorts still up and closed.

He was a big guy. He was over six feet tall and wide.

I could see a combination of muscle and bulk. I immediately felt small. And fragile. He wore sweatpants and a T-shirt. Obviously, he'd left class, because he didn't have a backpack or books, or even a jacket or coat on him. He looked down at me. I looked up at him.

"Dude," he said. He kept using that same word. He was such a jock kinda guy. "Dude, you're just sitting there. I gotta rub one out."

"I… um," I stammered. "I was gonna…"

He laughed. "Of course you were, dude. Why else would you be here?"

I had no answer. He didn't move, and I didn't know what to do. After staring at each other awkwardly for what was way too long, he shrugged and stepped into the stall and locked the door. My heart sunk.

"Come on," he said with a half-smile appearing on his face. "We'll share the wall."

He turned toward the concrete wall and pulled his sweatpants down. His cock and balls popped out. He was maybe half hard and started yanking himself immediately. I was frozen with shock. Oh, I mean, my head was swirling loving the moment, but I was stuck unable to move. My cock got so hard it hurt.

I looked down at his cock in his hand. Aw, it was kinda small. If I had to guess, it was maybe five inches? And in the complete opposite of me and my short stature and huge cock, this guy being so big, both tall and wide, it looked even smaller in his big fat hand.

He looked over at me. The half smile was gone as he focused his attention on his little willy. He nodded to the wall beside him. "Come on, you can have that side. We'll jerk 'em together." I couldn't believe what he was suggesting. I mean, I loved it. My head and my cock were

205

all in, but somehow, I couldn't get my body to stand up. "Come on, dude. It's not gay or nothing. You can't hold that shit in. You'll explode."

Finally, my head got my body to listen. I stood up and turned toward the wall myself. I gauged how close would be too close without looking too eager. He smiled, this time really wide. "That's it, buddy. Pull it out and jerk with me."

I reached into my own pants and pulled my huge throbbing cock up and out over the waistband. I tucked the elastic under my balls and grabbed my cock in one hand. I was harder than I'd ever been. Even if his cock weren't all that much to look at, he was a big bruiser of a guy. I looked at his muscular arms. His big chest was heaving up and down as he pulled on himself. He had a thick chest and a thick waist, and thick thighs. He was definitely some kind of athlete. Or just a gym meathead. What a fucking huge guy. Except where it counted.

I didn't want him to catch me perving out checking him out from head to toe, but I couldn't help it. After a moment, he noticed, because he finally looked over at me. He locked eyes with me. Was he trying to sense if I were gay? Wait, was he gay? I really didn't think so. The way he looked at me was more bro than that. I saw his eyes trail down, and his smile dropped off his face. His lips opened in a shocked look. He let out a grunt. He was looking at my cock.

"What the fuck, dude," he called out at full voice. If there were anyone else in the room, which there wasn't, we would have been caught right there. "Where'd you get that motherfucking cock! Dude, that fucking thing is huge!"

I blushed. In that moment, I was kinda proud and

flattered, but what do you say to a straight, muscle jock who is standing next to you jerking off and admiring your dick? "I don't know, lucky I guess."

He did not take his eyes off my cock as we both continued to jerk off. I have to admit, it was weird, but it turned me on like never before. I got both hands around it and jerked off with some vigor. I wanted to show off to my new bro buddy. I leaned back a little so he could get a better look at it. I saw his tongue between his lips. He was completely loving the show. I think I hypnotized him with my huge cock.

"Dude," he said. Then whatever it was he was going to say next stalled in his throat. His lips moved slightly, but no words came out. "Dude, what's it like to have such a cock?" he asked.

"It's the best, man," I tried to sound like him. "You can't imagine what it feels like."

Then he stepped back, and before I could react, he was standing directly behind me. He pressed in against me.

I didn't know what to say or what to do. He was standing so close to me I could feel his chest press against my shoulder blades. He was so much taller than me, I could feel his hard cock press against my lower back. His hand reached around and joined mine. "I have to feel what it's like. You don't mind, do you?"

I stuttered. I let go of my own cock and dropped my arms to my side, and his hand wrapped around it. He squeezed its thickness. His other hand came around and cupped my balls. "Oh man, I gotta feel what it would be like to have such a big cock. I wanna pretend it's mine, OK?"

He enveloped my body into his more, using his forearm pressed against my torso to tug me closer into him as he reached up and gave my dick a squeeze. I disappeared against his torso It was like I was no longer there. It was just him and my cock. I could feel his breath against the top of my head. He pushed it to the side slightly with his chin, and his mouth was closer to my ear. He breathed in and out, his head resting on mine. I could smell his breath. It was minty. His hips pressed into mine. He started to jerk me off and rub his own cock against my lower back to the same rhythm.

It was hotter than fuck, but after a minute, I felt like I wasn't even there. It was this jock and my cock sharing a moment with each other. His mouth pressed against my ear, and he moaned, "It's so fucking big. I wish I had a cock like yours, dude."

I was loving his big hands wrapped around my length, feeling someone else stroking me. It felt so fucking good. I didn't know if I should say anything. I didn't want to do anything that would make him stop. He started jerking me off faster, which got me really pulsing inside. I could feel his cock rubbing against me. Pre-cum had lubed up my back, so I pulled my shirt up higher. He was using the slickness to really get into sliding his cock against me.

I didn't know if I could take much more before I exploded, and that is just when he let out a huge moan, which put me over the edge. I felt his cock pulse and then blast all over my back. His lips were on my ear, and his moan went right through my brain. It was all I needed. I let out a loud exhale, and my huge cock erupted in his hands. I saw my stream shoot across the air and land on the Cum Wall. It hit higher than any other stain I could see. The first blast landed on the lettering above our heads. He must have opened his eyes, because my second shot hit just below that, and then the third, and then I was just geisering, cum spraying all over the place. I was painting the entire wall with my hot wet jizz. "FUCK DUDE!" He was definitely impressed. Finally, my head fell back and came to rest against his solid chest.

We stood there, his arms still wrapped around me, his hands still hugging my cock as it slowly came down off its high. He rested his head on my shoulder and then finally pulled away. He looked down at my back soaked in his cum. "Dude, I'm so sorry," he said and reached for the toilet paper.

He kept one hand wrapped around me and rested it on my slim, bare stomach. He was holding me there, and with his other hand he cleaned my back with the paper. It was almost romantic how he was taking care of the clean up. When he was done, he tossed the paper into the toilet and turned me around. My shorts were still down around my ankles, and his sweatpants were bunched around his knees, and he just kept looking right at my cock.

"Fuck dude, that is some goddamn fucking pud. You must tear up so many chicks. The girls must love that cock."

As we pulled up our pants, I didn't know what to say. I started to risk it, but I hesitated as my words came out, "Well, um, actually, I… um, I'm…"

He looked me in the eyes, and it wasn't lost on him what I was having a hard time saying. He just nodded knowingly. "Oh. OK. So maybe not the girls."

I nodded.

Was this the moment he punched me in the face? Was he going to immediately regret what we just did together when he realized it wasn't really just two bros helping each other out for me?

He looked right in my eyes. "Well, I bet the dudes love it then." He turned to the sink and washed his hands. I waited for him to finish and then washed my own, even though they were still clean.

"Well, buddy, that was fucking crazy," he said as he unlatched the door. It was the first time he'd called me anything but dude. "Maybe I'll see you here again. I gotta get back to class." And with that he walked off.

Before I left to go back to my dorm room, I turned and looked at my huge load of record-setting jizz dribbling down the Cum Wall of Senton Hall. And silently in my head, I thanked my new buddy. I didn't even get his name. I wondered if I'd ever run into him again.

Spring Break Buds

"Dude! You gotta come!"

Tony wanted to go. He desperately wanted to go. There was nothing he wanted more for his college experience than the opportunity to go on spring break to Florida. He'd been dreaming about it for a year and a half now. It didn't happen freshman year. His parents absolutely forbade it, because his cousin was getting married, and, as his mother put it, over her dead body was he going to miss that wedding to go to Florida with his rambunctious friends and cause holy hell.

He fantasized about spending an entire week at the beach, crazy parties on the sand, all his friends shirtless and dancing, raging music, everything he watched on television back when he was in high school. That was college. That was what college was supposed to be. But so far, it was nothing like that at all. It was studying and living in a crap dormitory and shared showers and research papers. And worst of all he hadn't gotten any pussy. Or dick. Tony would take either one.

He'd known that about himself since he was nine when he watched online porn for the first time. First, he started on the straight tab and scrolled through all sorts of videos featuring women. Women pleasuring themselves, women with a guy, women with two guys, two women together. He loved all of it.

But then he clicked over on a tab he didn't understand that had two intertwined male symbols. He learned quickly what those symbols meant, because he slid over into a section of the website that featured guys with big cocks jerking off, guys with another guy, three guys together, groups of guys sucking and fucking each other. He loved all of it.

The year Tony was 10 ended up mostly a blur of spending every waking moment holed up in his room, watching every combination of guys and girls, girls and girls, guys and guys. Until he saw a documentary about porn addiction. He wondered if that was him. He thought about the porn and realized he didn't get anything out of it. Except one thing. He wanted to be part of the action, not watch it. He couldn't wait to grow up.

And in the next year or two, Tony did just that. He grew up. His pits started to smell more, so his mom bought him deodorant. Hair started growing on his face, so his dad bought him razors and taught him how to shave. And in his pants, his little penis started to grow. He knew all about what was happening to him. His parents had given him The Talk, so all the changes to his body didn't come as a surprise to him.

But one thing that did surprise him was just how much his cock kept growing. And growing. *How big was this damn thing going to get?* he would wonder to himself. He'd always been what his dad called, 'the runt of the litter.' His cousins gave him the nickname Scrawny. Even his two sisters were taller than he was. His older brother would make him work out with him on the bench in the garage, but as much as he tried, he could never bulk up. He was just what the cousins called him. Scrawny. But now he was Scrawny with a huge cock. OK, maybe he had a little muscle on him, too.

It didn't do him any good though. On the outside, Tony was still a scrawny nerd. Through all of high school, no girl ever really paid him much attention. And no guys either. If there were any in his high school that would even consider doing anything with another guy, none of them were going to admit it. So, Tony graduated college, went off to college, aced his freshman year, and remained a virgin. A 19-year-old virgin with a big, fat cock.

"Dude! Are you even listening to me," his roommate was practically screaming at him. His mind came back to the present. "It's spring break for fuck's sake. You've got to come. You're coming. That's it. No arguments. You're coming."

Tony did not want to say no, but he also knew he had absolutely no money, and his parents were definitely not going to fund a Florida vacation for him to go off with five other guys on a road trip that would almost definitely lead to sunburns, drinking, raging parties, dancing, and with any luck, sex.

"Gio. You have no idea how much I want to. But I'm fucking broke. I don't have any money."

"Dude. Don't worry about it. Come on. I got you covered. We're splitting the hotel room six ways. It's gonna be so fucking cheap. And Sam is driving. He got his mother's SUV. Fuck you. You're coming."

Tony sighed. *Yes, yes, yes, fuck yes, a million times yes*, he thought in his head. But how was he ever gonna do it? He knew exactly what was in his wallet. A five-dollar bill and a credit card that his parents paid but with strict rules on what he was allowed to use it on and how much he could spend.

"OK. Yeah. Fuck it. You're only young once, am I right?"

"Dude, what? What are you talking about? We're young now." Gio looked at him confused. Tony rolled his eyes. His roommate Gio was the sweetest guy, but Tony had no idea how he managed college. He was such a moron. But a big, sweet moron. "We are gonna be on the beach all day, party all night, and we are gonna fuck hot chicks. Who needs money?"

Tony shrugged. "Well, we still have to eat."

Gio got up and walked to the door. "Fuck it. We'll figure it out. Dude. I'm heading over to the gym. You coming?"

For a minute, Tony didn't know if he meant the gym or Florida. "Yes. And yes." He got up off his bed and followed his roommate out the door. If he was going on spring break in a few weeks, he thought he better maximize his muscle beach body.

* * *

"Eighteen hours!" Gio hadn't realized. Tony wasn't surprised his roommate didn't know just how far it was to Florida.

"Gio. It's like 1,000 miles. You didn't know that?" Gio just sat in the backseat of the seven-passenger car all alone. He looked like a little boy when he was upset. Tony just took a seat in front of him and laughed. "Don't sweat it, G. You'll be fine."

Tony looked out the window and saw Sam pacing back and forth. He looked frustrated and annoyed. He was a handsome guy, a senior, usually in a pretty good mood, but not right at this moment. Tony got back out and walked around to stand next to him.

"Fuck these guys, man. I told them we wanted to hit

the road by 3:30. We want to get to Lauderdale by 10 tomorrow morning so we can get in a full day at the beach. Fuck this."

Tony didn't want the stress, so he tried to calm Sam down. "They'll be here any minute. It's all good. You know we won't be able to check into the hotel until the afternoon anyway."

Sam shrugged. "Yeah, I know. But we can park the car and head to the beach."

"Hey, I just wanted to thank you again for letting me come along. I'm really looking forward to this. I don't know how I'll ever be able to repay you."

"Ah, it's cool, dude. Tell you what, when you're a senior, do something like this for a scrawny, little sophomore. Pay it forward," Sam said, making fun of him.

Tony looked over at him. Sam had a grin on his face. "Gee, thanks," he said.

Sam grabbed him around the shoulders and dug a knuckle lightly into the top of his head. "I'm just kiddin' ya, buddy. But hey, you been working out? I guess you're not really all that scrawny really, are you?" Sam was feeling him up, groping his chest and shoulders. He liked the feel of this handsome senior's hands all over him even if it was in a joking manner.

As Sam let Tony go, he saw three guys lugging backpacks and roller suitcases along the sidewalk coming from the upperclassmen's dorm.

Sam yelled across the quad, "Well, you took your fucking time. Let's go!"

The three came closer and closer but didn't pick up the pace, making Sam more frustrated. "Fuck those guys," he mumbled to Tony and went around to the back of the car to make sure there was going to be room for all the bags.

Tony watched as they got closer. And then he started feeling a little awkward. He was heading to Florida with these five other guys, and the only one he knew really well was Gio, his roommate. He knew Sam a little, but they had never been that close. He was a sophomore, like Gio, but these other guys were all seniors. He just hoped they were all nice. They certainly weren't punctual, but he just hoped they weren't assholes.

From behind the SUV, Sam yelled out, "Come on! Come on! Let's go!" Tony walked around to join him behind the car, figuring he could help pack. He stood next to Sam. The three guys got closer, and turning his head toward them, Tony could make them out in a little more detail. And he almost blurted out a gasp.

The three guys approaching were, in Tony's mind, hotter than fucking hell. *Mother fucker*, he thought, *what the real fuck*. Three muscular, jock looking studs were getting closer and closer. Tony could see the bulging muscles through their shirts at a distance.

The one on the left looked like a tanned god. Latin, Tony thought, sexy and Latin for sure. He had on a baseball cap, but Tony could see long, dark black hair. And of course, the gym shaped muscular torso was just about bursting out of the tight white t-shirt he wore.

The one on the right was just about as muscular as the Latin guy, but he was so pale and white, he was practically see-through, Tony joked in his head. He must be Irish, he thought. This guy was blond, but in the sun, there was almost a reddish shine to his hair. What did his mom call that? His cousin had that kind of hair. Strawberry blond, that was it. *Man*, Tony thought, *that guy's gonna fry in the Florida sun*.

And walking in between them was a guy that Tony

216

thought looked like something drawn by AI. They were closer now, and Tony saw a strong jawline, big, rounded lips, a small straight nose, and round eyes that were looking right at him. While the other two had huge muscles, this guy was definitely muscular, but everything looked like it had been sculpted to match the perfect dimensions of human lust. Fuck, how did he have such a slim waist with that chest and those shoulders? And those thighs, what was he, a soccer player or something.

Tony realized where his mind was. And as the three new dudes joined them behind the car and started pulling off backpacks and tossing them at Sam, Tony started questioning just how 'bi' he really was. If all dudes looked like this, he would *definitely* be way more gay than bi.

"Who is this," the walking god said to Sam nodding at Tony.

"This is Tony. Gio's roommate. He's our sixth."

The pale Irish-looking guy smiled wide and extended a hand to him. "Cool, hey kid. I'm Kevin." Tony shook the hand presented to him and smiled back.

"Hey, I'm Tony. Nice to meet you."

There was an arm slung over Tony's shoulders from behind. He turned his head to see the bill of a baseball cap. "So, another sophomore. Ready for spring break, dude?" The Latin guy pressed his arm down on Tony's shoulders. "It's gonna be sick, man, sick."

"Can't wait," Tony said smiling at the guy.

"Carlos," the guy offered.

"Tony."

Carlos pulled his arm away, tossed his backpack into the back of the SUV. He announced, "Shotgun," and walked to the front of the car and got in the passenger seat.

"Man, fuck you," Kevin called after him. "We're taking turns." And with his bags secured inside, Kevin hopped into the open sliding side door and propelled his body into the far back seat beside a slouched Gio.

Sam had the bags fully stacked and was pulling the hatchback down. Tony turned to the last guy, the walking god. He was standing right next to him. Tony took in his perfect masculine beauty. This guy had not offered his name. In fact, he hadn't even looked at Tony.

"I'm Tony," he offered. This guy was either incredibly shy or an asshole, Tony thought, because he didn't even look at him. He just turned toward the door.

And then he finally mumbled, "Buddy." But he'd already turned away and pulled himself up and into the car and sat in the middle seat. Tony realized he'd be sitting next to him and hoped this guy was just shy and not a jerk, but his first impression wasn't going well.

Alone behind the car, he said to no one, "Nice to meet you." Then he got into the car and sat himself down next to the hotter than fuck Buddy. He had to reach between them to find his seatbelt. Buddy just rolled away from him without a word. He still didn't even look at him. Stupid name, Tony thought to himself. Who names their kid Buddy?

* * *

Hours went by. Gio sulked in the backseat. Next to him, Kevin was asleep. Tony kept trying to get a read on Buddy, but the guy had on his earbuds and was listening to music or something. Tony wanted so desperately to turn his head to the side and check him out more, but he knew it would be awkward. And with the headphones, it wasn't like he could strike up a conversation. Dudes were so closed off. Maybe it would be better to go after girls. Fuck it, that's what spring break was all about any way.

"So, this your first spring break, Tony?" Carlos had turned around to look at him. At least someone was interested in a little conversation.

"Uh, yeah. I couldn't go last year. But I'm really looking forward to it."

"Dude, I promise you, the girls are so fucking easy, you're gonna get laid no doubt. Trust me."

Tony didn't know what to say in response. "Cool."

Carlos was still looking back at him. "Sophomore? Really?"

Tony nodded, "Yeah."

"So, what are you, like 18 or something."

"Nineteen."

Carlos was shaking his head. "You're a baby. But don't worry. We'll corrupt you."

Tony laughed at that. "I'm looking forward to it."

Sam was driving and without turning his head from the road said, "So, that means you can't drink. And neither can Gio."

It dawned on Tony. Fuck, he wasn't gonna be able to get into bars. "Uh, no. Do they card down there?"

Carlos looked surprised at the question, "Uh, yeah, dude. They card at every bar."

"But we can try to sneak it onto the beach," Sam said.

"If we want to get arrested, dude," Carlos objected.

"We'll figure it out," Sam said.

Tony answered their concern, "Oh, I don't really drink any way."

And just then, from beside him, Buddy out of

nowhere joined the conversation, "Then what are you gonna do when we go out?"

Tony was surprised by the sudden question and turned to look at Buddy. He was still not looking at him. "Oh, I don't know, I mean, I guess I can just hang out in the hotel room or walk around or something."

Carlos asked, "Don't you have a fake ID or something? We can try to get you in. Hey Gio! Gio!"

From the backseat, Tony's roommate responded, "Yeah?"

Carlos asked, "You got a fake ID?"

"Yeah, of course, dude. Who doesn't?"

There was a moment of silence in the van until Gio added, "Wait, Tony, you don't have a fake ID? How you gonna get in anywhere?"

Tony was a little embarrassed of the attention. "Uh, I don't know. I didn't really think about it."

"Fuck dude," Gio grumbled.

"We'll figure it out," Carlos said. "Don't worry, Tony. Besides, you're a cute kid. The girls are gonna be all over you, buddy. We're gonna get you laid."

"Just not in my bed," Sam joked.

Buddy had closed his eyes and returned to his own world, but Tony took the moment to turn and look him over a little more. Fuck, he was so hot. His lips were so round and inviting. His chest was rounded and firm, begging to be caressed. His hips were round and small, and those thighs were so big and wide.

I'm in a van full of hotties, Tony thought to himself. *If only one of them were gay, or at least a little bit bi, like me*. He was still looking over at Buddy. He was staring at the impression of his nipple against his shirt when he realized Buddy had opened his eyes. For the first time he was looking right at Tony. *Sure, now you look at me.* He meekly pulled his eyes away and looked forward again, but he could feel Buddy's stare in the side of his face. He closed his eyes to try to nap.

Kevin must have woken up, because from the back of the van came the question, "Are we there yet?"

Tony, Carlos, and Sam all laughed.

* * *

The hours went by. The sun went down. Sam pulled off the highway, and at a roadside gas station, he refilled the gas tank. Tony went into the convenience store at the gas station to take a piss. While he was relieving himself at one of the two urinals, Buddy came in, paused for a second but then went into the one stall. Tony wondered if there was some awkwardness between them already. He hoped not, but of all the guys, Buddy was the one he could not get a read on.

Back out in the store area, he looked around for some chips or a snack. He thought he would use the credit card. His parents were not happy about his spring break choice, but they reluctantly came to accept it. They warned him again and again not to spend too much money, but he figured a snack on the road wouldn't be bad. He ended up the last one still in the store and didn't want to keep the other waiting.

By the time he got back to the SUV, Carlos had taken over the driver's seat, and Kevin had taken the opportunity to secure the front passenger seat. And Buddy had moved to the backseat where Kevin had been. *Was it because of him,* he thought? *He didn't want to sit next to me anymore?* Sam was closing the gas tank and putting the hose back, so Tony stepped in and took the spot Buddy had been in.

Sam came around and saw the last seat left, the one Tony himself had been in. "What is this, musical chairs," he joked.

* * *

Tony finally dosed off and after hours, he was roused awake by a cheering sound from the front seat. Carlos was pointing out the windshield. Tony saw what he was excited about. A big sign read, *"Welcome to Florida."*

Everyone roused awake. Gio joined the cheering, "We're here! We made it."

Sam laughed, "Dude. We still got like four hours to go."

"What," Gio exclaimed. "Are you fucking kidding me?""No, dude."

Gio was grumbling in the back. "How the fuck big is Florida anyway?"

Tony looked at his watch. It was 6:30 in the morning. They had made really good time, but he was just as eager as the rest of the guys to be out of the SUV. He was feeling sore and cramped all over. "Man, I can't wait to get out of this car," he said.

"You and me both," Sam agreed with him. "I can't wait to get on that beach."

Gio added, "I just wanna get laid."

Tony wondered about that, "So what exactly are the sleeping arrangements then?"

"Well," Sam said. "We only have one room. Two queen beds. So, either we'll get an extra bed or two of you are gonna have to sleep on the floor."

"Well fuck me," Gio said. "I know what two you guys are gonna toss to the floor."

Carlos laughed, "Fair is fair, sophomores."

"We could take turns," Kevin offered. Tony was momentarily relieved by that.

"Fuck that," Sam said. "Sorry, no offense, boys, but I planned this trip, I got the car, I paid for the room. By the way, you all still owe me for your shares. I'm sleeping in a bed. You all can fight it out for the other spots."

"But," Gio asked. "How we gonna get lucky if we're all in the same room?"

Kevin chimed in first, "Dude you gotta go back to hers."

"But what if she's sharing a room?"

There was silence. Nobody knew how to answer Gio's concern.

Sam finally said, "Dudes, we'll figure it out. We can have a code or a sign, like a hanger on the door or something."

"Well, nobody better do anything in my bed," Buddy added in.

* * *

After another tedious four hours, the SUV filled with six college dudes pulled into a parking space at a small, white motel a block from the beach on a quiet side street in Fort Lauderdale. One by one they fell out of the car and followed Sam to the reception office.

Tony stretched. Gio yawned. Kevin bent over to touch his toes, stretching out his lower back muscles. Tony dared to look at his hot, round bubble butt for a split second. Damn, another fucking hot muscle stud. He was surrounded. *Fuck it*, he thought, *I don't think I'll be able to even look at any chicks surrounded by all these hot dudes.*

As Kevin stood back up straight, Tony saw Buddy staring right at him. Was this guy forever going to be staring him down? He thought he was about to get called out, but Buddy just turned and walked off into the motel office.

When Tony got through the door, he heard the woman behind the counter yelling at Sam. "Four person maximum. You can't have six people in the room. You can't do this."

"Oh, come on," Sam was arguing. "We just drove 18 hours. What do you want us to do? We're not gonna mess up the place."

"No," she kept yelling. "You spring breakers are all the same. This is not happening. I don't care where your other two go, but you're not all staying here."

Sam looked like he was about to punch a wall. Kevin and Carlos were standing behind him equally frustrated. Tony felt like it was all his fault. He and Gio shouldn't be there.

And in that moment, Tony saw Buddy step forward. He looked like a different person. Rather than the quiet, sullen look he had sported the entire trip, suddenly a smile beamed across his face, and he directed it at the woman behind the counter.

The other guys stepped back and let him take charge of the conversation. "I'm sorry," he looked at her nametag. She seemed like she was about 40 or so. "I'm sorry, Michelle. We really didn't know. Is there anything we can do? We're not going to have anywhere else we can go." Tony saw a mesmerized look come across the desk clerk's face. Buddy was smiling at her, and when Tony looked at that face, he too was struck by the intense beauty of it. Who could resist that face? Buddy was fucking insanely gorgeous.

Michelle's mouth stayed open as she looked into Buddy's eyes. He put on a bit of a sad puppy dog look and leaned an arm on the counter. Tony noticed his arm muscles bulging a bit, straining the sleeves of his shirt. He was sweet-talking this woman, and it seemed to be working.

"Look, I'm Buddy. This is my pal Sam. Kevin, Carlos. And this is Gio." He paused. Tony felt excluded, but then Buddy turned full around and grabbed his arm. "And this sweet kid is Tony." Buddy put an arm around him and hugged him in close to his side. "He's Gio's roommate, and we didn't want to leave him behind. It's his first spring break, you know?"

Michelle's eyes switched over to Tony. He smiled at her. Buddy was looking at him. He looked over at Buddy and then back to Michelle. He gave her a big smile. Michelle melted. She looked back and forth between Buddy and Tony.

"You guys just better not trash the place, you hear me? This is so not OK. You could get me fired."

Buddy released Tony. Tony felt the sudden loss of the touch. "Thank you, thank you," he said to the desk clerk. "We will be complete gentlemen. I promise. You won't hear a peep from us."

"Well," she said with a smile. "You seem like nice guys. But I can't give you a rollaway or anything. You're either gonna have to sleep three to a bed or on the floor. And no extra towels."

"We brought our own," Sam offered. "It's cool. We'll be fine. Promise."

* * *

Outside back at the SUV, the six guys were quietly cheering.

Sam was patting Buddy on the back, "Dude, that is so fucking insane. It's like you hypnotized her. How the fuck do you do that?"

Carlos was almost laughing, "Seriously. I thought she was gonna cream herself when she looked into your eyes. Dude, it's like a gift. You are the ultimate stud, man."

Kevin suddenly wrapped his arms around Tony from behind. "Don't forget this hot little fucker, too. Buddy, I don't know how you do it, but then you added in this boy right here, and I think poor Michelle will be blowing her load tonight fantasizing about a good old tag teaming from the two of you…"

"What?" Tony was shocked by Kevin's comment. "Me? That was all Buddy."

"Nah, man," Carlos added. "We brought the hotness and the cuteness with us. The chicks are gonna be creaming themselves. Buddy, I don't know how you do it."

Me? Tony thought to himself. *What are they talking about?*

He turned beat red. Heat pulsed from his face. As the luggage was being pulled out of the back of the car, he turned to find Buddy staring right at him again. Silent and focused, his eyes were glued to Tony's. He nodded without a word. Tony's heart leapt in his chest.

"I'd bang her," Gio said, and they all made their way to their room.

* * *

The room was tiny. Sure, the two beds were queen sized, but they took up most of the room. And one bathroom, of course. How, Tony wondered, are six dudes gonna share one bathroom? And then looking around the room, resigned to the fact that he was going to be one of the two on the floor, he wondered where he was going to fit. There wasn't much room between the beds. *Maybe between the bed and the window*, he thought.

He didn't want to think about it. They would have to make it work. He found a place in the corner to put his backpack. He would just live out of it. There weren't going to be enough drawers for all their stuff either. Oh well, a week of cramped living, sleeping on the floor. But at least they'd be on the beach and in the sun.

"OK, boys, we have got to hit that beach," Sam announced. They all found spots along the walls for their bags. Sam and Buddy commandeered most of the drawers. The rest of them propped their bags here and there against the walls and on top of the dresser and on the small desk.

Tony pulled out a bathing suit from his bag, and when he stood back up, he was met with a completely naked Kevin standing next to him. He was caught off guard by the sight. Kevin was so incredibly pale from head to toe. He was almost a literal white. *Pink white*, Tony thought. And as the sweatpants hit the floor, Tony got a glimpse of Kevin's huge pink cock dangling between his legs. *Holy fuck*, he thought, *that's almost as big as mine*. And again, like clockwork, he turned to see Buddy staring right at him. *Fuck me*, he thought.

Tony announced, "I need to take a leak like crazy."

227

He escaped into the bathroom with his bathing suit in hand and took the opportunity to change with a little bit of privacy. Coming back out after a moment's breath, he re-entered the room in just his bathing suit to find all five other guys had pulled on swim trunks.

Buddy was still shirtless, and his sexy muscular body was on full display. His torso almost shined, his skin looked so soft. He was hairless except for a wispy line of fuzz below his belly button that led down into his red trunks. His chest was so well-rounded, it looked sculpted out of marble. Tony caught himself again staring down his new bros and resigned to stop.

But Carlos was commenting on just what he had been ogling. "Fuck me, Buddy. I don't know how you do it. You've got like the perfect body. No wonder Michelle melted."

Buddy shrugged. "You've all got muscles. Not just me." He looked over at Tony and stuck his chin out in his direction. "Even the kid over there." They all turned to Tony who again got beat red.

"Oh, I'm just a scrawny nerd. That's what my family calls me."

Kevin put a hand up for a high-five. "Dude. You're rockin' it. No kidding. Watch out, bitches! We're coming."

Tony turned to look at himself in the mirror. OK, maybe he had put on a good amount of muscle. *Fuck it*, he thought, *I don't look like these muscle studs, but I guess I'm not too bad after all*. When he turned back to the other guys in the room, he realized Buddy had been watching him look at himself. He felt immediately self-conscious and went for the hotel room door and was the first one out of the room.

* * *

The beach was packed. College aged guys and girls filled the sand. Tony had never seen so many people together in one place outside of sporting events or concerts. He was surprised they even found enough space on the sand to put out their blankets.

They spent the day in ultimate beach bliss. In and out of the water, spread out on their towels on the sand. Carlos was chatting up a group of three girls to their right. Kevin was standing near him, trying to pull the attention of one of them away, but all three seemed like they were flirting with the sexy Latin.

Sam and Gio were ogling another group of girls to their left, but Buddy was lying flat down on his back taking in the sun on his towel, sunglasses on, earbuds in. He was in his own world. Tony was mesmerized by his body. He could not stop looking over at Buddy again and again. His chest, his arms, his stomach, that line of treasure trail hair, fuck he wanted to know what it led to.

He had to stop. He had to stop eye-fucking his travel buddies. Maybe he should focus on some of the girls around them. So, he did, and they were good-looking and young, but they were just not as hot as the hot maleness he was surrounded by. Maybe they were all straight and totally unattainable, but he was enjoying getting to take in the visions of Carlos and Kevin and especially Buddy. Sam wasn't all that bad either. Gio, well, that was his roommate, and just not his type, but he knew there would be girls that would go for him. Big dumb jock. Lots of girls went for that.

Yeah, he had to stop. He said he should stop. He should stop. "I'm gonna go down in the water," he announced. Gio and Sam just nodded at him. Buddy didn't even open his eyes. Tony trotted down and threw himself into the waves. He had braced himself for a crisp coolness, but he was met with the warm, sun-drenched waters of Fort Lauderdale Beach. It was the temperature of a bath. It felt awesome after that long car ride, and he floated and waded until his mind forgot about abs and chests and bulges and treasure trails.

Tony bounded up the sand back toward his mates. He was soaking wet, of course, and when he got close, Sam was pointing at him with a wide expression of surprise on his face, "Dude!"

Carlos and Kevin looked around at the loud exclamation from Sam and saw him pointing at Tony. They all got wide-eyed. Gio looked up and burst into laughter.

"What?" Tony looked at them. They were all pointing at him. Some of the girls with Carlos and Kevin also let out shrieks. He looked down at himself. His wet bathing suit was plastered to his body, and his huge, long cock was perfectly outlined by the clinging fabric. He immediately pulled the fabric away from his shaft and sorted himself out so it wasn't so obvious.

The girls were laughing. Some had hands over their mouths. Tony threw himself down on his towel, embarrassed.

Sam was beside him on his own towel. "Dude," he said, with a smile on his face.

Tony rolled his eyes. "I'm so embarrassed."

"Embarrassed?" Sam said surprised. "Did you see the way those girls looked at your cock? You can have any one of them, guaranteed." He put out a fist for a fist bump. Tony begrudgingly met it with his own.

Gio chimed in, "My boy's got the goods, am I right?"

Sam nodded. "It's bigger than Kevin's." It was, Tony knew.

Buddy woke up and lifted his head. "What are you guys talking about?"

Sam, Gio, and Tony all burst out laughing, but no one told him. Tony wished out of everyone that Buddy had seen his outlined package, but he hadn't.

* * *

After hours on the beach, they were back in the hotel room. They'd eaten a fast dinner of crappy burgers at a walk-in brew pub by the beach and were getting dressed for a night out in the bars.

Kevin was moaning in the bathroom. "Dude," Sam was scolding him. "Why the fuck didn't you put on sunscreen?"

"I did! I just burn real easy." He came out, and Tony got a glimpse of his shining red face and shoulders, arms, chest. "Fuck my life. It's so fucking painful."

"Dude," Tony said surprised at how beat red the Irish guy was. "That's gonna fucking hurt!"

"It already does!"

Sam made the proclamation, "OK, we got to get Kevin here drunk, so he can sleep with that burn. Is everyone ready?"

He was met with nods and final looks in the mirror. Gio was the last ready, pulling on his t-shirt.

It was about 12 blocks from their motel to the bars along the beach. They'd already made the trek twice, so they were pretty used to the route. As they got closer to the beach, there were more police all around, keeping eyes on all the spring breakers. Barricades stopped pedestrians from crossing other than at designated crosswalks.

"Geez, it's like a police state," Gio complained.

"It's all for safety," Sam said. "No big deal."

They made their way up to the doors of a very crowded bar. A ton of people were converging on a couple of bars in a row on one intersection.

"You sure I'm gonna be able to get in?" Tony asked.

"Come on, with all these people," Carlos said. "How are they gonna notice? There's no way they're carding." But as they made their way closer and closer to the doors, they saw security, and sure enough, they were indeed checking IDs.

"Fuck," Tony said. But Sam was already showing his and going through the door.

"Come on," Gio said. "At least try."

Kevin and Carlos were through, and Gio was nervously showing his fake ID to the doorman. Somehow, it worked, and he joined the others in the crowded bar.

Buddy was standing next to Tony. The doorman was looking at Tony expectantly.

"Uh, I forgot my ID," he said sheepishly to the big bruiser of a man blocking his entrance.

"Then you don't get in," he said abruptly.

Buddy was behind him. Tony looked at him and said, "Oh well."

"What are you gonna do?" Buddy asked him.

"I guess I'll just walk on the beach. It's beautiful out. And then I'll just go hang at the hotel."

Buddy had his ID in hand, and the doorman was

looking at it. "You gonna be OK? You have one of the room keys?"

"Yeah, yeah. I'll be fine. Have fun." Tony walked out of the mass of people trying to get into the bar. Buddy was left in the doorway watching him go before he pushed through to join the others inside. All alone, Tony went to the intersection and crossed the street to the beach side. Turning north he started strolling, and after just a short minute or so, his mind took in the sight of the beach, the sound of the waves, and he sighed out in a serene calmness. This sure beats being smushed in a crowded bar anyway.

After just a half a block or so, Tony heard a voice behind him calling his name. "Tony!" He turned. Buddy was jogging up to him.

"What are you doing?"

"You know, what? I don't drink anyway, and it was super crowded in there. They're already doing shots," Buddy said. Then after a moment, "Is it OK if I join you?"

Tony's heart soared inside of him. "Yeah," he blurted out through a big smile. "Yeah, sure. I was just walking, you know?"

"Sounds great."

"I mean, you don't have to babysit me if you don't want to," he offered.

"No, it's cool," said Buddy. "Look, I kinda wanted to apologize. I know I've been kinda stand-offish. He stopped walking and turned to look at Tony who also stopped. "It's just, well, I am sometimes a little shy, but also, this trip just got out of control. You know it was just gonna be Sam and me. But then he invited Kevin and Carlos, and then somehow Gio got invited, and..," he paused. "And you. Not that I'm complaining. It's just, I

233

didn't think it was gonna be all the craziness. I just wanted to relax on the beach."

Tony nodded, "Yeah, I get it. I'm sorry. I didn't mean to weasel my way into your trip or anything."

"No," Buddy blurted out. "It's good." He paused then added, "I'm glad you're here."

Tony didn't respond right away. They fell back into a very slow pace and made their way along the white seawall separating the sidewalk from the sandy beach. Tony didn't know what to say to this insanely hot guy walking with him. "I kinda thought you didn't like me," he admitted.

"I know, I'm sorry, I just was, in a funk. Forgive me?"

"Of course," Tony blurted out. "Sure. We're cool."

"Cool."

They made their way slowly, step by step, side by side. They didn't talk much. They just enjoyed the ocean breeze and the sounds of the waves. As they got a few blocks away from the cacophony of the bar scene on the southside of the beach strip, it got quieter, and they both were relieved at the peacefulness of the night.

They looked across at the giant hotels and resorts. They looked out across the beach at the ocean shining in the moonlight. Tony couldn't think of a better way to spend the evening, especially with this incredibly hot guy sharing it with him. He just didn't know if the other guy was feeling that same way or not.

"This is my idea of a vacation, you know," Buddy said at last. "Just enjoying the ocean, the quiet. Can you imagine being stuck in that bar? Drinking and screaming over the music. I guess I'm just not a partier. Is that boring?"

"No, not at all," Tony said. "I totally agree with you. I love the beach at night. I love the quiet. It'll be good before we have to cram back into that one small room. I'm not looking forward to sleeping on the floor, I can tell you that."

"Sorry about that, man," Buddy said nicely. "Sucks, but hey, we're young, and we're poor, right? What do they call this? The best four years of your life?"

"Yeah but tell that to my back tomorrow morning after sleeping on a hard floor. Let's see how I feel then."

After several more blocks, the craziness of spring break crowds was behind them. The beach was serene. Buddy stopped and pointed at the white seawall. "Want to sit for a minute?"

"Sure," Tony said. They stepped up and put their feet over the wall on the beach side and faced the ocean. Buddy sat down next to him. Really close, Tony thought. He liked it.

"This is nice," Buddy said.

"Yeah. Thanks for, thanks for joining me."

"I'm glad I did," Buddy said. "I didn't want it to be weird between us. I know I was a snob on the car ride. I promise I'll make it up to you."

"It's OK. Like I said, I get it. It's cool."

Buddy leaned into him and gave him a little shoulder to shoulder shove. Tony pushed back, and they smiled at each other. Was Buddy flirting with him?

The beach was beautiful and serene. Two men were walking down to the water. Tony commented, "Oh, I don't think the beach is open at night, is it? You think the cops will chase them off?"

Buddy shrugged. "I'm not sure. I think they're more concerned with the crowds down by the bars." Just then the two men near the water's edge turned to each other and started kissing.

"Oh," Tony said, surprised.

"Oh," Buddy repeated with a laugh. "I think we're at the gay beach."

"Yeah," Tony said, "I think I just figured that out." They both laughed. Tony kept watching the two men, but Buddy was watching him.

"Tony?"

"Yeah?"

"Can I ask you something?"

"Sure."

Buddy sighed and then asked his question, "You're gay, right?"

Tony froze. He turned to look right into Buddy's eyes. Fuck, he was so close. "Um, well, yeah, I mean, well, I'm bi." He said but added, "But yeah, recently, I think I've been more focused on guys."

Buddy was nodding. "Yeah. I could tell."

Tony felt embarrassed and flushed with warmth in his face. He knew he was blushing. "I hope you're not freaked out or anything, I…"

But Buddy interrupted him, "Dude, it's cool. I mean, it's just I could kinda tell. The way you looked at me. But then you were checking out Kevin's giant cock, and..," but after saying those words, they both started laughing again.

"I knew you caught me looking. And it's just, well, you gotta know you're like hot as fucking hell. You're like so, so perfect, I mean your body, and I should stop, I'm sorry."

Buddy fell quiet. Tony didn't know what to say next. He looked out at the ocean but then couldn't take the silence anymore. He turned his head and found Buddy just staring right at him. He was so close to him. Buddy's lips moved, "So you didn't ask me."

"What?"

"You didn't ask me if I'm gay."

Tony's mouth opened, surprised by the comment. He didn't think there would have been any chance. He suddenly realized, he just assumed the whole time that Buddy must be totally straight.

But before he could ask anything, Buddy reached up a hand, put it on the back of Tony's head, pulled him forward, and planted a kiss right on his mouth.

Tony was taken by surprise. Blissful, ecstatic surprise. He let out a quick moan before Buddy's tongue eased out and pressed between his lips to explore his mouth. He reached up and grabbed around the older guy's chest and pulled him in closer. He needed Buddy to know he wanted it. Of all the people he could possibly get kissed by, Buddy was absolutely hotter than anyone he could have ever hoped for.

They wrapped their arms around each other and kissed deeply and passionately and forgot about the world around them. They moved their legs out of the awkward position they were in when they first twisted toward each other. Buddy pulled his legs up onto the seawall and slid one on each side of Tony. He wrapped himself around him, arms around Tony's upper body, legs around his waist.

Finally, they separated their lips from each other and took a moment to look into each other's eyes. Buddy was breathing heavily. "I'm so sorry I was such a weirdo in the car. I just didn't know what to say to you. You're so hot. I wanted you as soon as I saw you, and I didn't know if you were gay or not, and I didn't know what to do, and then you were sitting right next to me, and I was so nervous, and..," he was going on and on.

Tony let out a laugh. "Are you kidding me? I was feeling all that just the same. No way I thought you were gay, or bi, or like anything other than a total straight dude, and you're so fucking hot."

They both turned their heads to notice most people walking by looking over at them. Most took one look and started smiling, but a few were taken by surprise to see two young dudes in a full embrace. One older couple, two men, walked by, and one called over, "Aw, you guys are so cute together."

Both Buddy and Tony seemed to blush at the comment. They gave the guy a smile and a nod. Buddy turned back to Tony, "You want to go back to the room? The boys won't be back for hours."

"Yes," Tony just about screamed. "I can't think of anything I'd want to do more."

Buddy pulled his legs out from around Tony. He stood up on the seawall and extended a hand down to help Tony stand. They kept their hands together as they hopped off the seawall. Tony made a turn to the right to head north toward their motel, but Buddy hesitated.

Tony turned to look at Buddy standing still. Buddy waited a moment, then said, "So there's a CVS over there. I'm thinking I might want to pick up a few things."

"Oh, yeah, um, sure," Tony said.

Buddy still didn't move but looked right into Tony's eyes. "Like maybe some lube." Tony didn't know what to say, but he was bursting with excitement inside. Buddy finished his sentence, "So you can fuck me. If you want to."

Tony nearly blasted out of his skin like a rocket ship to the moon. "Fuck yeah," he exclaimed.

Buddy pulled his arm firmly and launched both their bodies back toward the crosswalk. "Oh good, I was hoping you were a top."

Tony's mind was tumbling around and around and around. This unbelievably hot senior with the rock-hard, perfect body wanted him to fuck him? How could this have all happened so perfectly? And on the very first day of spring break.

The two young men got through the very crowded CVS. The cashier knew exactly what they were going to be doing when she rang up the bottle in Buddy's hands. Buddy paid with a credit card. The cashier put the tube in a bag, and they were off back to the hotel. No two guys ever power-walked so quickly with so much purpose than Buddy and Tony in that moment.

Tony had the key in hand and opened the door, his hands almost shaking. Buddy seemed as eager as a boy on Christmas morning. Once the door swung open, Buddy bounded into the room. Tony stopped to lock it and turn the deadbolt. He added the security chain for good measure.

When he turned back into the room, Buddy had already tossed off his shirt and thrown it on the dresser. He'd kicked off his sneakers, and he was unbuttoning his shorts. Tony was loving the show, but he wanted more. "Hey, let me do that."

Buddy stopped and stepped toward Tony and threw his arms around his shoulders and pulled him in for another passionate kiss. Tongues intertwined. Lips pressed firmly together. Tony could not believe the feeling of Buddy's naked torso against him. The kiss was

239

the hottest thing he'd ever experienced, but he had to take his shirt off so he could feel Buddy's skin against his.

Without breaking the contact of their mouths desperate for each other, Tony pulled his shirt up. Buddy helped, and when they had to, they pulled apart so the shirt could come up over his head. Buddy grabbed it from him and threw it on the dresser to join his.

They pressed back together. Tony could not believe how firm but how soft Buddy felt. He reached his hands down and grabbed his firm round ass cheeks. Fuck, they were meaty and firm and so incredibly round.

Tony's cock was hard in his pants, and he pressed forward with his hips. It hung out to the side, stuffed in his underwear, and when it made contact with Buddy, the other guy froze and pulled out of the kiss.

"Oh fuck," he said. He reached a hand down to Tony's crotch and found the bulge. His hand slid along the length of it. "What the fuck is all that?"

Tony smiled and felt warm. "Surprise."

Buddy's hand folded around the shaft through Tony's short. "Fuck me," he gasped.

"I intend to."

Buddy started shaking his head, "What did I get myself into? Holy fuck. You are going to have to take it real slow, mister."

Tony smiled, "Well, you said we have a few hours."

Tony kicked his sneakers off and reached out for Buddy's shorts. "But I want to see what you've got to show me, too."

Buddy laughed, "Well, I don't think it's going to measure up to this," he squeezed his hand firmly on Tony's cock again. He couldn't seem to let go. "But I think you'll like it."

Tony took Buddy's hand and pulled it off him and urged it to the side. He took a step back and looked at Buddy from head to toe. He placed his hand on Buddy's neck and started caressing him. Buddy stood with his hands at his side and let Tony explore him.

Tony's hand rubbed over the broad, round orbs of Buddy's chest. He was such a muscle stud. His chest was so big and round. Tony's hand slid over to one nipple. Dark and ever so tiny, Tony circled it with a finger. He squeezed softly, and Buddy let out a quick breath.

Tony's hand continued down to feel his stomach. His abs were like a washboard. Tony looked at them as his hand kept going south. He pressed his hand into the line of hair at Buddy's navel and kept going further down until it rested at the undone button of his shorts.

He pulled the zipper down and opened the shorts. As they expanded around Buddy's thin waist, they lost their hold on his hip and fell in one quick plummet to the ground. Tony looked down and saw the tiny, white bikini briefs. Buddy's cock was pressing against the fabric, the bulge of it sticking out nicely.

Tony put his hand on it and pressed firmly. Buddy moaned and closed his eyes. Tony fingered the elastic and slid his fingers inside. "I need you naked now," he whispered and pulled the briefs downward.

Buddy's cock had been pointing down, and when Tony eased the briefs down, it sprung out suddenly to bob into open air with a bounce. Tony's eyes widened. It was already fully erect, and it was beautiful. It stuck out poker straight. It had a firm girth to it, and it was probably at least seven inches long.

Letting go of the briefs, they too fell to the ground. Buddy stood completely naked in front of him. He stepped back and took in the vision of it. Buddy opened his eyes and smiled at him. Tony could not believe how perfect the guy was. He had a body like Michelangelo's David, he thought at first, but then he revised that. Buddy was even more muscular than the sculpture. And there was no comparison in the cock department. Buddy had that work of art beat by a landslide.

He put his hands back on Buddy and started caressing and touching him all over. He walked around to his side. He slid a finger up and down the side of Buddy's torso, along his lats. Ever so softly, his fingers barely touched the soft skin of Buddy's side. He flinched as the tingling sensation pulsed through him from the touch.

Tony kept going and stood fully behind him. He looked down at his back. The V of those lats was incredible, but looking lower, Tony could not believe how beautiful Buddy's ass was. So smooth and soft, the orbs of his ass were big and round, and dotted on the top with two rounded dimples. He took both ass cheeks in his hands and groped them firmly.

"Fuck yeah," he moaned. Buddy pressed his ass out to welcome the grabbing hands.

"I want you so bad," he whispered breathily. "I'm all yours."

Tony came back around in front of him. Still caressing him, he said, "Lie down on the bed."

Buddy obliged and spread out on his back in the middle of the bed closer to the window. Tony stood over him. Buddy leaned up on both his elbows to watch him.

Tony unbuttoned his own shorts and pulled them down. He knew his huge cock was going to be obvious in his own underwear. It was pushing out to the left, barely able to stay inside his underwear. He dropped the shorts and kicked them away. Buddy's eyes were boring into his bulge. He reached down and pulled the underwear down, too. And his huge cock popped out into view. He'd never been so horny and so hard in all his life.

Buddy's eyes went wide. His mouth opened. "Fuck me," he said again. "Fucking hell, how big is that?"

Tony smiled. "It's about nine. Maybe a little more."

Buddy's hand came forward. He grabbed around Tony's waist and rested them on his now bare ass. His face directly in front of Tony's waist and that huge cock, he pulled him closer. He opened his mouth and immediately sucked in the head.

Buddy went to work immediately. He moaned loudly and slid down inch after inch into his mouth. *Mmmmpphhhhh*, was the only sound he could make as he pushed as far as he could, and the cock lodged deeply into his throat. He tried to keep it there, but he had to let it slide back out.

He let out a little gagging sound but did not waste a moment and pushed the cock right back down his throat hungrily. He kept his hands firmly on Tony's ass and pulled him in toward his face. Tony could tell he was trying to relax his throat, and he saw more than a full extra inch slide in the second time.

Buddy would not let up. He kept it in his mouth and tried to push down further and relax his mouth. Finally, he let it slide out again with a huge gasp. A long slick string of spit remained connected from his mouth to the head of Tony's cock. He looked up at Tony who could see Buddy's eyes tearing.

Tony reached over for the bag from the drugstore that Buddy had put on the bed. He pulled out the lube and opened it. Buddy watched him with a huge smile on his face. "I want you inside me so bad."

243

Tony got the lube open and squeezed out a huge gob of it. He slicked it all over his cock. Up and down the shaft, the lube and Buddy's spit slicked it until it shined. Buddy's mouth was open like a hungry animal.

Tony put the lube down, and Buddy stood up. "Can I sit on it," he asked.

Tony nodded, and Buddy urged him to the bed. Tony laid down on his back, and Buddy stepped up onto the bed. He squatted over Tony who could not believe how beautiful he was. Beautiful and horny, Buddy was more than eager. All the standoffishness that he seemed to have in the car was gone. Buddy was cock hungry and horny, Tony could tell. He knew he had the power over him now, and he was going to give it to him so good.

Buddy held the huge cock straight up underneath him. He had a foot on each side of Tony's hips, and he was squatting over it. He eased himself down, and the head touched against his warm butt.

"We're gonna have to take this real slow," he said.

"As long as you need," Tony said. "Cuz once I'm in, I'm going to fuck you good."

Buddy sighed as the head pressed into his butt. "Oh, fuck yes, I want it so bad." He urged the weight of his body down, but his ass was hesitant. He held the cock straight. Tony was rock hard and looking up at Buddy's sexy body. His cock pulsed with anticipation. And finally with a loud moan, Buddy pushed down, and his cock slid into the tight hole. "Fuuuuuckkkkk," Buddy moaned.

Tony reached up and squeezed one of his nipples. Buddy closed his eyes and moaned even louder. "Yes. Fuck, yes. Tony, wait, wait, let me relax." Tony's cock was only halfway inside, and Buddy paused there in a half-squat.

He reached under and cupped Buddy's ass in his hands. He touched a finger to the side of his cock. He wanted to feel it sliding into this stud. Buddy's hand still gripped it as well. Buddy breathed in and out again and again. And with the third deep breath, he pushed himself down, and Tony could feel another two inches of his cock slide deep inside.

"You OK?" he asked.

"Fuck me," Buddy sighed. "Yes, it's so big." He opened his eyes and smiled down at Tony. "Fuck you're so big."

Tony loved hearing that. "You can take it, baby. Take it all."

"Fuck yeah. You're so deep inside me."

Tony felt his cock with one hand. There was still an inch or two to go. He wanted to be as deep inside Buddy as he could go. He wanted his entire huge cock lodged inside this muscle hunk. Damn, he was so hot. He wanted power over the stud, and he knew he had it.

"Come on, baby. Open up. Take it," he said with a little more authority in his voice. He was starting to feel like he was the man in charge, like Buddy was his. He was younger, he wasn't as well built, he was a sophomore, and Buddy was a senior, but he was the one in charge. He was the one with his huge cock pushing deeper and deeper into this hot, muscle stud. He repeated, "Take it."

Buddy moaned and let out a whimpering sound, but he pushed again, and at last the full nine-inch length of Tony's cock eased deep inside his ass. He let out another gasp and then let his weight fall down, impaling himself on it.

"Oh baby," Tony said with a huge grin on his face. "That's it." He pushed his hips upward, and he felt his cock urging Buddy's ass to relax and to open up more and let him in deeper. Buddy started to moan and didn't stop. Tony started thrusting, and Buddy took it. He put his hands down firmly on Tony's chest and held his ass in place so Tony could start sliding in and out of him.

Tony grabbed his hips and pushed him down as he thrust his hips up. Fuck, he could not believe how deep inside Buddy's ass he was. He had used a lot of lube, and he could feel the slick, wet, warmth wrapped around his cock.

"I want you on your back," Tony ordered. "I'm gonna fuck you, and you're gonna take it."

"Yes, sir," Buddy said. Tony's cock pulsed hard at the words. Fuck, he liked that.

Buddy slid off and sighed loudly as Tony's cock fell out of his ass. He laid down on his back and lifted his legs in the air. "I want you back inside me. Please. Fuck me. I need it."

Tony spurted more lube onto his throbbing hard cock, and then he obliged. He grabbed Buddy's legs and kneeled between them. He put one on each of his shoulders, and his cock pressed back into Buddy's ass where it so desperately wanted to be. He pushed firmly, and this time, the entire huge cock slid in deep in one thrust.

Tony pressed against Buddy's ass until his hips were pushed hard against Buddy's ass. Buddy's eyes were wide open, and he looked up at Tony with a look that made Tony want even more.

He started sliding in and out of Buddy's ass. Harder and faster. At the end of his thrust when his cock was pressed deep inside, he pushed a little more. He loved how that made Buddy's eyes open even wider. He loved the whimpering moan it caused him to expel. He started banging into Buddy's ass so hard, it was making a loud slapping sound with each thrust as his hips pounded against the flesh of Buddy's ass cheeks.

Buddy reached down and started stroking himself. Tony was now pounding and pummeling his ass. He let loose like an animal. Buddy was getting plowed by his massive cock, and he had a huge grin on his face. Tony loved looking right into his eyes.

"Oh, fuck oh fuck," Buddy moaned. "I think I'm gonna cum."

"Don't," Tony ordered.

"Oh fuck, I don't want to. I want you to keep fucking me. Oh, fuck me."

But the dirty talk brought Tony to the edge, too. "Fuck, I'm gonna cum, too."

Buddy was jerking himself off fast and hard. Tony slammed into his ass again and again.

Buddy was breathing fast and hard, but he was able to gasp, "I want to see you cum. Pull out and cum all over me. Please?"

Tony pulled out. Buddy let his legs fall, and Tony straddled over him. He gripped his slick, lubed cock and started jerking himself. Both guys were jerking. Both cocks were aimed at Buddy's beautiful, smooth, muscular body.

Buddy gasped first, and a huge torrent of cum shot out and hit him square in the middle of his face. He closed his eyes quickly, and another blast shot out and hit himself right in the mouth. Tony loved the show, and it brought him over the edge. With a moan, his own huge cock exploded. He aimed right for Buddy's face, and a huge burst of jizz splashed out, covering and coating Buddy's lips. Before the second shot could escape, Tony leaned in even closer. Buddy had his mouth wide open with the gasping breaths of his last shots of cum that were spreading out over his abs when Tony's second blast shot right into his open mouth. Followed by the third and a dribbling fourth, Tony's cock erupted all over Buddy's face and mouth. Cum rained down on him, Buddy smiled widely.

Tony loved it. Buddy was even more beautiful completely smeared in cum. He pushed his cock against his mouth and slid inside. Buddy moaned and sucked on it, and then Tony pulled out and collapsed on top of Buddy's slick, wet body.

He wrapped his arms around Buddy. Both guys, completely spent, laid there quietly as their breathing slowed. Buddy wiped his mouth with the back of his hand. Tony traced wet circles around his nipples and the hollow at the base of his neck. He then put his hand on Buddy's chin and turned his face toward his. He planted a firm kiss on his lips and pushed his tongue into his mouth. He could taste the salty cum, and they shared it with a passionate, deep kiss.

"I want to do that to you all week. Can we?"

Buddy smiled and laughed lightly. "You better believe it," he said. "I can't believe it really happened. I wanted you so bad."

"Me, too," Tony said. "I could really get used to this."

"Oh," Buddy said emphatically. "You can fuck me as much as you want with that cock, mister. But," he paused. "Think I can return the favor, too? Before the week is over?"

Tony smiled. "Fuck yeah," he blurted out.

They lay there arm in arm for a while longer then went into the bathroom to shower together. But when the warm water hit them, Tony's cock got hard, and they did it all over again.

About the Author

Matthew Cooper is an author, editor, and publisher. He writes both gay and straight erotica and edits anthologies. He lives in Florida.

Other Riverdale Avenue Books Magnus Lit Titles You Might Enjoy

A Starr is Born
By Ryan Field

Sleepless in San Francisco
By Ryan Field

Pretty Man
By Ryan Field

A Christmas Carl
By Ryan Field

Fangsters: Clan of the Jersey Boys
By Ryan Field

Fangsters 2: Gangbang Fangsters
By Ryan Field

Valley of the Dudes
By Ryan Field

Stepbrothers in the Attic
By Ryan Field

Dancing Dirty
By Ryan Field

Jockboys 2
By Simon Sheppar

The Jockboys Saga: The Director's Cut
By Simon Sheppar

Other Titles by Matthew Cooper

Frat Boys and Dorm Rooms
Surprising Myself